Revenge of the Wolf

A novel written by Wyatt Michael

4

For Rayna
Happy 16th Birthday

Contents

For as he thinketh in his heart, so is he.
Proverbs 23:7a

Chapter 1

1841 𝔄.𝔇.

𝕭lack clouds moved quickly across the London sky at midnight and opened to reveal a Full Moon hovering over the city. Beneath it, within a secret basement, was a laboratory filled with rows of tables that held an exhaustive collection of experimental equipment. Beakers, test tubes, glass bottles of chemicals over fire along with copper tubes and wiring were all dimly lit from above by gas lights that were along the outside wall. One window, positioned at ground level, sat high at the ceiling and let in the light of the moon. An iron fence along the street outside kept its secrets hidden from prying eyes.

A ferocious black wolf growled and bit at a scientist who watched him through a cage made of wide iron ribs that sat upon a table against the far wall. The wolf wore an iron collar attached to two heavy chains that led to the top of his prison. In a fit of rage, he jumped and attacked at the bars, wishing to loose himself and kill his tormentor.

Doctor Phillips watched on. Other than his widening eyes his face was without expression. He turned quickly to the table behind him and took hold of a clear glass phial that contained a silvery chemical, almost like mercury. He poured it into a large syringe and then fixed the needle to a gunpowder charge at the end of a long iron pole. With it, he turned to the wolf which then crouched and growled in madness, showing its teeth. The scientist stabbed between the bars of the cage with the needle and pierced him. It exploded with violence and burst with fire and spark. The wolf thrashed in the cage and roared in pain, but then writhed as he quickly began to slow in anger and become docile. He breathed heavily and stopped, trembling, sedated. While growling with his eyes fixed upon the man, he laid himself down into an induced sleep.

The scientist stared on with stunned reaction and shook in his excited breathing. He turned away and began to write quickly in a thick brown leather-bound book with a brass latch.

W hen the sun arose from hiding his face from the evils of the night on his following morning, a thin man with medium length black hair that he kept combed straight back with occasional strands that dangled onto his forehead, walked down a green lane in the English countryside. The place sat five miles outside of London city and was surrounded by forests of oak, yew, and goat willow that stood afar off from the grass fields along the dirt road that led him. He was nearly forty years old by a few months and appeared to be poor by his drab brown clothing and carried a small sackcloth bag filled with his only earthly possessions over one shoulder. Somewhat melancholy traces of a hard life of physical labor lined his clean-shaven face and were in his dark green eyes, but it was all he knew or cared to. He was not thin without brawn, but had development of strength resulting from years past. As always he was tired, but had never a chance to find true rest. He had the appearance of a traveler, one who either could not or would not find his place and the shoes on his feet were worn of it. There was a tiny light that lay deep within and could sometimes be seen by some, but in the trudging forward was frequently blanketed with despondency - his long-time companion. He carried the weight of the world in his sackcloth bag and could not lay it down…even if he knew a way.

The nearest town was yet a few miles to the east and he headed towards it. As he went, a loaded farm cart rolled past beside him going the opposite way on its usual course. After some time crossing the rising and falling hillsides, an empty one, driven by an old farmer who was going in the same direction, drew near and stopped.

"Ride, sir?" he said softly.

The traveler nodded and jumped onto the open back and the rickety thing rolled on.

In the period of twenty minutes, the farmer's cart arrived at the only small town in that area outside of the city. Buildings lined both sides of the main street which housed blacksmiths, tanners, markets, taverns, inns, and the like. It was both simple and developed and the traveler found it to be acceptable if possible. He looked upon the proprietaries with a somber face, jumped from his transport when it rolled to a stop, and turned to the old man.

"Can a man find work nearby?"

"There is a farmstead estate two miles west…Mister Breggins' place. He does hiring on his site," the farmer said.

"How do I find him?"

"The Watermill Inn," he answered, pointing ahead. "Mister Holling is the keeper."

"Obliged, sir," the stranger responded with sincere demeanor and a nod.

The farmer whipped the horse and rode away as the man traveled along the unpaved street, moving through laborers, artisans, and traders going about their day's business. The little town was old, like most of England, and the people who resided there were the great grandchildren of those who had great grandparents that also lived in that part of the world. It was slow and deliberate in its lethargic comfort, clean and well manicured. The greenery of the wild countryside had found a place in the corner pots and windowsills where summer cornflowers and buttercups flaunted their colors to passersby. He did not even know the name of the place nor did it matter. They had all just run together in his mind. It was morning and the movements of the entire day were already foreseeable by the actions displayed by the people there. He passed several practical establishments and discovered the sign that he was seeking, hanging from the second story of the building. He entered and at the front room of the modest inn was greeted by Mister Holling who was pleasantly smiling.

The gentleman kept his face shaved clean and had bushy brown hair that he brushed over to one side. He was in his sixties, judging by the wrinkles that gathered on his face near his faded blue eyes and was in good physical condition as a result of his running to care for his company. He was dressed sharp and prepared and gave the impression of a respectable establishment although it would cater to the less privileged with impartial respect. It seemed quite well enough for one who had no place to lodge.

"A good morning to you, sir," the innkeeper announced as he approached.

"A good morning," the man responded somewhat dry. "I be in want of a bed."

Mister Holling prepared his aged leather Registry and took up his feather pen. Certainly, sir…and where, might I inquire, be ye hailing from?"

"How should one get to Mister Breggins' parcel to appeal for work?" the man interrupted.

Mister Holling quickly left his questions to his own pending inquisitiveness and answered. "I've got a young gentleman that can carry you shortly if ye be in need…Now, sir, for your quarters," he said while hurrying away.

His guest nodded with a straight face and followed.

An hour later, Mister Holling's company rode upon a single horse-drawn wagon alongside a boy who was in his teens. They traveled a couple of miles from town and both were silent as the wagon drew up on a large farming operation at the end of the road. The boy drove the horse through a gate opening in a rock wall that surrounded the property and headed towards the giant farmhouse that sat deep within.

It was a solitary second generation home with rectangular windows of twelve panels each that seemed to be in three conjoined sections. There were two stories that spread throughout the space, but took on various forms as they went. On one end, the upper master bedroom opened to a large viewing deck on top of an open air patio. The place was home to many several century year old trees with long and diligent boughs and large active barns that housed both animals and their stores.

The man studied the place as they went and watched the thirty men or so that were across the acreage doing various types of work. Laborers were driving horses, shoveling bedding into barns, stacking bales of hay, watering livestock, and all other sorts of farming tasks. In the distance all around the reliable outside walls he saw many acres of wheat and corn growing with men working in them. The wagon stopped at the side of the beautiful white house where there was an entrance beyond two steps on a raised wooden deck.

"I'll wait for you here, sir," the boy said courteously.

The man climbed down from his seat, stepped onto the platform, and knocked on the timeworn maroon door.

Inside the great farmhouse a large gray-bearded man in his mid-sixties, neatly dressed, looked to the door from his office desk. He wore a cream colored linen shirt with a low standing collar and a dark blue cravat that was tucked into an ivory silk waistcoat with enameled gilt buttons. Dangling from a golden chain he carried an eighteen carat gold Swiss open face quarter repeating pocket watch that stated it was precisely eight o'clock AM.

"Enter."

The man walked into the office room and nodded. "Sir, I seek Mister Breggins."

"You have found him," the large man said with raised eyebrows, tilting his head back. He placed his pen into the holder and folded his hands together. His visitor spoke softly.

"I am Mister Cecil Griffiths. I was graciously delivered here by Mister Holling of Watermill Inn. I am looking to be hired, sir."

Mister Breggins paused for a moment and sized up the man in front of him. "Are you able to present yourself daily, no later than sunrise, whenever that may be, ready for work, whatever that may be, and fill complete the day's toil, however that may be?" Mister Breggins said critically.

"I am, sir," Cecil answered.

Mister Breggins flashed a glimpse of anger and it was clear upon his face. "Thieves will be punished to the full extent of the law, Mister Griffiths!" he said with a long hard look from beneath his brow.

"I understand, Mister Breggins. You will suffer no evil by mine hand...upon my word."

Mister Breggins took a deep breath and sighed as if appeased by Cecil's soft answer. "There will be no drunkenness on my stead."

"Of course, sir," Cecil responded, respectfully and steadfast.

Mister Breggins spoke again with warmth. "You're in luck, Mister Griffiths. I do have a place for you by reason of the season and I am not one to turn away a man in need. I pay a pound sterling at each week. Start to day. See Mister Wycliff on your exit."

"I thank you, sir."

Again, Cecil nodded, but remained expressionless. He put his hand to the door and turned it when Mister Breggins spoke once more.

"What has brought you to Ramsbury Barlow, Mister Griffiths?"

Cecil turned and paused at the door for a moment. He looked to the ground and then into his new employer's eyes.

"I suppose...I am looking...for myself," he said in repose, softly, with intense meditation.

Mister Breggins turned his head slightly to one side and kept his gaze upon Cecil; a man that became something of a small mystery, whether good or bad he could not tell. "And when you find him?" he asked with a stern and penetrating voice.

Cecil looked to the floor and then back to him. "I know not."

There was a long silence and Cecil did not move. He stared to the floor again in thought and then turned and went out.

At ten o'clock in the night, a dark wooden door at the end of a long hall sat quiet in the Watermill Inn. The room number upon it was unclear in the faint light that was given off by the gas lamps that burned along the walls. Within, the room was dark, lit only by a single candle's flame that sat upon a small table beside a bed. Next to it was a deeply worn black leather-bound book lying open to the back pages. Cecil stared down onto it as he sat on the side of the bed in the silent room. The simple walls and floor were exhausted planks of dark woods settled tightly together, but absent in the darkness.

He gritted his teeth together and breathed heavily in anger. Upon it was a list of names handwritten on the blank page and penned immediately beside each one was another name. His hand shook as the words burned in his mind.

Cecil took a drink of liquor from a large bottle and stared wide-eyed at the page. Rage built stronger within him as his mind cycled the impossible images. He threw the partially filled vessel and smashed it against the far wall near the invisible window which had the inside latches closed and locked.

T he crop fields of the estate were filled with working men at nine o'clock in the morning the succeeding day. Cecil strove alongside others employed by Mister Breggins, cutting down Spring Wheat with scythes and piling it high upon large horse-drawn carts. He stood and wiped the chaff and sweat from his forehead in the morning sun, drawing intense breaths from the level of physical labor. He looked around and upon the other men who shouted orders to one another. He took up the heavy blade again and began to swing.

That evening, Cecil sat himself between the bumpy roots of a large old yew tree that grew beside a wood fence that ran the length of a long country lane. It was an ancient height of twenty meters and its reddish-brown bark was peeling. Within its long dark green conifer needles, large clusters of white-yellow anther, like balls of flower, grew. They decorated its arms like shining pearls tossed into bowls of leaves.

It was one hour before dusk and he rested at the end of the day's toil. He enjoyed the solitude of the place that sat part of the way between the town and the farmstead. It was somewhat secluded and he could see that the lane went slightly downhill and turned around a bend up ahead to the right, away from the fencing.

He pulled a beautiful harmonica from his pocket and rubbed the mouthpiece with his dirty hand. He put it to his mouth and very softly, almost inaudibly, played a single note. He was sad and sighed as the sound of the soft breeze blew through the bending needles above his head.

O n the following day, Cecil and the men of the farm worked to separate a large herd of goats, male and female, for milking. Several nannies had their heads locked into stanchions in a row down the fence line as men were filling buckets with their milk. While Cecil worked, another man alongside him made conversation.

"Burney Yarborough," he stated, reaching out a gloved hand to shake while bent over with his other upon his knee. He was a hefty and large fellow with amber brown and white hair kept safely shaded beneath a wide brimmed straw hat, aged somewhere in his mid-fifties.

"Cecil Griffiths," he said with a dry face, shaking hands with the man.

They continued to work and there were no words between them for a moment.

"Is your heart right with God?" Burney said plainly while wrestling a goat into place.

Cecil stopped and looked at him with a single raised eyebrow, taken aback by the execution of the question. He continued to work and, without looking up, spoke a response. "The God of this world is not concerned with the affairs of man whether they be good or bad."

"Nay, sir. This is not true," Burney said with a big smile. "For God loves all and does not desire that any man should perish. Jesus Christ, His only Son, came that we all should have life…and have it more abundantly." He had an honest voice and some inner gleam about him that would reveal itself.

Cecil gave Burney a short moment of pause for it and squinted his eyes at him. Burney continued.

"Come with me and a few others to service Sunday, the Sabbath to God, and you shall see for yourself," he said, standing tall and looking Cecil straight into his face.

Cecil snorted, slightly shook his head, and blew off the words as he continued with his work. "I must decline, respectfully, Mister Yarborough," Cecil said to him and then turned and walked away.

In the evening, much to their delight, the men were released from their labor earlier than the day before. Again, Cecil found himself between the roots of the old tree along the fence which had become a place of tranquility and contentment. He took the harmonica from his sack and looked upon it for a moment as the Song Thrush picked among the seeds overhead. He put it to his mouth and as he always did, made a single soft note upon it. A young boy came walking around the curve on the dirt road and he looked up and noticed him with a tiny, almost unseen smile.

He was thin with blue eyes and neatly combed dark brown hair, age eleven or so, dressed well as a normal schoolboy and carried two school books strapped together by a leather cord. Cecil appeared happy as if meeting a long lost friend as the boy approached him.

"I heard a fellow play one sharp tune on one of those! You know any?" the boy said, very friendly.

"No. I don't," Cecil answered, looking down with a soft smile.

"My name is David. Me mum an' dad call me Davey. What's yours?"

"Cecil."

"I've seen you here before, sir."

Cecil nodded. "I have found it to be no small comfort to me here," he said.

"It is the road to my house," said Davey.

Cecil turned and looked in the direction the boy was heading with a serious face. "I see."

"May I look at that French harp?" Davey asked.

Cecil handed the boy the harmonica with a melancholy smile and the boy sat down beside him.

"It was made in Vienna," said Cecil. "It was my father's."

"A very pretty thing. Is it real silver?" the boy asked.

"It is."

Davey admired it closely with a great smile. "Well, if you know no tune, it is well enough to look upon it, I says."

Cecil got a small smile on his face, but within, his heart was full of sadness over the thing.

"My father has never played instruments of music, although, upon observation, I expect it interests him," said Davey. He gave the harmonica back to Cecil with careful attention.

"My father only played it in secret," Cecil began. "When I was a lad, the same as you, I caught him alone once in the forest of our place making a beautiful song. It was slow, like the lament of a creature of the wood that was hidden from the eyes of all men who had lost the way home. Its sound traveled deep into the woodland and seemed to echo into the earth's hills themselves. I was drawn to it...not only because of the aberrant sound, but because of its loveliness." Cecil snorted softly as the thoughts became real to him again. "I can still hear that song. It's as a vanished haunting call from a faraway place and a faraway time." Cecil looked down upon it and paused a moment in his memory and then returned. "My brothers and I did not know of it. I don't know why. I figured it to be something he wanted for himself. When he saw me, he smiled, seemingly embarrassed, and said, 'Now you've learned something you would not expect about your father to day. Come,' he said, 'try it for yourself.' I blew into it and he laughed. He rolled it in a cloth and hid it away inside a fallen tree. I smiled and he said, 'It'll be a secret only between you and me.'"

Cecil looked down, solemn, and the boy listened carefully.

"I never told my brothers," he continued. "After my father died, I went back there to his secret place and took it to remember him by."

The boy looked on with wide eyes. "When did your father die, sir?"

"Before his time…when I was just a lad…not more older than you."

Davey looked down, disappointed. "How?"

Cecil looked to him and then down as he replied. "He was killed in an accident…my mother and father both…they had no daughters. I was the sixth of seven brothers."

Davey stared upon him with much consideration for his story and then rose to his feet with a small token of sentiment. "I am sorry, sir, to hear such a tragic tale."

Cecil returned his eyes to him. "Live your life to its fullest, lad," he said calmly. "You'll never know when all is spent, whether ye be young or old. Do that which is right and pray what is right will be done to you in return."

The lad nodded with a pause and a small smile and then walked away, down the lane in the direction of his home – somewhere past the forests and the fields.

The scientist, like clockwork, consistently performed tests upon the wolf in his dark basement laboratory in the night. His subject was sedated and still, lying down, perpetually held by the shackle around his neck. The man inserted his hand into the cage through the bars and injected chemicals into the wolf with a syringe. He turned to his table and wrote notations of the Periodic Table of the Elements in his brown leather book. With a swab, Doctor Phillips collected saliva from its teeth and took it to his tables. He studied the movement of the strange living cells from the sample under a microscope. They seemed to grow into long strains and mutate into new and different cells. He dripped a deadly poison onto the slide plate and discovered that the wolf's cells were unharmed. He shook his head, perplexed. He pulled the plate out and held it over a kerosene flame for ten seconds and then re-examined the specimen. To his astonishment and confusion, the cells were unchanged and had not been destroyed.

"No reaction? How can this be?" he whispered to himself.

In amazement, he raised his head, turned, and looked upon the motionless creature.

Rain poured down upon Mister Breggins' property. It was time to eat and Cecil and the other workmen of the estate ran into a great barn and sat at a long wood table that had been placed in the aisle. The massive loft on both sides above them was full of hay that dampened the sound of the drops overhead like heavy blankets. Plump women, cooks of the kitchen, served the men their daily lunch under the cover of the wood shingle roof barn. The meal set before them included boiled potatoes, garden greens of cabbage and kale, halved onions, fresh biscuits and fresh butter, raisins and goat's milk.

Cecil entered last and found no place for room at the table. Burney Yarborough waved to him from the furthest end to come. He made a spot on the very edge of the bench and Cecil sat down with him, expressing a thankful nod.

Mister Breggins, who sat at the head of the table, said the prayer.

"We thank Thee, O Lord, for Thine abundance we are to receive and give Thee thanks for the rain that waters the land. Remember the poor, the destitute, and the hungry. Let Thy Grace fill us and carry us all our days. Amen."

"Amen," the men at the table concurred.

They began to eat and speak to one another in cheerful communion in the cool that circulated through the open doors. Burney turned to Cecil who sat beside him on his right.

"Have you secured lodgment, Cecil?" he asked.

"I have....a room at the Watermill Inn," he responded.

"Mister Breggins only keeps enough rooms here for overnight work...men who have been hired to the position with no family to go to," said Burney. "They are all occupied for the moment, but there is a house with rooms to hire I can show you. If you should decide to make a stay of it...called the Fitzgibbon Rooming House. From there, a wagon stops to fetch the men who come here from it day by day. I'll take you there on

Sunday to situate you after we gather with the saints on the Lord's Day. Would that suit you?"

Cecil stopped chewing and looked seriously at Burney. "For the moment, Mister Yarborough, I am quite suited where I am and do not desire to remove," Cecil answered.

"Well, how about my standing offer at the Ramsbury Church of St. John the Baptist?"

Cecil was straight-faced and still and finally yielded in part because of Burney's continued kindness and consideration. "Very well," he responded.

"The Parson is Minister Eckelhorn Cooke, a man after God's own heart," Burney said, being very pleased.

There was a short moment where the two men did not speak and ate their meal. Burney then stopped and turned to Cecil with a very serious demeanor and spoke.

"He is able to do exceeding abundantly above all that we ask or think."

Cecil stopped and looked Burney in the eyes, then turned and continued to chew his food, looking down onto the table. He was troubled and felt a pain of guilt within.

The Sunday morning that Burney had been anticipating had finally arrived. At ten o'clock Cecil found himself sitting on the aisle of the fifth row in the small but crowded English Protestant Church. His dress was modest, clean clothes, but would barely pass as decent. As Minister Cooke was speaking a prayer from the simple white pulpit, his somewhat nervous gaze traveled over the room at the other people. He saw a beautiful nineteen year old girl with red hair beneath her delicate lace cap, smiling at him. In the sunlight of the room her bright green eyes were in keen reflection. Her skin was noticeably sleek and elegant like the creations of the mulberry grower's silkworms of West Bengal. He could not help but to immediately notice her divine lips that were worthy of the gods. This in accord with a tiny turned up nose, he was profoundly distracted.

She sat with her father, an older man with a long gray beard who appeared outwardly kind and gentle and her mother who seemed a perfect match for him. Cecil's face temporarily lit with only a subtle smile and he quickly returned his head downward to keep from being seen not in reverence.

The minister closed the prayer and made a final statement before a tall sculpted cross of bronze that hung on the wall. "Amen. Remember, in the words of Christ our Lord: 'Whatsoever entereth in at the mouth goeth into the belly and is cast out into the draught...But those things which proceed out of the mouth come forth from the heart; and they defile a man. For out of the heart proceed evil thoughts, murders, adulteries, fornications, thefts, false witness, blasphemies - These are which defile a man, but to eat with unwashen hands defileth not a man.'"

With piercing eyes, Minister Cooke looked upon his congregation with a hard and somber face. For his own reasons, Cecil looked down to the floor, avoiding the messenger and the message.

Outside the church when the service had concluded, the members of the body stood lovingly socializing with one another. Cecil shook hands with several good-humored and happy men and climbed into a horse-drawn wagon with Burney Yarborough. He turned and saw the young lady smiling at him from among the faces and it made him lightly smile in return. He nodded to her as they rode away from the property in a succession of many others on the short ride to town.

Several days passed and The Golden Serpent Society, a secret club comprised of rich men, mostly men of science and study, convened in the night at the great whiskey room of a millionaire's estate. The place was long and tall, decorated with exotic polished woods with carvings of huntsmen and their hounds, filled with fine leather chairs, mahogany tables, two large ornate fireplaces of marble, and a high library wall of books along one entire side opposite the abundantly supplied bar. Game trophies lined the walls above - caribou, elk, and American buffalo. Several bear and tiger rugs lay on the floor with teeth showing, forever frozen in the moment of their swan song. The forty or so men in attendance enjoyed themselves by smoking cigars and pipes and drank bourbon from lead-crystal glasses. Gambling was certainly encouraged and indulged by many in the form of gentleman's cards and a roulette table with highly focused silent players.

An attentive guard stood at a podium at the entrance to the room and upon it was a golden sculpture of a biting snake. A gentleman entered the doorway in front of him, pulled the gloves from his hands, and placed his right hand upon the head of the adder. He spoke aloud as the man at the podium carefully watched and listened to his words.

"I swear an oath upon the Golden Serpent and before God to guard the Society's secrets of meeting, its members, and its ideas…to hold all spoken words in utmost confidence upon pain of death…sworn upon my life."

"You may freely enter, Doctor Stratton," the society guard stated.

Doctor Phillips sat in a high-backed burgundy leather chair around an oval coffee table with several other colleagues. He was dressed in a black tail coat evening suit as all men there were. His hair was a rich brown, which he kept styled with a center part and was long enough on the sides to tail into slight curls. He donned sophisticated whiskers that grew long at the sides of the jaw but the face of his chin was shaved clean. Along with this, he carried a down-turned mustache, but it was not overbearing and did not connect with his beard. A dapper gentleman server approached him carrying a silver tray and he took the single glass of bourbon from it. Doctor Ashcroft made a statement.

"We have made some significant advances in electric shock treatment in not only the mentally ill, but for physiological medicine as well," he said.

"Demons are no longer exercised by beatings in shackles secured to the walls in Doctor Ashcroft's offices of practice?" Doctor Bentridge said, jokingly. The men in the conversation laughed.

Doctor Albert began with an observation. "Increasingly, to the lay public, such therapies that are violent are disliked... For instance, the spinning Darwin Chair... blood will issue from the nose, eyes, mouth, and ears, but in many cases the subject professes to have been cured," he said.

"With such opposing public opinion we are pressed to experiment with chemical and electrical methods," Doctor Ashcroft responded, vigorous in his manner.

Doctor Phillips had been listening for some time and then spoke. "What if an illness of the mind could be introduced in measurement to an already suffering patient that could then be abated by mathematical formula?...Therefore being made manageable."

"Madness by equation?" Doctor Sutherland asked while smiling with curiosity.

"I have been experimenting with a wolf...by injections," Doctor Phillips continued. "Chemically, I have introduced a controlled insanity."

The scientist's associates were most intrigued although their thoughts were mixed with unbelief.

"Now that *is* a curious something, Doctor," Lachlan Ashcroft added.

"Why a wolf?" Doctor Bentridge asked him.

"Because of similarities in their social structure to human society, the way they mate for life, institute hierarchy, and govern dysfunctional behavior...among many other notable human attributes," Doctor Phillips responded. He looked down and shook his bourbon so that the liquid spun in his glass. "In this process I have discovered that once every thirty day cycle the wolf experiences uncontrolled fits of madness...something totally unrelated to the course of the experimental behavior that only one element will subdue. The secret is the metal, silver."

"Silver?!! A costly remedy!!" a joking Doctor Sutherland cried. The men chuckled, but respectfully, with much interest. "Could you not have settled on a more practical antidote?!" he added.

The men chuckled again.

Doctor Phillips responded with a half-smile. "I have discovered a disorder under certain conditions in which a defect forms when an atom leaves its place in a crystal lattice, creating a vacancy, and relocates nearby where one did not preexist...which I plan to submit to the Journal of Chemistry Science as my findings become conclusive," he added with a smile. "It is this imperfection in a silver bromide crystal by the presence of extra atoms in an otherwise complete lattice which causes the crystal to become unstable when heated within one hundred degrees Celsius of its melting point. For reasons I will not yet reveal, when I introduce a very small measure of silver into the bloodstream, all adverse effects or violent tendencies are quelled and the creature returns to a natural state...both psychologically and physically."

"And if there is no antidote, Doctor Phillips?" Doctor Albert asked with much concern.

"This monthly illness has been noted to subside within eight hours, before daybreak of the morrow, when left unaided," he replied.

Doctor Albert grew puzzled with some measure of dismay. "A side effect or a mischance?" he spoke aloud, but intended it for his own thought.

Doctor Phillips became quite serious and drew a deep breath. "I answer you gentlemen," he stated, "that my findings are turning out to be something I did not foresee...a discovery that will set the scientific world on its end."

Doctor Blake, a younger doctor of science with an interest in astronomy who had been sitting directly to the left of Doctor Phillips, listening carefully, spoke for the first time.

"When did you begin these experimentations?" he asked without expression.

"I began instituting injections some three months ago, Doctor Blake...on the 6th day of February," he answered.

Doctor Blake stared intently into Doctor Phillips' eyes. "The night of a Full Moon," he said.

Doctor Phillips looked down again into his drink with a half-smile and raised it to his lips in thought, realizing this for the first time. He became meditative and his face went long.

"Indeed, it was," he said and then finished his glass.

Chapter 2

$\mathfrak{C}$ecil sat awake in his room in the night at two o'clock. In the light of the single candle beside his bed, he stared at the harmonica as it sat upon the black book that lay face down. It would seem to call to him from his dreams and rouse him from deep slumber. When it was not drawing much of his thought it was merely waiting in sight. He twitched and gritted his teeth in a continuing and unstoppable rage.

$\mathfrak{A}$ dead body of a man lay on its back on a thin and dirty straw-stuffed mattress on the floor. It decomposed in a dingy dark London flat in the seedy part of the city and was covered in blood. His neck had been cut. The floor was black and disgusting with filth, illuminated by the white light of mid-morning from a nearby window.

Two London constables stood in a rundown alley guarding the door to a stairway of the dismal apartment building. A police carriage rolled up on the cobblestone street, drawn by a single horse. It stopped and the Police Commissioner, the Chief of Police of London's West Side, came out through the carriage door.

He was forty-two years old, young for his esteemed position, but earned the title with much capability. Well liked by all other men of his division as well as neighboring ones, he was quite shrewd in his dealings and demanded respect. He wore a graying brown beard, which he kept closely confined to his features that streaked heavily with silver throughout. He was not overweight other than what was natural for men his age and stood six feet tall with a husky build.

He quickly walked forward into the stairwell in his characterizing uniform of duty without stopping, past the guards.

He briskly ascended the decrepit staircase to a flat guarded by another officer and went in. The windows of the room were open, letting in the only bit of light and to let out the revolting stench of decomposition. Four detectives scoured the room and some of them held handkerchiefs over their faces to keep out the smell. The body was on the floor near a tiny closet and a window.

"Commissioner Howe," Detective Allcott said with a nod from a kneeling position beside the body, standing in the now dried pool of blood.

The commissioner looked upon the dead.

"He was slashed here across the neck and was then stabbed repeatedly in the heart and lungs," said the detective.

"Any witnesses?" asked the commissioner.

"None, sir. No one has seen the victim enter at any time, so he must have come in the night...by the decomposition, sometime in the past four days, Commissioner. The nearby tenants know him not... By the location, I'll warrant a whore brought him here where the killer lay in wait." Detective Allcott pointed to the open closet door at the edge of the mattress where the victim's head laid. "Probably over money by the looks of it," he added while raising his eyebrows.

"Not something uncommon here in London," said Detective Halsey, who stood nearby.

"A robbery turned murder," Detective Allcott stated.

Detective Shipley, who was looking over the room, spoke from a corner. "Lured to his death over lust," he injected.

Commissioner Howe turned to him with a stern face, glancing again to the body. "Lust sprouts from man in many forms...some more readily seen than others," he stated. The commissioner immediately turned to the gentleman who remained kneeling by the body. "Find our perpetrators, Detective Allcott. Put their heads in a noose."

The detective looked at him, expressionless and still.

The commissioner headed towards the door, but looked on. "Get this vile spectacle out of here," he said as he turned and walked out.

Mister Wycliff allowed for amiable game play on the surface at a certain appropriate juncture in the field that had been newly cleared of Spring Wheat. The area was an ideal location for a competition of engaging Rugby football, the rules made famous by Rugby school in Warwickshire, and it was no coincidence that the man had enough hands to fill the opposing positions. With

Mister Breggins' approval for a short hour of non-personally destructive sport, the combative forces that were once at longstanding peace with offerings of concord went to war.

The created ball was an inflated pig's bladder and spherical in shape; a desideratum, an aforethought of necessity from mid-summers past and had been carefully stored on the property out of sight, but not out of mind for the welcomed matches of merciless crushing humiliation. The losers would not live down the outcome for another entire year. The game was, unbeknownst to the master, much more than a simple advantageous recreation or score; it was the determining factor of social standing.

It was not an option to abstain from or to shun the oncoming slaughter for fear of relentless eternal harassment. The men gathered at their lines, well rehearsed in the method and Cecil prepared himself alongside Burney, his ally on the front. Their purpose was clear – protect the confederate who holds the ball and strive to not be killed doing it. There was a silent set of rules in place, but the men recognized the unspoken and most observed rule first – there were no rules.

"Cecil! You did not know that you had signed your own certificate of death at the Breggins farmstead did you?!" shouted Mister Wycliff in a taunt from the opposing line.

Cecil did not smile and prepared to destroy anyone that got in his way of the goal line if the ball were to land in his possession.

"There will be no pity for the weak!" cried Burney, nearly foaming at the mouth with retaliation, much to Cecil's surprise.

The drop-kick-off sailed high from Cecil's team, the *Red-eyed Goshawks*, that started an hour long trampling and bruising that none of the players were soon to forget. In a moment of heightened violence in the struggle for the goal lines, Mister Wycliff and his *Sun Bears* executed a scissors move. The ball was short passed to Theodore Tillmire, a *Sun Bear*, and he immediately veered to the right in Cecil's direction. Instead of charging him, Cecil waited to calculate the play. Burney was drawn in alongside Everard, the covering defender, as a second defender in Tillmire's diagonal assault. Mister Wycliff ran across and forward in the other direction, just behind Theodore. He received a pass as they crossed and then ran directly towards the point of the disruption in the defense. Cecil saw his moment and without a warning, tackled Mister Wycliff to the ground with ruthless potency.

Mister Wycliff groaned under the weight of six men that landed on top of him and his face was ground red with the hard elbows and palms that everyone used to exact coercion from their enemies.

The *Red-eyed Goshawks* cheered and Burney lifted Cecil into the air by a hug to his waist with accolades and laughter.

Again, Cecil and Burney had an opportunity to shine when the *Sun Bears* left them room to maneuver. In a *Goshawks* play of their own offense, the players distinguished by being shirtless, Cecil had captured a *Sun Bears* kick and ran toward the edge of the field. Burney, his defender, came alongside and traveled slightly behind. As Cecil jumped the low cut grassy wheat stems that created an uneven playing ground, he slipped through the side edge of the sliding defense into the path of danger. Daniels Delaney, a brick wall, came at him for the takedown. Burney slipped through the opposing line, ripped himself from Mister Wycliff's clutches, and was at a favorable length for a floated pass. In the assurance of being considerably crushed,

Cecil cried out.

"Burney!"

He tossed the ball backwards, away from trouble, and Burney ran into it at pace with a solid catch. Unfortunately for Cecil, Daniels Delaney executed a late tackle out of spite and drove him into the ground, but the sensation was worth it. Burney broke free with the insides of a hog and, like cultured livestock, set himself to freely graze on the desirable stalks of the in-goal. He was ankle tapped from behind with a mean shoe just a second too late and fell forward onto his face inside the scoring bounds, giving his team the points. He had literally eaten dirt and slowly got to his two shaking feet, but it seemed to Cecil and the others it was one of his greatest life moments. Cecil laughed at the soil that had smeared across Burney's lips as his team shouted with laughter and cheers. The old man was hurt, but enjoyed every minute of the shooting pain.

When their hour drew to its close to every man's dismay, the *Red-eyed Goshawks* finished with the highest score in equal number of plays. It was time to give up the playing field for the plow and planting of corn and beans for the inevitable fall harvest and in the pain of joint swelling and strained muscle the men were temporarily satisfied to yield to it.

Mister Wycliff, who was not much for being a sore loser, other than physically, had a word to say to the newest member of their annual club.

"Welcome aboard, Cecil. You played well. I know who surely won't be on the opposing team next year," he said with a soiled sweating face, an aching shoulder, and a smile.

Cecil sat gently with his back against the old tree in the serene setting in relief from his hard work and harder play. It was quiet there in the evening. There were hardly any calls of birds or rustling of surrounding wildlife as they all seemed to be settling for the oncoming night in their various residences. The ants had their lull in the twenty-four hour work day and retreated to their elaborately designed, but silently booming metropolis under the earth to later emerge stronger onto the surface than the day before.

After some time at pondering the ways of survival among the living things of the world, Davey came along again carrying his books.

"Hullo, Cecil!" he shouted.

Cecil nodded and waved to him with a smile as the boy approached.

"Taking your rest again?" he asked.

"I am…when I can get it. Sometimes when they call for supper I excuse myself to come here instead. The final stop before I go…home," said Cecil.

"What is it you eat if you ignore supper?"

Cecil looked around on the ground at broken sticks and fragments of bark. "Oh, I always find a spider or two that tastes fairly good," he answered with a smile.

"Ha!" Davey laughed. "Cecil! What do you really eat?!"

Cecil laughed at him. "Each night when I get home there's a pelican on my windowsill with a giant salmon in his beak to deliver it for my supper. I ask him what's his name, who sent him, or where did it come from every time, but he never answers."

"Cecil!"

Cecil laughed again.

"Mind if I give you company?"

"Not at all," Cecil responded with a small smile and soft voice.

Davey sat down on the big tree roots. "What brings you here day by day?" said the boy.

"I've taken hire at the Breggins farmstead for the time being."

"I know of him, an acquaintance of my father's. Whence have you come?"

"Yorkshire...in a roundabout way...here and there."

"Is that where your family was from?...where you were raised?" Davey asked, becoming serious.

"It was."

"It seems my father's family was from thereabouts. I would not know for sure. I've not seen it," Davey said.

"Here," said Cecil, "a gift for you to day." He reached into his sack and pulled out a lime and gave it to the boy.

"A lime?! I've not seen one of these in a good while!" Davey shouted with a big smile.

"You may never see one again!" Cecil said in high spirits. "Best you take it and eat it soon! I kept it from a ship captain I know in London. He gave me a box of them upon the Greenland Dock, but I'm sorry to say this is my last one. I have no idea where it is from."

Davey gazed upon it with an even greater smile and then looked to Cecil. "Some tropical island, no doubts!"

"You know," Cecil started, "the men who go to sea for extended amounts of time, like the whalers, are rationed limes in their meals. The whalemen go out for sometimes five years at a time to hunt for the oil! So, by eating limes it keeps them from getting scurvy. The British navy became so known worldwide for it that the sailors of the seas call the British men 'limeys'."

Both of them laughed loud.

"Did you ever work on a whaleship?" asked Davey.

"I did not...only upon the docks to repair them and to load them."

Cecil became deeply reflective and spoke after a pause in thought. "Once you sail away on some ships you cannot change your mind and come back. Your decision is absolute. I've not been able to make many decisions of such weight in my time with as much confidence. Who knows what tomorrow holds? Or, who knows what a day may bring?"

"What reasoning has brought you to this place now?" the boy asked him, somewhat cheerful and in an earnest tone. There was a silence before Cecil's reply.

"I perceive that you are an intelligent boy," he said. Cecil became very serious and looked Davey in the eye with what almost seemed to be a warning. "When you decide what you will do, do it without remorse, without regret, and do it with boldness."

Davey looked on Cecil with a sincere but happy face, pondering the words of his newfound friend. He looked down to the attractive glossy lime in his hand with a new appreciation for the simple thing.

At midnight, some days afterwards, a cellar door at the top of a rock stairway slowly opened. Doctor Phillips came through it wearing his white chemical smock and carrying a flame. The darkened laboratory below began to reveal itself in the flash and flicker of fire as he pulled the door closed and traveled down the stair. He put the torch to the gas lights high on the walls and they began to burn. He turned up the flames with a knob protruding from a copper pipe and looked upon the black wolf.

The creature was motionless on the floor of its dark cage. Doctor Phillips became alarmed and was stricken with panic. He set down his light and took up a long pole. Quietly, he slowly aimed it between the bars and crept forward. The tip of the pole inched to the wolf's neck and the man quickly electrocuted him with it. The beast did not move under the high voltage of electricity and appeared to be dead. Doctor Phillips removed the prod and put on thick leather gloves. He pushed his hand between the bars, quickly tapped the wolf, and recoiled.

There was no reaction and he reached in again, took hold of the animal by the fur, and dragged him around so that his iron collar could be better seen. The wolf's dry tongue hung out over its teeth and no breath passed over it. Extending his arm, he tried to unlatch a lock on the collar with his gloved hand, but could not. He removed his glove, but then put it back on, looking upon the creature in both suspicion and fear. He made a fist and punched the animal in the head and quickly backed out of the cage. The wolf's head flopped up and back with no consequence. Doctor Phillips, being reassured, removed his glove, reached in slowly, and took hold of the latch. He moved his head down closer near the floor of the cage and tried to find the pin that eluded him. His brown hair ruffled against the black iron bars as he pressed fully upon them to reach. He pushed away the wolf's neck and brushed the long fur aside to move the metal into position. To see better, he squinted his eyes in the poor lighting as he fumbled with it. The pin finally came free from a latch and the collar swung open on a hinge and fell off.

The wolf bit him in a split-second, snapping up the doctor's hand into his teeth. He jumped to all fours and growled in rage, wrenching the man's arm in further with great strength. The scientist cried out in both fear and pain as the wolf held his entire right hand in a powerful bite and pulled on him. Doctor Phillips reached for the electric prod of his invention with his other hand and the wolf released him, barking and hissing against the bars.

Doctor Phillips fell back onto his laboratory tables, holding his trembling bleeding hand with a scream among broken glass. He turned and fell to the ground, got back to his feet again, and ran up the stairs in terror.

The wolf growled and panted with fury in a scowl. His lips quivered upon his red blood-soaked teeth and his purposes were executed.

Albern Partridge was a man in his late forties with a dull grim look that was continuously on his greasy unshaven face. He was tall and strong with perceptible arm muscles that were always used to intimidate lesser citizens or worse. Everything in his world was simple; it was his way or Hell to pay. He was born without a soul and the organ that pumped the poisoned blood that slithered through his veins had never been fused to feeling. Not an ounce of sympathy or empathy was ever instilled into his animated corpse by anything above, but below there was plenty to be had. He was the right arm of the devil and a scourge to humanity. In his inebriated eyes was another foggy window into Hell and it was his custom to send the unwary there.

His ritual was the same almost every day. Because

of his careless temperament, he was a drunk and the ship docks that abused him day in and day out did not care. He could not drown his own private miseries into oblivion although he tried effectively without rival and he purposed to inflict them on others. But for now, he was at home in the assuagement of the Turnspit Public House with the other brawlers and working ne'er-do-wells in the evening of the gamblers' glory. In behalf of the Parliament of the United Kingdom implementing the Cruelty to Animals Act of 1835, the clientele were pressed to enjoy the accepted sport of the rat pit. Down the creaking black steps through a jagged doorway cut in the rock in the back, mass crowds of hopeful men from all classes would file to the basement where the tiny arena was standing to make some richer. The racket was profitable for the Turnspit and they could hardly keep enough ale and lager to support them; even in readiness. The white smoke of tobacco hovered in the gas lights over the stale smell of blood and beer as the excited and whining dogs jumped at their masters' leash.

"Gentlemen! Place your bets! Place your bets and win a prize!" cried the announcer. "Put down your pounds, shillings, and pence for a take that will purchase an endowment for the lady or a trust for the ragamuffin! Don't be left cold on poor man's lane when this is your big opportunity to go home with the leprechaun's pot! Or not go home atall…and find another woman!"

All of the men laughed and their movement formed a rolling sea of gray, brown, and black cloth and silk top hats by those who wore one. The crowd had gathered around the waist-high barriers that enclosed a twelve foot square ring where the killing would be done. Handlers took hold of barrels that made loud scratching sounds from within.

"Here to amaze and to make some richer is seven

dogs, starting with Shadrach Wesley Pinsmail's Black and Tan Terrier, Doll - winner of six competitions and counting!" The announcer resumed over applauds. "Another contender hails from Leicester; John Harker Leggett's Bull and Terrier, Olympus - with five wins!" he shouted. "Mindful! Do not give your hearts away to these only for Chandler Swaddle's Bull Terrier, The Prince, is sure to give 'em a run for it! Now, for an introduction worthy of the monarchy!" he shouted. "Our unsung true gambler for the night! Give us a cheer for our principal rat-catcher who alone delivered one thousand five hundred of the little villains for our fancy – our rodent royalty - Jack Black!"

The audience gave huzzahs and whistled as the most peculiar man stepped out alongside the announcer, raising a hand. He wore a striking coordinated outfit of scarlet in a top hat, topcoat, waistcoat, and breeches. Over his shoulder as a banner to his profession and obsession, he displayed a wide leather belt inset with large cast-iron rats. He smiled from a face ringed with a thick brown beard that was cut to travel under his chin and up around his ears like a bib. On each fingertip were small wrappings of cloth which he used as a defense for being bitten. The managers had allowed for him to give a short business endorsement.

"Rats is not all me game," he stated, "although I make a bit of a thing of it!"

His audience laughed.

"When you have a want of birds, unusual fish, or a fine-bred pedigree dog that is second to none, I'm your John! I mean Jack!"

The onlookers returned with their dependable laughter.

"And," he continued, "I fancy meself on magnificent specimens of taxidermy that your company will find first-rate!...Creatures you'll fear will make off and run away from their displays!"

He bowed low to the floor and removed his hat and received one final cheer.

The handlers proved the strange man's worth. Two men lifted a barrel to the side of the enclosure and tipped it over with heavy shakes. Precisely three hundred large black and brown rats fell into the arena and went scrambling in all directions. Some of them were so large and fat that they dwarfed all others. The men scraped the clingers out of the barrel with spades, careful not to cripple the valuable merchandise. The announcer laid out the rules and regulations.

"Each dog will have a weight handicap! A combination of the quickest time, the number of rats sent to their eternal rest and the dog's weight will decide the victory! The timekeeper will calculate in mathematics the final tally! Gentlemen, make ready!"

Albern took all the money that he had made that day in eleven hours and handed it over to the collector, a sizeable deposit into the bank of the insane. His face was hard and he gritted his teeth in a fever of unsighted greed, newly confident in a righteous return.

"The Doll," he stated squarely with his usual scowl.

The referee climbed over the barrier into the ring. He wore an official red waistcoat and a black top hat and kicked a rat away from his special knee-high boot.

"Mister Pinsmail, are you ready?!" he shouted.

The breeder gave a nod as he held his terrier in the air over the rats and the dog growled and showed her teeth.

"Go!" the referee cried and the dog's paws hit the floor.

The men began to shout for the Doll as she immediately herded a terrified crawling mass of them into a corner. Within two seconds, she started picking the frightened strays that bolted from the wriggling pile alone in her needle sharp teeth. She quickly bit down on them in their mid regions with homicidal compulsion and threw their twitching bodies against the walls. As they collided, she would already be finishing another screeching biter to the same fate. She went mad in a killing frenzy and took up two and three rats into her death grip at once, crushing their bones and their organs in a swift single bite. The larger ones, who were more intrepid, turned with a temporary stay of execution and bit onto her ears. She was only minutely delayed and dealt with them harshly with a clawed push from her paw against the ground. The vermin were slung wildly to the left and to the right as the condemned had nowhere to hide from the reaper of rats.

The men were neurotic in the captivating bewitchment of death. They shook their fistfuls of money over their heads as the lingering smoke's still placidity was violently disturbed.

Doll's head and face was covered in gore and she seemed to get stronger as the minutes stacked up. Albern screamed at her to kill with rigor, destroy with ferocity - deliver without fail. The pupils of his eyes flared with deep red and at that moment the normal black was eclipsed.

The timekeeper called the match at one hundred rats with a chime and the master quickly lifted his prize from the slaughter. The dog dripped with blood and chunks of flesh and he set to cleaning her off. The gamblers' furor echoed from their den to the outside streets. Each man had his own count and they hassled each other in the debates.

"One hundred rats – Time: eight minutes forty-five seconds. Five point two seconds a rat!" the timekeeper shouted.

Albern and the others who had bet on the Doll cheered and readied themselves for a payoff while their keen opponents claimed an infraction.

"Two of 'em are movin'!" a few men cried to the referee. "It's a foul!"

Albern turned with a look, clearly desiring to strangle the 'rats' and became furiously enraged with shouting riposte.

"There is no foul, you rotten cheats! Shut your mouths or I'll rip 'em off your face!" he screamed with a red appearance, but was not heard under all the other more shallow threats.

The referee saw fit to agree as two of the count, mistakenly, very slowly hobbled forward, dragging their hind legs in smears of blood.

"The Doll will have to re-enter the arena and finish off the remaining rats! Her new time at this will be added to her original time! You know the rules, gentlemen! All bets remain in place!"

Albern was beside himself in outrage and could barely refrain from satisfying his temper with stabbing and maiming human victims.

The dog was led by its master to the suffering remainder and seven seconds was added to the time.

Mister Leggett's Bull and Terrier, Olympus, was given his chance and one hundred deranged English rats later, beat the Doll's final time by four seconds; a lesser dog of the same weight, but still the champion.

It was an upset that most rollers were willing to except in the thrill of the game, but Albern wanted his own blood. He finished the alcohol that he held in his hand and shattered the glass against the wall and the floor.

To his surprise, in the seconds before requiring a payment of vengeful restitution from those who put him out of his reward and the entire day's toil, the West London police commissioner and several of his top detectives entered from the back, dressed in their uniforms and smiling, ready to do business. Albern decided to let it go before he became cornered by the police and bitten just like one of those doomed rats inside the ring. He passed behind them, taking his anger elsewhere and slipped away without trouble with enough sense and they did not notice him.

In a slum in another part of London, Albern climbed the dirty staircase to the door of a flat. He turned and walked down a dim unexpressive hallway, past a couple of forest green doors that appeared black, and stopped at one. He beat on it with his fist.

"Open this door, you hag!" he shouted in a deep and drunken voice.

A frail trembling woman unlocked the door and let him in. She moved out of the way and kept her head down as he stomped past and sat at the old kitchen table by the door.

She was thin from depression and destitute with little more than rags to cover her. Her eyes clung to dark rings above her cheeks as one reduced to a life of continued bare necessity.

With slurred speech he shouted again. "What food have we to eat, woman?!"

She went to a wood box on the shelf and nervously brought him a plate of cold victuals she had previously prepared. He stared long into it, slightly rocking and attempting to focus. A small boy stood, afraid, against a doorway and peered around at him. Albern became angered.

"What is this?" he said in a calm tone.

His wife, nervously with trembling lips, answered him, stuttering, "Albern, I had expected you earlier...I d'didn't n'know you'd be out as long...I tried to k'keep it warm for you as long as I could."

He became enraged. "This is burnt! Not fit for a dog!" he yelled.

"Please, I am sorry...I didn't mean to..." she pleaded.

"You tryin' to poison me? You tryin' to make me sick?!"

He threw the food against the wall and grabbed her by the hair. She screamed out and the boy hid in fear. Albern stood to his feet and drug her straight through the adjoining room to a small door that was battered and dark.

"No! Please!!" she screamed.

He threw her to the floor inside and turned to the wall. Taking up a thick leather whip, he stretched it in his hands and slammed the door behind him.

Through the door, the boy heard the man beat her without mercy. Her screams were unendurable and blood curdling. He stood, quaking with terror, staring at the door of the closet room, unable to do anything. His mother screamed so terribly that he turned and ran out of the flat into the dismal hall. The boy frantically beat upon two other doors that stood nearby.

"Help! Help!" he cried desperately. No one answered him and he turned down the stairs into the street.

He traveled around a block to the main street and found two London constables walking together in the light of a street lamp.

"Help! Help, sirs!" he shouted.

They followed him to Albern's door and pounded on it with clubs. The boy hid down the hall against a door, watching in fear. The officers heard a woman scream deep inside the walls and then become silent. They took hold of the knob and found it to be locked. They beat hard upon the door and were ready to break it in.

"London Police! Open the door!"

There was a moment of silence and the door swung open wide. Albern stood sweating and breathing hard.

"What is this?" he said to them in a whining voice, angry.

"You Albern Partridge?"

Albern tilted his head back with wide eyes. "That depends…what is it to you?"

The London policeman stared at him with a look that could kill. "You're disturbing the peace."

"Who says?" he answered slowly with building indignation. Albern staggered, holding onto the door frame. His wife came from behind him, pulling a Shaw up over her arms and neck. Her face was red and her eyes were swollen from tears. She pretended nothing was wrong, but could not hide her shaking.

"What's the matter, constables?" she said calmly.

"Madam, are you well?" the officer asked.

She snorted and laughed. "Why wouldn't I be?"

The constable looked at Albern. "You come with us."

"Whither to?...and why?!" he shouted furiously. He backed away from them.

"We are arresting you for household disturbance," the officer said, stepping forward across the threshold.

Albern became enraged. "By what witness?!!"

The two officers grabbed him and the three men began to wrestle to the ground. The woman screamed in horror. Albern put up a great fight and the men fell back against the eating table.

Albern shouted as he tried to get loose. "Unhand me! I know the commissioner!" He raised forward and punched one of the constables in the chest with so much force that he flew back against the dinner plate shelves and broke them.

The other law officer smacked Albern across the

head with a truncheon and he went to his face on the floor. They got his hands in shackles behind his back, pulled him up under his armpits, and dragged him out the door into the hall.

They passed by the boy who was pressed into a door frame, shaking. Albern, who was dripping with sweat, realized it was him who had brought the police.

"You," he said to the boy softly while trembling with rage and gritting his teeth.

The boy covered his face in the door as they pulled him down the stair, face down. His mother screamed in a fit down the darkened passageway.

Chapter 3

$\mathfrak{I}$t was the six o'clock hour of the evening when Cecil finished his work with the other men. About fifteen of them began to head back to the farmhouse and walked alongside a large horse-drawn cart stacked high with hay, carrying their grass hooks over their shoulders. One black man, with a deep and handsome voice, sang a slow song for the men to hear. They were silent in contemplation and listened intently to him as they walked along, weary at the day's end.

> *"How good is the land to give us its increase*
> *By the sweat of his brow God blesses a man*
> *One woman, his helper to make him with children*
> *And The Lord to bless them and make them to stand"*

He began the chorus, which he sang in a higher register.

"The steps of a good man do not seem so easy
But the steps of a good man are solid and true
The God of Creation of these He shall order
Till among all the angels we follow and go"

He hummed softly a tune in the same key and then began again, using the ending melody of his chorus.

"Would you not lean on One who can hold you?
Lean on The Lord if you've nowhere to go"

Cecil walked with his eyes to the ground, reflecting on his life and his feelings in a solemn mood.

After the men had finished with closing for the day, Cecil strolled along the simple double-tier wood fence to his favorite place, carrying his sack over his shoulder. He made his way to the old tree and discovered Davey sitting in his usual spot ahead. Cecil made his way to him across the field.

"Hey there!" Cecil called with a smile.

"Hullo, Cecil!"

"It's becoming quite common now to find you here!" Cecil said playfully as he came near. "Like me!"

"I've been waiting for you."

"Have you now?"

"Yes," said Davey.

"Whatever for?"

"Come and sit," said the boy with excitement.

Cecil got down to the roots beside him.

"To day I received a Merit Award for a science study that I did!"

Cecil got a big smile on his face. "A science study?! Well done! Why, that makes me very proud to hear indeed!" he replied with sincere appreciation and admiration.

"Did you ever receive one of those?" Davey asked.

"No, I did not!...not as clever as you, Davey!" He rubbed the boy's hair and messed it up. Davey smiled. "It is good that you excel in your studies. A man's life is more livable when he is an educated man. With hard work and determination, your dreams will certainly come true," Cecil said with a short nod.

"Maybe I'll become a sea captain! Ha!" the boy exclaimed.

"Ha! I think not! Keep your feet on dry ground and only write the adventures in a book about it if you want my advice!" Both of them laughed and then Davey became slightly serious.

"What about you, Cecil? What are your dreams? Or, what of your brothers? Did any of them have any adventures?"

"Me? I never had any. I figure to have only a home with a loving wife..." Cecil paused. "...and a child to call my own. Maybe that would be my dream."

Davey looked attentively at Cecil, listening.

"As for my brothers," he continued, "I know not. I have not spoken to them in many years. They are farmers, merchants, proprietors of business and the like..." Cecil became dark for a moment. "...living out their lives as they will with their families, I'm sure."

"Why do you not speak to them?" Davey asked.

Cecil paused, looked at Davey, and then away. "My brothers believe that I am dead."

"Dead?! Why?" said Davey, troubled and surprised.

Cecil did not answer or look back to him.

"Why won't you tell them you are alive?"

"It wouldn't change anything."

Cecil paused again. "The world is a puzzle, Davey. It is sometimes all we can do to make reason of it."

There was a short silence and Cecil spoke again with a smile, changing the mood. "It is good you were rewarded to day for your achievements. It is not often one is acknowledged for his ability."

Davey smiled again and felt important when he was around Cecil who patted him on the shoulder.

At twilight on an overcast evening on the Old Forest Road, a horse-drawn farm cart rocked along, pulled by a single horse. One man drove it down the narrow lane through the center of a very dense and dark forest where only few ever traveled. He wore a stained and soiled hooded cloak that covered his head and face. His left hand held the reigns in front of him and his right was kept beneath the cloth, hidden in his lap. The driver brought the horse to a stop and sat silent and still. There were no sounds in that place. A distant thunder rolled over the trees above him and touched their uppermost branches.

After a few minutes alone, two horsemen rode toward him from around a bend in the road ahead. He did not move. The riders approached and halted. The man pulled the hood slightly back with his left hand, only to reveal his face. His skin was white from lack of recent direct sunlight and his dark beard was cut back into thick bushy strips along his cheeks. A curly black mustache joined his pointed chin whiskers. He was a forty-four year old incentive for substantial trouble and his appearance was a peculiar indicator.

"Anyone aware of yourn absence?" one of the horsemen asked.

The man in the cart slowly shook his head.

"Well, let's have it," the horseman said. He jumped down and walked to the driver's left side, near his seat, and began to look into the cart from the edge. Under the hood, the man's eyes were wide with anticipation. "I want to see what we've paid you for."

Instantly, the driver elbowed the horseman directly in the face and knocked him back. The man who was mounted immediately went for a pistol at his lap and got his hand on the beech hardwood stock. The driver fired a crossbow with his right hand, hidden in his lap, and the arrow pierced the man on horseback in the chest. It continued through his back and he fell dead from the saddle to the ground.

The man on foot staggered back and turned. He darted into the trees as blood flowed from his broken nose and busted mouth.

The driver jumped from his cart and chased after him.

The horseman turned over a hillside in the fleeting light and crossed over the decaying floor of the forest in the shadows. He was unarmed because of the security of the man who left his wasted body on the road.

The driver went swiftly behind and was just far enough to lose sight of his target as he turned into the dark rows of ancient pillars.

The escapee stopped and hid against a twisted trunk and held his hand to his bleeding face. He tried not to make the sound of panting for air, but in the resounding still it seemed that his efforts were useless. As he stopped, the sounds of his pursuer immediately ceased and all went hauntingly silent. Blood flowed rapidly onto his hands and would not abate. He searched for a reliable sanctuary, but there were none to resort to.

The horses stamped and snorted on the road alone, looking to each other and upon the edge of the quiet forest.

The hooded driver advanced from cover and crept over the softly crackling undergrowth with carefully placed steps. There was no movement beyond and he sought the slippery absconder with heightened anxiety. He went forward and peeled his ears from beneath his rugged hood as he stood still. The distant roll of thunder pressurized the air in the treetops overhead. He was in a hurry to get back to the unattended horses in the middle of the road and his mind went to them. As he remained motionless and ready to withdraw, the sensation of being watched crawled onto his skin.

The hunter slowly turned his head to his right and twisted with planted footing to look behind him. There, against the broad camouflage of a tangled tree, his victim stood with a raised arm.

The horseman threw a heavy jagged stone and struck the driver in the chest as he spun away and darted further into shadow. The driver took the painful blow in his stride, a pointed corner seemed to embed into his frame before it lost momentum, and overtook the man in his focused agility.

The driver knocked him to the ground and he cried out in fear. He held the man down by the hair on the back of his head and beat him in the face, repeatedly, to death with his bare fist. The murderer stopped, breathing with great labor, and stood upright. He took hold of the body by the ankle after catching his breath and dragged it over the obscure paths toward the failing light.

The road was clear and the horses lingered. Looking both ways, he quickly got the two dead men into the cart. He rolled each of them in a canvas bag and pulled a cord that cinched them closed. He removed the saddles from the horses, threw them into the back on top of the bodies, and covered everything with a large soiled canvas. The horses were quickly tied to his cart and he turned around, going back the way he came.

The cart of bodies rested inside a large enclosed smithy as two hours had passed. In the center of the room was a raised stone fire pit for heating metals. Along the rafter beams hung rope, tools, pokers, hammers, wedges, pins, and all manner of devices used to assist a blacksmith. Hugo Faulkner, the driver of the cart, lifted the canvas and took hold of one of the body bags. With relative ease, he pulled it to him upon the grime and grit that lay in the bed and stopped at a sound.

At that moment, there was a heavy knock upon the crude wooden door of the establishment - as thick as one would find at the gates of a medieval stronghold. He quickly covered his cargo, ran to the door, and pressed his face against it with trepidation.

"Who calls?!" he shouted.

A visitor spoke softly on the other side. "The road to find out."

The cloaked man unlatched the locks and slid open sizable iron bolts on the door and opened it only a few inches. A young man stood, hooded, in the pouring rain outside.

The visitor spoke again, softly. "Are the children asleep?"

"Forever," he responded with an unaffected stare.

The blacksmith handed the hooded man that stood in the dark storm outside his door a small leather pouch. In return, the visitor pushed an envelope of paper through the small opening and he took it quickly. The hooded man turned in haste and disappeared into the darkness of the night. Hugo shut the door, locked its latches securely behind him, and returned to his cart.

He grappled the body bag and dropped it to the ground. He dragged it by one end across the room to a burning furnace and threw it into the fire. The second body was then managed across the bed and pulled half way to where it bent at the waist and hung down from the edge. As he put his hands upon it for a firmer grasp, a young boy, filthy and ragged and wet from the rain, ran into his room from an opposite heavy door in the back. The blacksmith was startled by him and quickly moved in front of the open cart.

"Hey now! What is it, boy?" he shouted in a harsh voice.

"Mother sent me to help with the work."

The man remained stern and pointed to the door. "Go on now! Have your way! Your duties are spent for the evenin'! Tell your mother I will be some time yet more here!"

"Yes, sir," the bedraggled child said as he ran off.

The man returned to the cart and towed the body across the stale dirt floor to the furnace and threw it in. As he looked on, his face flickered in the light of the fire as it flared up and roared.

Outside the laboratory of Doctor Phillips, the thunderstorm raged. Water poured down the high window at the ceiling and flashes of lightning brightened the room. Thunder rattled the glasses across the tables. The man hurriedly opened the creaking cellar door at the top of the stone stairway and rushed down it. He cast his eyes upon the black wolf that paced frantically and wildly in his cage. The doctor appeared to be ill and lay back against the lower steps, staring upon the wolf with both fear and turmoil. His shirt collar was loosened and he rubbed his neck with invisible irritation. The man's eyes were changed with some unrecognizable subtlety and his face twitched, revealing several sharp elongated teeth that he could feel opening his gums.

The wolf stopped his frenzied pacing and lowered his head, showing his teeth, making eye contact with the fevered and sweating doctor. By telepathy, the wolf spoke to him in a harsh whisper.

"Release me!"

The scientist heard the wolf's hissing voice in his head clearly and was filled with frightened dreadful repentance. He lunged forward and staggered to the iron cage, guiding himself along the tables. He breathed erratically and the wolf moved side to side with fixed wild eyes. The lightning flashed throughout the room from above and thunder shook the walls around them. The man, with crazed eyes, inexplicably understanding his past victim now with new and unnatural sympathy with perplexed fear, threw open the cage door.

In an instant, the wolf leapt out, dashed over the tables, and jumped to the window ledge. He turned and looked again to the scientist for a moment with transformed convictions and busted through the window glass into the lightning filled sky of the stormy night.

The man fell back against the stairwell, violently trembling as the rain water traveled deep like a river down into the sewer drain of the cobblestone street outside.

Chapter 4

$\mathfrak{M}$inister Eckelhorn stood in the pulpit behind the podium and delivered his sermon to his Sunday congregation. He was an austere man since birth, which coupled appropriately with his occupation, and deeply regarded the significance of an honest life. The attire of his weekly recognized priesthood was a robe in draping black segments lined with gold Pekinese stitching; from afar only a subtle embellishment, but undoubtedly praiseworthy within close inspection.

A peaceful settling emitted as he read from God's Word. Cecil sat still as he listened, wearing what he usually wore, clothing that would agree as work attire. Upon searching the room, he noticed the young lady again, who was listening intently to the message, and then brought his eyes downwards to the floor.

"Then came Peter to him, and said, Lord, how oft shall my brother sin against me and I forgive him? Till seven times?" the minister read. He paused a moment and looked up to everyone with raised eyebrows and then back again to his Bible. "Jesus saith unto him, 'I say not unto thee, Until seven times: but, until seventy times seven.'"

Cecil held his black book on his lap, which was opened to the back pages. It was a Bible and there upon the last leaf was the hand-written list of names. He stared at them with a quiet look of anger. The words spoken in the room faded away and he heard no more.

When the reverend had finished speaking, Burney Yarborough climbed into his wagon and took hold of the reigns. Cecil came to him.

"I'd like to walk, Mister Yarborough."

Burney nodded with a small smile. "Enjoy your day, Mister Griffiths." He whipped the horse and his wagon rolled away and left him.

Cecil turned and went past the side of the old church building to its backside. With genial direction, he went under the giant yew tree that had been planted in the churchyard a hundred years before and its shadow crossed over him.

Before the small white church got very far behind, a wagon pulled up alongside him on the commonly abandoned road. It was the young lady and her parents. The man upon the driver's bench was alone and the ladies were seated on a smooth board along the back behind him.

"Good afternoon, sir," the older gentleman greeted him.

Cecil nodded pleasantly.

"Allow me to introduce myself. I am Graham Windham, farm owner of Chestfield Pointe, my wife Cynthia, and daughter, Marie."

"Cecil Griffiths. Good to meet you," he responded, shaking hands. Marie nearly blushed.

"Sir, we understand that you are a newcomer to

Ramsbury Barlow and that you are employed by Mister Breggins?" Mister Windham said politely.

"I am, sir," said Cecil.

"We would like to extend to you a welcome to sup with us to day, whereas you may ride with us and I shall deliver you to your abode after. Would you do us the honor of accepting, sir?"

Cecil glanced to Marie and she smiled and looked down. "I will," he said with a subtle smile.

"Very good. Climb on," Mister Windham said cheerfully.

Not far off, Davey walked across the churchyard alone and saw Cecil ahead. He raised his hand to call him, but did not as Cecil climbed aboard the wagon and rode away. Davey was disappointed in missing the opportunity to speak to his friend and in seeing him with a young lady.

The day was a calm and lovely one. Cecil was entertained with much enthusiasm and conversation to which he learned much of the history of Ramsbury Barlow. He took a short walk with Marie at her father's approval and request over the vast property while the food was in preparation. She was intrigued by Cecil's sometimes poetic nature even though he was usually very quiet and kept his feelings private. She made him somewhat nervous for the simple fear of getting to know someone new with other purposes in life, dreams, and her young age. She was from another world; one of brotherly love and respect - one that he thought was foreign to him.

The Windham acreage possessed a treasure that was well hidden and yet sprawling. A rich vineyard of many grapes created an enchanted walk through lanes of trellises overburdened with bountiful clusters of fruit. It had been a while since Cecil had seen an atmosphere so pleasant and it made him smile.

"My father does nothing more with these than simply savor their beauty," Marie said. "He is not concerned with their worth as goods, but rather an avocation intended for personal pleasure. He does not let them become part of a chore to which they would be spoiled, but of something that he is free to merely enjoy. It is his secret and that thing that he holds for his own."

"He has accomplished something of great cost, more than the cumulative gold reserves of man could buy," Cecil remarked, pondering them, but then turned to her with implication as he spoke slowly. "...A hidden rare jewel without measure of value." She looked at him and understood his meaning with a red face and admiring smile.

In the evening, Cecil sat to dinner with the family in a modest farmhouse, invited for a second meal after spending the day at the Windham Farm. As they spoke together, the sun began to set and darken the landscape outside. The table sat beside windows that looked out to the barn that was situated across the farmyard. As the master of the house put food onto his plate, he established conversation.

"It was mid-winter in Roddendale when Misses Windham and I first met," he said. "Our fathers had business together when we were yet children - mine, a farmer with many acres of property and hers, a wagon-smith of impeccable skill. As fate would have it, on a journey homeward from the city to deliver grains for the storehouses, the wagon we rode upon deviated from the lane in the snow and was rent upon an embankment of stone. The horses were even pulled to the ground and struggled to stand again. My father and I traveled alone and were thrown into a great drift of snow and were miraculously unharmed. As my father hauled out the horses, we discovered the front wheel axel and its housings were crushed and our means of transportation was ended. The temperature was quite cold and for good fortune, another wagon came immediately by. As my father stayed with the horses, I was taken to the wagon-smith to bid for his assistance. When our Samaritan discussed with Mister Edwards a resolve for our situation, I saw who would be my wife for the first time, standing in a doorway peering back at me."

Everyone at the table smiled.

"She was a tiny thing," he continued, "ten years old with very long curls and I the same age. I will admit to it now, but not then, that I thought she was beautiful. Cynthia's mother quickly took me in and set me to food and warmth as the men went to recover my father. As I very gratefully devoured my plate, the little girl sat at the table and stared at me as I ate. Some years later, our paths crossed again when I was a young man and she remembered me. This, in turn, led to the conversations that ultimately brought us together. Thank God for a broken wheel axel on a snowy lane and an over-curious little girl."

Everyone laughed, but Cecil became somewhat reflective and solemn.

"I say that even now, to this day, she still watches me when I eat to be sure that I'm getting enough." Again they laughed, but harder than before and the host posed a question. "A truly notable man would oblige her, would you agree, Mister Griffiths?" He said with a joking smile.

Cecil nodded, smiling, as he ate and then revealed his thoughts with a gentle melancholy tone. "The story of how my father and mother met was told to me for what seems so long ago that, sadly, I do not remember it. But I do remember something - When I was young, my mother became seriously ill. Thankfully, it was a passing affliction and she recovered, but during that time I could see my father's suffering in his devout and unwavering love for her. I knew then that if something had happened to her he would not have recovered and would not have returned to the same man. Their affection was never plainly demonstrated as I was a lad, but it was something quite deeply sensed and understood by us all." Cecil paused for only a moment as he looked down to the table. He spoke softly and slowly. "I've hailed from northern England and have never married. The lines of work I have adhered to in my life never allowed for much discovery in such deep affections. Even years after I had struck out on my own as a young man, I have always yearned to go back and relive those feelings that pervaded me by my parents. I feel that in your circumstance and in mine that the effective power of love can cross over all reaches of distance and time to fulfill its purposes."

Mister Windham smiled with much admiration as he looked upon his new guest. "I can see that there is some good in you...Cecil," he said with a nod.

Marie looked to Cecil and radiated with a beaming smile.

Fatefully, at that moment, there was a long and terrible squeal of pigs in the barn outside. The farmyard was dark. Graham quickly spun in his chair and gazed out through the window behind him. A piercing squeal of a pig came again from the barn.

"Cynthia, my gun! Marie, fix a light!" he shouted in worry.

Immediately, everyone leapt from the dinner table and the women ran from the room. Cynthia returned in only a few short seconds with her husband's flintlock musket and Marie brought to Cecil a lighted lantern.

The men bolted from the front door with speed into

the night and could hear the noise of tormented pigs inside the barn. Graham threw open the swinging barn door and Cecil followed close behind with his light raised.

Graham was in the lead as he and Cecil ran up the center aisle of the old barn in the dark. Immediately, straight ahead of them, inside a pen filled with dozens of large pigs, a massive wolf-like humanoid creature raised fully up on two legs holding an enormous two hundred fifty pound squealing kicking pig in its teeth.

The monster stood eight feet in height and was completely covered in long dense brown hair. Its head possessed the exact features of a brute wolf, but its body was similar to that of a giant man endued with tremendous muscle mass. Long hard claws protruded from its brawny fingers and immediately roused dread upon those who witnessed it. Its legs and feet were shaped like that of a wolf, but its hips were developed in a way to where it would stand upright like a man.

Graham and Cecil's mouths dropped open in total fear and amazement. Graham, trembling, quickly brought the gun to his shoulder and fired. The burning powder flared over his hands, lighting the men's faces, and the shot ripped over the pig's back, splitting the skin, and struck the creature on the cheekbone.

In an instant, the giant wolf roared in pain, dropped the mutilated pig, and jumped over the stall gate towards them; not killed by the direct hit to the head. As the beast touched the ground, Graham, with no time to react, turned the gun in his hand and attempted to defend himself with it as a bludgeoning weapon.

Cecil dropped the lantern to the ground and got hold of a pitchfork that was exposed in its enduring fire – the closest thing at hand.

The wolf creature swiped across Graham with its left arm and threw the gun from his grip to the hay loft far above and behind them.

"Cecil!!" Graham screamed frantically.

As Cecil ran forward to help him, the beast continued his motion and slashed Graham across the neck and face with the long claws of his right hand - ripping them open and killing him instantly. At that moment, as the wolf was twisted in his swing to his left, Cecil stabbed every prong of the pitchfork into the creature's rib cage and pushed it in to the foot with all of his strength. The monster roared out in agony and brought his right arm down, straightening his body, and pulled it out with one quick continuous motion. The wolf yanked on the pitchfork, pulling to his left, and Cecil did not let go. He bit down on Cecil's forearm and ran him backwards into a wood wall, smashing it down, while punching and throwing him with the backside of his right arm like a doll.

The back of Cecil's head was the first thing to break the stall. He landed inside on his back upon a pile of scattered straw among the broken chunks of lumber. He lay completely motionless and his eyelids were closed and did not twitch.

The beast pivoted and quickly came upon him with malice when Cynthia's voice resonated from outside. The wolf looked upon him in the jumping light of the lantern that burned nearby for only a short moment and turned away, toward the barn doors to escape.

Within the dining room of the Windham house, Marie stood, nervously watching her mother walk closer to the barn through the window.

Cynthia held a flintlock pistol and crossed the farmyard towards the barn with fearful tension.

"Graham?! Cecil?! What's the matter?! What's the noise?!" she shouted.

Marie watched her mother walk slowly around to the other side of the barn, out of sight. She waited anxiously for what seemed like an unnatural amount of time to hear from anyone. Looking side to side in surmounting worry, she could not bear it any longer and stepped out onto the porch. She searched in all directions where she stood, afraid, and heard nothing. In the light of a Full Moon, she reluctantly ran forward across the farmyard to see. As she neared the barn doors on the other side, she heard her mother's buffered screams on the air. She immediately walked up on the wolf creature that was standing over Cynthia's dead and bloody body. It was breathing heavily; the sound of its long draughts ripped the air - and dripped with blood.

Marie screamed with horror as she turned and desperately ran to the farmhouse. The creature dove forward and chased her with unimaginable speed as she got to the porch and put her hand to the door knob.

The wolf drew near with short bursting growls as it ran on all fours like an ape; closing twenty feet away in his massive stride and then jumped at her.

Cecil lifted his head and rolled his eyes as a shrill scream penetrated the walls behind him. He dropped his head and blacked out as the sound pierced that of the squealing pigs and echoed and echoed in his ears.

Graham Windham's farmhouse was silent and nothing moved as the sun began to rise. Cecil opened his eyes. He lay in the same position. Painfully, he lifted his head and felt the back of it with his left hand. He stared at his hand and saw no blood, but discovered that his arm was injured and covered in dried blood; appearing to have been bitten by some large animal. He suddenly remembered what had happened.

Immediately, Cecil sat up and cried out in fear. He hurried to his feet and stumbled out into the aisle way in the first light of morning that came through an open barn door. He turned and saw Graham's bloody body lying on the ground where he was attacked. He went over and shook him and realized that he was dead.

Cecil ran to the farmyard and came upon Cynthia's body immediately outside the barn door. He softly cried out in fear. He turned towards the house and, as he got to the porch, found blood slung on the doorway. Marie's body lay just inside the threshold, covered in blood. He entered, quickly rolled her over, and found that she also was dead.

"No, no, no...Marie," he said softly in deep sorrow for the young girl. He looked over the room as he held her head and did not know what to do. He rubbed his forehead with his bloody hand in intense debate and shook. Rage flashed over his face as he was choked with immeasurable grief and dread. He was a newcomer to that place. The impossibility to explain it and fear of having his secrets discovered, forced him to leave her there uncovered and cold. He carefully, with deep regret and escalating indignation for his decision and for fortune, laid her head to the floor, rose, and turned to the door. He looked upon her sweet face and knew that it was too good to be true.

He dashed out to the well and pumped the handle. Water flowed into his hands and he washed his arms and face of his and Marie's blood. He tore a piece of cloth from the tail of his shirt, tucked it back in, and wrapped the bite injury completely. He stood, trembling, then ran off in fear, down the lane and away as the sun was climbing.

Cecil ran through the fields and lanes on the way to

the Breggins farmstead without slowing. He ran in despair. He ran to stay and not to leave. If he would only make the cart he knew that he would be safe and sound. With desperately summoned strength, he ran for nearly twenty minutes and came up on a split in the road. Ahead, he saw the farm wagon full of men coming up the road toward him. A partial feeling of relief came over him and he slowly walked to it for some five minutes while catching his breath with level composure. He jumped onto the back as he was covered in sweat, alongside the other men that took the transport to work with him each day.

"Hey now, a good morning, Cecil!" one of them said softly.

"Ready for Monday?" asked another.

"It's good you're here...there's much of me work that needs doin' to day!" one of the older men cracked.

Men laughed as they rode along to Mister Breggins' farm - some smoking pipes, some whittling wood.

"Are you awake this morning?" a man beside him asked.

Cecil turned around, partially. "Am I ever awake in the morning?" he replied with a serious tone and face.

The men laughed out.

"What have you done to your arm, man?" another worker beside him asked.

"Uh...I was bitten."

"Bitten?!!" all of them exclaimed.

"A dog," Cecil said plainly with no expression.

"You out'ta teach 'im some respect! And you?! What you expect?!...takin' from his bowl again?!"

Everyone laughed hardily and a few men around him patted his shoulders. Cecil nodded quietly, distracted, and subtly trembled, staring off to himself in worry and fear.

Chapter 5

Le Club Des Haschischins was loud with laughter, music, and carrying on at night in London. French women prostitutes, dressed accordingly, were drinking with the men and some sat on their laps. A man played the piano in the center of one end of the room and a crowd gathered around him, singing a drunken song. One of the men sang boisterously like the others as he held a small glass of clear liquid in one hand with his other arm around the shoulders of a woman.

> *"Forty days we were aboard the wine filled ship - the Misty Lynne,*
> *and there each night we floated on the liquor of the Chinamen,*
> *but after all I came to shore, and put to work upon dry land, ...and boy, Oh boy how it was dry!,*
> *I turned around and signed away my soul to sail upon the Misty Lynne,*
> *and now my troubles are sunk to the bottom of the sea of licorice root gin,*
> *And I hope they never swim again as I drown...down...down."*

Everyone in the place laughed, cheered, and tipped back their bottles and glasses. The whore with the man turned to him with her powerful seductive manner amidst the clamor.

In a soft alluring voice she said, "What about you, Jack Todd? You want to go down with me?"

A drunken smile grew slowly across Jack's face and she led him through the bustling room into a dimly lit golden hall with red velvet tapestries pasted against the upper walls. Her hair was auburn in color, pulled up into a bun on the back of her head and her eyes were an irresistible blue. She wore makeup on her face reminiscent of Asian culture past and was a woman that did whatever she wanted.

Jack was a thin man, but not underweight, used to the constant substances that would abuse a man's physical betterment. For forty-three, he was an effective man of the night and was for as long as he could remember. His lifestyle did not abide without requiring its tax and he did appear older than his age. In order to continue with the youthful temptresses that had him wrapped around their bejeweled fingers, he would keep his beard removed and shaven cleanly. His face was generally a happy one in mingling with his kind and his days were spent waiting for the nights. There were no week ends and no week days for they all melted into one day after another day. It was all he ever knew or cared to.

Within the enticing décor of the sex and drugs room of the brothel, the whore made herself comfortable and removed her outer jacket. She turned a key in a locked wooden case on top of a mahogany credenza of unparalleled extravagance - richly bestowed with bronze sculpture portraying cherubim among grapevines and drawers fastened with cornucopia fruits. Inside was an opium and hashish pipe that was fashioned into the form of a dragon. She lit fire to the deep blue Cloisonné enamel lamp and puffed the smoke into Jack's face. She passed it to him as they sat in pleasure upon a beautiful green chaise.

"And down we go...," she said, drugged and slowly, pressing her face against his cheek.

Jack smiled with smoke flowing from of his nose and mouth like the dragon himself. "..Down into the darkest sewers of London..," he said.

The mixed drug burned in the pipe and the fire turned to gray ash.

A police carriage rolled up on Graham Windham's property early in the morning. There were several officers combing over the yard, searching for anything that may have went unseen. The commissioner of Ramsbury Barlow borough, a stout heavy gentleman with bushy bands of grey whiskers on the sides of his face, stepped out and met his lead officer near the body of Cynthia.

"Good God," he said softly with confounded pity as he approached her.

"Triple murder, sir," the officer stated with reverence.

The commissioner looked down and sighed in frustration as the officer explained the situation.

"Cynthia, Mister Windham the same way in the barn, and his daughter lies in the parlor of the house," he said.

The commissioner blinked his eyes hard and sighed

even greater. "Mercy of God," he said under his breath.

"We are dumbfounded," the officer continued. "Could it have been a beast of some sort?"

The commissioner was dismayed and shook his head. "You certainly have me, constable."

The officer turned and walked him to the house while pointing. "Not seen the like in all my years. And to come through a door like so…with the carnage to the victims...Too large to be a dog…and wolves have long been eradicated here...A man would be out of the question, likely."

There was a short pause of thought before the Ramsbury Commissioner spoke again. "Nevertheless, I'll notify Commissioner Howe in London," he answered.

The officer nodded as he looked down upon the corpse of the young woman who had been sliced across the chest.

At ten o'clock that morning, a police carriage pulled up and stopped outside of West London Police Headquarters and an officer stepped from it and went in, carrying a letter.

Commissioner Morton Howe sat at his desk in his private office, a lengthy room with very tall windows reaching from floor to ceiling situated on the building's corner as well as the street. Along the walls on two opposite sides was an expansive library of books with much wood shelving and design to house them as well as promote display. He was well lit by natural light as his tall English tenné draperies were usually always drawn. He wrote on legal forms with pen and ink when there was a knock on his door.

"Enter," he responded.

The courier officer appeared in his room and spoke

with a courteous nod. "Commissioner Howe."

"Officer Lotney."

"I have word from the Ramsbury Commissioner."

He handed over an envelope.

Morton opened it and read the brief message written within…

Commissioner Howe,

Greetings to you, sir. There is a triple death at Windham Farm, a location 5 miles outside of London. Mister Graham Windham, his wife, and daughter have been killed. We know not the cause as of yet, but will keep you posted as details emerge in our investigations. At first glance, it appears to be from a wild beast, but in the probability of something more sinister, I thought you should be aware.

Signed,

Commissioner Belamie ~ Ramsbury Barlow ~ 4th Watch Division ~ England.

Commissioner Howe quickly scribbled down a quick note on paper and gave it to the courier officer.

"Thank you, Officer Lotney. Your message has been recorded. If Commissioner Belamie should require my services they are at his disposal."

"Thank you, sir. Good day," the officer responded with a nod. He turned and left the commissioner alone.

Morton looked up from his desk and gazed out his window in thought. He wrinkled his brow, baffled by its strange quality.

Upon completion of the work that evening, Cecil immediately made his way back into town. He walked briskly and distrustfully looked side to side into the surrounding trees, curves in the valleys, and hills around him. The shadows appeared to move and take tangible forms. His eye was always pulled away to seemingly unnatural threatening shapes in the landscape. He was uneasy and did not want to be going alone, yet did not want to be with another. He pressed with an urgency to get to his room, a business that was long overdue, and did not stop or go his customary way.

Near sunset, Davey stood tossing a leather ball into the air, alone, and looked down the lane and over the fields for Cecil, but he did not come.

Cecil entered his room at the end of the hall and quickly shut the door behind him. He turned up the gas on his walls and light moderately filled his room. He was afraid of what he would find after neglecting his wounds for so long in concealment. There was a knock on his door after a short moment. He opened it to Mister Holling who entered with the teenage boy, carrying a large wood tub to bathe in. They placed it in the middle of the room. The boy stepped into the hall and returned with a large tin bucket of hot water which he dumped into it and then went out again for more.

"Good evening, Mister Griffiths," said the innkeeper with a nod on his way out.

The boy immediately returned and poured again into the tub. He bowed, respectfully, and exited the room, closing the door behind him.

Cecil began to quickly undress, nervously, from his filthy sweat-soaked clothing and climbed into the tub. He was perspiring with anxiety and dunked his bitten arm into the water. He gritted his teeth and breathed through them with bursts as he examined the wound with a trembling hand. It seemed partially healed, but a call for a doctor was not an option. He splashed water onto his face and stared down, motionless, into his wavering reflection.

The Saint Mary's Church of England Schoolhouse was an ancient structure. Built of flat stone and brick in 1622, the steep roof was gabled and coated with Collyweston slate limestone shingles. There was a tooled stone wall that encircled the yard which was very busy with children running through it during an after-lunch recess. Around the side of the moss covered building, in the shade of a large oak tree, several boys were gathered, including Davey.

"Did you hear?" Ralph said, whispering to the others in a circle.

"Hear what?" Michael asked quietly.

"Ol' man Windham and his family are dead!"

"Dead?! What happened?" Howard said, amazed.

"...and his daughter, Marie," he continued.

"You lie," said Alistair.

"It's true. Me dad told me. He heard it. Someone killed all of them on Sunday!"

A teacher walked around the side of the school house building and caught them.

"You lads return here at once!" she shouted.

The boys ran off, but Davey stood alone – still and in disbelief, staring to the ground, wide-eyed and reeling in disordered thought.

℧he Ramsbury Commissioner approached Doctor Stratton in a great open laboratory of study within Saint George's University of London. The space was lofty with every type of preserved specimen known to science along its walls. The place had quite a history, in use for some one hundred years, wherein men of medicine and zoology pried at their curiosities. As he drew near to an examining table in the center of a corner prepared for lecture, the doctor pointed to a mutilated pig's corpse upon it.

"What is it that you can reveal to me, Doctor Stratton?" the commissioner said to him with serious intent from the stairs that he descended to reach him.

"Commissioner Belamie," the doctor started, "it would seem to one practiced in the discipline of zoology that the bite marks are the direct result of a brush with none other than a beast of the Canidae family...the genus: Canus."

"I beg your pardon, Doctor?"

"A wolf, Commissioner…and a rather large one I suspect," he replied, poking along a row of bloody puncture wounds in the pig's dead flesh.

"That creature? …Here?"

"My argument exactly, sir."

Commissioner Belamie sighed and stood silent. He could see such large holes penetrating deep through layers of fat and muscle; large enough to spy into without assistance or prodding.

"If it were, could or would such a beast be expected to set itself against a family and execute such devastation?" he inquired, troubled for such a question to come from his mouth.

"We are yet to find out, I'm sure, Commissioner Belamie," the doctor responded as both men looked upon the carnage inflicted to the shredded and gutted animal.

The field workers assembled together and sat along the lengthy tables in the open yard of the farmhouse ready to eat when Mister Breggins made a grievous announcement.

"There is ill news that I must relay, gentlemen. Mister Windham of Windham's Farm, not many miles from here, was found dead…he and his wife and daughter. They were murdered."

The men began to speak among themselves in complete amazement.

"At this moment there are no answers for how or by whom this evil has transpired. There is some speculation that it was by some wild beast. I would ask of you to keep yourselves alert when in the field for any such suspected creature. Our prayers go to the families affected," he said, saddened.

Cecil, whose face was grim and angry, stared upon Mister Breggins with a cold gaze. The men around him began to talk and become anxious, but their words were blurred to him.

ℭommissioner Howe rode alone in an unmarked police carriage through the countryside, leaving London. He proceeded past forests, ponds, quiet homes, and many open fields as the sun traveled to its place in the late evening hours. He thought of his wife and her happiness with recent events regarding the settling of the home and it made him smile. Images of her dressed so beautifully for the dinner balls that were expected later in the year took turns in his mind and it made him pleasantly anxious. He wondered what he would be without her; if he would have even amounted to so much in so little time. When they were not together she was still with him in heart. He wanted to see her, but there was always a call to business.

Forty-five minutes into his journey, he entered the door of the Ramsbury Ale House and Commissioner Belamie stood from a distant table to greet him. The place was somewhat filled, but the patrons were merrily reserved.

"Commissioner Belamie," he said as the two shook hands.

There was complete darkness; the kind so heavy it made sound. A small scratching came from the blackness ahead. Cecil was afraid and stared into it with disturbed wonder. He stood from his bed and moved forward into its void, but he himself was illuminated in light. He slowly came nearer to the soft scraping sounds that seemed to be right in front of him. He went deeper and deeper toward them in foreboding, knowing that there was something black-hearted behind them, like a strong voracious dog on the other side of rice paper.

Immediately, an enormous black face of a wolf jutted from the darkness with a deafening roar.

Cecil jumped awake on his bed, breathing hard and exuding great drops of sweat. He pulled up on his sleeve and looked upon the bite mark on his arm. It was nearly completely healed and gone. His hand burned and he turned it over. In his grip, he realized, was his father's harmonica.

Cecil quickly dropped it to the floor and it spun to the foot of his bed. His palm had what appeared to be a subtle burning rash in the faint shape of the harmonica. He held his wrist in his other hand with a grimaced face of pain.

He sat up and then stood to his feet in agitation and ailment. He turned and stared at his hand and then upon the harmonica by the bedpost. He wondered why. After getting into his clothes, Cecil quietly exited the front door of the Watermill Inn unnoticed and turned out into the street in the night.

Commissioner Howe and Commissioner Belamie sat in a booth against a wall quietly speaking. Two nearly empty glasses of pale lager sat before them on the table.

"It was something I have not seen before," the Ramsbury commissioner said softly. "Even some of the hogs were mutilated and eaten. This leads me to believe that we are dealing with some wild beast. It seems by its size quite possibly a lion in nature...but with the calculating vengeance of a man...most puzzling. Upon further examination by a doctor of science, we have possibly concluded that it was some type of large wolf."

Morton's face changed and he was shocked to hear such a conclusion.

"At this moment, I have nothing else that I can believe," Commissioner Belamie said. There was a moment in which he went silent in his thoughts. "The location of the Windham farm made it impossible for neighbors to see or hear anything...even under the circumstance. He had even fired his gun," he reported.

Commissioner Howe looked at him with a new and greater surprise, but immediately, upon closer concentration had no theories to suggest.

"Our search for further clues has turned up empty," Belamie continued. "The residents here are afraid to go out at night I am sorry to say. The Windham family...just massacred. I don't know what to think of it. Perhaps it will be something familiar, commonly encountered right under our noses or perhaps it will be something that no one has ever imagined, save in some godless nightmare." Commissioner Belamie sighed and looked to his glass. "I pray this one is promptly resolved and the damnable, worthy of condemnation, are dealt swift judgment."

"It is all of us who are guilty. There are none innocent," said Morton with a meaningful look into his old friend's face.

Commissioner Belamie looked at him with a half-smile and became silent. Amidst an understanding nod of his head, he snorted softly with no small agreement with Howe's words.

"We are forced to live in such evil times," Belamie responded.

The men paused and took another sip of their beer

as they ran out of probable suggestions or further words that they felt to describe the theories and actions of man.

"How is Julia?" Commissioner Belamie asked solemnly, changing the subject.

"She is well. Her sister came into an inheritance and has bought her new furniture for her reading room," he answered with a short smile.

"Oh, very good."

"It was something that she desired for quite some time and I am very happy for her to achieve it."

The men paused a moment again and Morton finished his drink.

"Dispatch any details you further acquire and, as always, you'll have my total involvement if needed," Commissioner Howe said with a reassuring nod. "If there were anything relevant to surface on my end I will be sure to inform you."

"We are threshing all leads with paramountcy."

"The night waxes. Best be on my way, Floyd."

Commissioner Belamie nodded. "It was good to see you again, Morton. It's been a long time. I'm sorry under such terrible circumstances."

Commissioner Howe stood, shaking hands, as his company remained seated. "My love to Rosalie." He turned and walked around the bar into a small coat rack foyer room, the entrance to the Ale House, and placed his hand on the door.

As he did, it swung open wide to the outside and there, holding it open, was Hugo Faulkner. The men stopped in their tracks and stared at one another eye to eye without moving. Neither man spoke as they stared for a moment, seemingly startled. Commissioner Howe then moved through the door, Hugo watched him as he passed, and both men continued a little longer on their way.

At the witching hour, the city was totally silent. Only the wind of portent blew through the gathered council of whispering brick chimneys on the rooftops, delivering the hand that would write upon the wall. A half moon hung above in the night sky and Jack Todd was unlucky enough to be having his life beneath it.

Beside him in deceit was Tisiphone, one of the three Erinyes, guardian of the gates of Tartarus, punisher for crimes of homicide, disguised as the blue-eyed harlot and clothed in a blood-wet dress of red scarlet.

"Come now, Jack," she said sweetly. "Come with me to see the Witch of Strasbourg. She is travelling with her wares to briefly visit London."

"A witch?" said Jack with suspicion. "What they got a witch doin' in London?"

"A medium, Jack. She's quite harmless," she laughed at him. "People been doin' it for centuries and its catchin' in France, I hear."

He smiled, being somewhat disarmed by her beauty.

"She speaks to the dead and it'll be fun, Jack. She won't be here long and I want to go."

"But you're not allowed to go," he answered with a small tease in his truth.

"You can take me. We can sneak away through the back hall. I know! Let's chase the dragon there, Jack. Ha!"

A smile grew on his face and he liked the idea of it.

"How terrible would it be to go for that?!" she laughed with licentiousness. Her smell alone had gained mastery over Jack and he would have followed her with spellbound enchantment into the very caverns of sheol.

"You, my liberal temptress, have persuaded me," he smiled while kissing her hand. "Lead me to thy ghostly lairs of manipulative bidding."

After the two of them ceremonially conjoined by the fires of the old serpent's breath, they slipped away out the back and made their way, laughing, to the privately hosted and privately disclosed parlor of Madam Brouilouille.

They were quietly hoarded into a haunted foyer lit by candelabrums of many rows after their payment had been procured. The living seekers of the dead waited with them with silent folded arms and crossed knees like made up corpses in caskets in a home where time was clicked out in seconds by the echoes of a mantle clock. Jack's object of his brooding kept her hand on his lap with a smile as they were called by the hostess.

"Come. It is time," the woman said with a pale smile. She wore a white flowing gown and held the single flame of a candlestick as she led the group of five into a dark door situated at the resolution of an ominous hall. As she stepped, it was lightly and floating like the specter of a murdered woman calling sailors to weep with her upon soundless waters. They followed by her flickering orb that caused the shapes in shadow upon the walls to reach down and try to take them.

The intrigued customers, by direction, were seated at a round table that was comfortable enough for a hand to be taken on each side. The kerosene chandelier above them was at unrestricted brightness, but was soon to be smothered for the reassuring of the spirits. To their fascinated concern there were two dolls that lay flat on their backs together in the middle of the table. One was in the form of a young man, dressed in plain brown breeches with a buttoned overcoat and the other was a young female in an ordinary cream colored dress with a dark blue kerchief that was pulled over her dark brown curled hair. Both had large painted eyes within fixed lids of attached eyelashes and stared up at the chandelier as if they were waiting for something to happen.

Their necromancer entered the room as the hostess curtsied away into the mysterious paths and shut the door behind her. She was an older woman in her fifties with a large build, not dainty or frail, and her light raw umber brown hair was very abundant. She held it in giant pinned loops all over her head and around her neck, over her snow white muslin gown, was a deep blue scarf with long threaded fringes.

"I am Madam Brouilouille, communicator to the spirits of the dead," she said with her French accent and only the slightest hint of a smile. "I welcome you. We will commune with those who have passed before us and seek of them solace, answers, and guidance to good fortunes. They are our eternal lights that oversee us from the beyond and our beacons to navigate us into safe asylum."

The guests looked to one another with stimulated enthusiasm and Jack smiled nervously in his inconspicuous intoxication at his partner at the table.

"The dolls are instruments to which the summoned spirit will bridge with us," the medium explained. She went between two at the table and took hold of each one. "They are not attached to strings or managed from beneath your table. To assure you that I have not tampered with them I invite you to touch them and inspect them thoroughly to your satisfaction and confidence."

She passed the dolls around in opposite directions and the witnesses turned them about in their hands with much amusement.

"Place them in the center and we shall commence," she said. "I will sit in this chair behind you and you shall see that I do nothing to interfere."

Madam Brouilouille reached to the chandelier and turned the knobs at each flame and snuffed them out to individual vacillating wisps like tiny dancing apparitions. Their faces went dull and all would have been darkened but for four remaining lights upon candles that were placed in each corner of the room.

"Ladies and gentlemen please join hands with the person beside you," the medium said from her velvet chair. "We shall now call them." She took a deep breath and breathed out slowly and everyone was silent in expectation.

"We sit here in unity to call upon any spirit of the near present or long past that wishes to speak to us," she started with her eyes closed in meditation. "We wish to speak to you. We wish to hear from you. Will you answer us? Will you speak to us now?"

There was no sound and the guests stared upon the dolls and upon each other in suspense. Madam Brouilouille continued, but in a louder voice.

"We wish to commune with the spirits of the dead. Will you speak to us and grant us your direction?...For we desire it."

Immediately, in the yellow light of the candles, the male doll began to wiggle and move. Everyone's eyes widened in fear and delight. It slowly leaned forward at its waist and sat upright with its strange eyes. Jack and his companion's face lit up with astounded grins as the surreal scene was greatly enhanced by their influenced frames of mind. The doll levitated upwards as if pulled by a string and its legs straightened beneath it. It quietly hovered in mid air a few inches above the table and stayed completely still. The sober guests thought to seek out an invisible string of fraud, but found none.

"I sense that you are a male spirit," said Madam Brouilouille. "Who are you and what is your name?"

A timid voice of a young boy came from the open mouth of the doll with long echoes as if from bottomless tunnels.

"My name is William," it said.

The onlookers gripped each other's hands in amazed disbelief, but genuinely knew it was no trick or hoax.

"How old are you, William?" she asked softly.

"I am ten," he said nervously in a sorrowful voice. "I don't 'ave a light and I can't see down here in the dark," said the frightened boy.

"Is there any way you can get a light, lad?" asked Madam Brouilouille, tenderly.

"No. They won't let me. It's too dangerous down here. It could cause an explosion. It's so dark and...and ...I'm frightened."

"Don't be frightened, William, we are here with you now. How did you get down there?"

The doll did not move as it faced the witch and the voice whispered through from a hollow deep.

"I'm a trapper. I sit in the darkness in the tunnel of the coal mine, alone, against a trap door and when I hear men comin' up with a cart of coal on the track I open it for 'em. You can't stand in here, the tunnel is too low. The men who push and pull the carts have to keep their heads down under the cart to shift out. I am alone in here with me thoughts, hour after hour 'fore I see anyone again, and I can't see me own hand in front of me face in this god-awful dark."

"How long have you been down there, son?"

"Do you think I could come out?" asked the boy in a whine.

"I would like for you to come out, William. My name is Madam Brouilouille."

"Sshh! Wait now!...somethin's movin'!"

The witch stopped and listened quietly.

"I got a ghost down here with me on the other side of me door. I can hear 'im in the dark. He's faint, but I can still hear 'im," said the voice.

Everyone became even more frozen than they were before.

"I'm afraid of him, Madam B, he's from the very down deep. He's from down further than the others in my tunnels. He never comes up so far. Not whiles I've been in the tunnels."

There was a pause from the voice and they waited.

"He says he has no cart of coal to bring through, but wants me to open to him so that he may come out."

Madame Brouilouille prepared to speak and before her words were exhaled the doll spoke.

"This one knows Jack," said the little boy and the doll turned slowly as it hovered and faced the one it had indicated. Jack's smiling face instantly fell away and he was afraid.

The witch looked to her consorters. "Do any of you go by that name?" she said softly.

Jack did not move and kept his gaze fixed upon the eyes of the conscious doll that had deliberately sought him with a pounding heart.

"His name's Jack," said the woman that brought him there.

The others in the circle looked at one another and marveled with wide eyes.

"Let him out, William, so that he can speak to Jack. Jack is right here sitting beside me. It may be important, William. Will you let him out so that Jack can speak with him?"

There was no sound from the doll and the room went silent.

"William? Are you there, child?"

"Yes."

"Can you open your trap door for Madam Brouilouille and for the ghost? It may be that he means no harm at all. Maybe he wants to help Jack."

"He scares me. I don't want to."

"Maybe you should have no reason to be afraid. We can do it together. Will you try for me, William?"

"Yes."

"Very good, William. That's a wonderful boy."

Everyone sat in razor sharp captivated anticipation and did not move a muscle as a candle quickly sparked and stuttered behind them causing some to nearly jump.

From the mouth of the little distorted caricature of a human a long echoing creak came from the door in the darkness. Everyone at the table held on with sweating palms and breathed loud in the air of the room. Jack tried to gently pull his hand away from the woman who relished in his torment, but she would not let go and gripped him tighter.

He did not want to know any more. He wanted to leave. He had his fill and his fun, but was ready to go before it was a terrible mistake. It was not his idea to come there to the witch. He wanted it to be over and he trembled in great drops of sweat.

The distant boy cried out with a terrible scream and was quickly silenced. His voice ran away, far into the chasms of the earth, alone. Immediately, there was a long hiss that came from the mouth of the smiling toy.

"Raaamseeey!!!"

Jack Todd fell back in his chair and broke from the circle. As his body disconnected the chain and his shoulders hit the floor, the doll fell dead to the table in a heap. As he leapt from the chair and ran for the door, he screamed out and frightened everyone nearly to death.

"Leave me be!!!!"

The circle, as well as Madam Brouilouille, stared on the spectacle in horror. Their mouths hung open in complete surprise as Jack tore away at the door and dashed from the house as fast as he could go.

The strumpet gasped in excited and entertained surprise and then distantly watched his exit with a cold-blooded face and vacant lifeless eyes that were something not of this world. In the near darkness it went unnoticed.

Morton Howe rode alone inside his carriage by the moonlight down the road to London. As it rolled along, creaking with the movement, he was startled by a sound in the nearby forests that closed in on each side. He pulled his flintlock pistol, spooked by the conversation he just partook of, and nervously stared through the windows into the soulless mists.

Cecil went far on foot and walked the dark London city streets in some unnatural insomnia, but things were different in his perception. His sense of smell was greatly enhanced, delivering to him the stagnant rot of the sewers below the ground, the unnatural putrefied fluids that dried into the cobblestone crevices, and the faint implication of things that were dead and under the ground far off in some macabre place. He wondered if his senses were truly heightened or if the city was more leavened with gross offence than its usual obscenity. He could trace the scents of baked grain breads and fish entrails, body odor of coster mongers and spices of the departed food market that had been in some whereabouts earlier that day. The perfumers' artistry accentuated the amalgamation with separate choices of bergamot, rose, jasmine, clove, labdanum, and ambergris; all of which left their indisputable mementos on the midnight air. It was unmistakable. He could smell the embodiment of these things like an invisible but tangible trail that led through the dark.

Private conversations were no more left to the discretion of their partakers. Their uninhibited flair rose with contempt against their solicitors and lovers through the windows far above him as if he were standing within their chambers.

Dark shadows were no longer covert and willingly confessed their revelations. With robust clarity taken from dismal ash, Cecil was armed to make the starlight his instrument of instinctive perception.

It was odd to him, but he knew that the bite had what seemed like a mysterious and valuable effect. He wondered what would continue to transpire and at that point felt no fear to find out.

In the night, he looked beyond and two men appeared in a dark alleyway a city block away at a very great distance. They spoke to one another softly in a whisper and Cecil could hear them.

"She comes. Get her."

Cecil turned his eyes ahead and saw very clearly in the dark, a woman walking quickly to get to her home. She left the main street and turned into another course, nearly running to get where she was going and Cecil could smell her fear. One man in the darkness retreated into a door and closed it behind him and the other ran off into the shadows.

The attacker, who was wearing a top hat and long coat that disguised his features, appeared in the same alley as the woman and charged her. She cried out, turning away in panic as Cecil swiftly ran past her, coming towards them both at a great unnatural speed. The stalker's eyes widened in amazement and, unknowingly, his mouth dropped open.

Cecil hit him like a bull and snatched him up by the throat in one motion. He was twice as big as Cecil, but it did not matter. Cecil lifted him into the air with little effort, ran him backwards with overwhelming strength, and pinned him against a brick wall. Cecil's eyes enlarged and he gritted his teeth, testing himself and his power.

The man reached into his coat pocket and uncovered a long blade and tried to stab him. Cecil caught his knife hand and squeezed the man's fingers against the handle, keeping him from letting go. He twisted the knife upwards and pressed it to the man's face. Slowly, for the sake of his own amusement, he nudged the tip into the skin and jerked his arm, causing the man to slash open his own cheek. He pulled him forward and beat his back against the wall until the breath was knocked out of his lungs. Cecil dropped him to the ground and took him by an ankle as he gasped for air. He turned and sprinted up a wood stair at the side of a building to the rooftop, brutally dragging the man backwards behind him. Knives, surgical scissors, tourniquets, and a scalpel fell from the man's pockets through the steps as they went and clanged to the ground below.

When Cecil reached the top, he bent over and ruthlessly beat the man in the face with his fist and nearly incapacitated him. He grabbed him again by the foot, walked him thirty feet to the edge of the roof, and dangled him upside down over the side with one arm. A large crate sat against the wall in the alley far below. Cecil raised him higher, slapped his face, and wrapped his other hand around his victim's throat and squeezed. The man was barely conscious, but quickly revived as Cecil choked him. With wild vengeance, he looked down on him and spoke in a whisper as their eyes met.

"You will not try to touch a woman again...if you do, I will find you and kill you."

Cecil forcefully threw him downwards with both hands. His hostage fell two stories and broke through the crate at the bottom with his head. He was knocked unconscious and the compression to his neck nearly killed him.

Cecil stood above, looking down with the wide eyes of unlimited power and executed judgment, breathing hard with fearlessness within. He was new, reborn in a light of superior strength and absolute control. His options had changed and he knew exactly what he would do.

He quickly remembered to look around to see if anyone had witnessed him and then ran away into the incognizant darkness.

Davey went toward his house in the evening, walking down the dirt lane after his day of schooling had ended. He did not see Cecil anywhere ahead and was wary and went cautiously. He did not know what he would say or do if he should see him and a greater part of him did not want to find out. The tension was too cumbersome and it was unbearable. As he got right upon the tree where Cecil normally sat, Cecil came around from the other side.

"Davey!" he said cheerfully, happy to see him.

The boy jumped back, frightened, with wide eyes. Cecil became puzzled.

"What's the matter? You look like you've seen a ghost."

"Oh, n'…nothing," said Davey, nervously. "You startled me."

"I'm sorry," he said with a chuckle and then became sincere. "Do you not have an escort that can carry you home each day? Must you walk alone?"

Davey was troubled by the question. "Why is it you ask?" he said with uneasy suspicion.

"Never mind it. There is no reason to concern yourself. A mere observation," Cecil responded. "It would not matter. I am faithfully along your path if there was ever any cause to need someone," he said with a confident smile. "Have you gotten along? How do you fare?"

Davey gave Cecil a serious and somewhat apprehensive look into his eyes. "Well.....Cecil."

Cecil sat down on the tree roots and Davey watched him. "Come now. I have a story for you to day. One you are sure to enjoy and remember…that is if you'd be in want to hear it?"

"Yes," Davey answered in doubt, curious to know what it would be about now in light of recent events. He remained standing and kept a short distance which Cecil did not notice. The confidence that had been an indispensable part of their relationship was, sadly, now shaken.

"Once, long ago," Cecil began, speaking slowly and softly as he stared off over the gentle hills that lay still in front of them, "a fellow went to market to buy fish for his family. When he was nearly finished with his business, he looked and saw, tied to a cart, a small dog, barely weaned and blind. He, for some unknown reason, had compassion on the thing and determined within his heart to purchase him and take him home to his son. 'It's a useless thing,' the merchant said, 'You can have him for nothing.' So the man took him home and gave him to his boy. The man's wife was amazed and said, 'What will we do with this thing? What is it good for?' 'I do not know,' the man would only say, 'but there is something about him.'"

Davey sat down beside Cecil, unarmed and emotionally involved with the story.

"After some years went by," Cecil said, "the man and his wife were pressed to journey to a neighboring town for three days and they left their son behind. As it happened, in the night while they were away, the house caught fire and burned as the son slept. He was pulled from his bedding in a room blackened with smoke and dragged to the ground. It was that blind dog that had found him and pulled him along the floor, down the stairwell…and into the darkness of the farmyard."

Davey listened intently in astonishment.

"It was the blind dog that saved the life of that man's son."

Cecil looked down to the ground in a thoughtful moment of silence and then spoke. "Sometimes…it seems…there is a reason for everything."

Cecil took a small twig and drew circles in the dirt at his feet as both weighed the story.

"Who was the boy?" Davey asked, like his curious self again. Cecil looked up to him with a sentimental and sad smile.

"He was my father."

Davey had a very small half-smile and stared into Cecil's face very intently. The look in his eyes was somber even though he was cheered by the story. He slowly looked down to the ground, never sensing danger or anything other than straightforward honesty, while in his uncertain and intermingled thoughts.

Eaton Barrett was now a man of integrity. At this phase in his life the days were busy with raising the seven children that depended on him and his wife. All were beneath the age of eleven and he thoroughly enjoyed the experience. He even believed it changed him.

Sarah, his wife, was the daughter of a poor farmer in northwestern England and he met her in mass of all places. He had been affiliated with the occupation all of his life and she seemed to be cut out for him. They had met seventeen years before when he was twenty-nine and she, twenty. He was an easy man to love by everyone in his household and he did well to always keep it that way.

Eaton's farm, a couple hours' travel from the bustle of London, was a simple and ideal place to raise them. It was built by his own hand for he had no family to lean on and he was proud of that. He stayed with friends of the church for one whole year as the construction of his house was in process. Soon upon its finish he met her and it could not have been better timing. He knew nothing of interior decorating and did not have the time to be concerned with it. During their courtship she devised its comforts from afar and by the time they were married it was ready for her to enjoy.

Profits were made by renting out acreage to nearby dirt farmers as well as the sale of his own production. The operation was not in large proportion, but was humble and fitted neatly with the number that he was concerned with. The fields were not going anywhere and he set down his design and would work it for as long as he was able.

The turnout was unexpected and not something that he would have imagined early on, but it suited him - the new him. His present was reminiscent of the good past, but that was another life and he never thought about it.

As the girls were with their mother, he and his three young sons determined the well being and time of harvest for the endless fields that circled his plot. They stood by him and he gently pulled away a portion of corn husk and exposed the plump yellow kernels inside.

"We look for the corn borer on the underside of leaves. First, I inspect the three leaves above the ear, then one at the node, and the three below the ear for evidence of eggs," he said, pointing, as the boys looked up and listened. "I also inspect for young larvae feeding on the leaves or leaf axils and the leaf collar. If these worms infiltrate the crop, they will tunnel into stalks and bore into the developing ears, ruining them."

He then gave them an eternal lesson within his instruction. "It is important that a man be ever watchful for anything that would try to come and destroy what he has sown. There will always be an enemy that seeks to devastate the work of your hands...and sometimes it will succeed."

The boys followed their father away, mounted the farm wagon, and were returned again to the yard.

"Go on and play. Inform your mother that I will be some time more in the field at work and will return when finished," he commanded them.

"Yes, father," the boys responded in obedience. They climbed down and immediately went running like wild animals over the grass.

"Mind your mother!" he shouted to them with a smile. He gently whistled and tapped the horse with the reigns and she pulled his wagon away.

He went on, down a lane that was cut alongside fields of corn, alone. Not very far from the house, just out of view over a small hill, he stopped. Eaton climbed down and went walking over a pleasant path of grass in the sun to a nearly completed project of white quartz stone. His tools were already alongside it: shovels, hammers, chisels, and a dwindling heap of material. It was something that he had been secretly working on for many weeks as his time allowed with much joy. Its placement was perfection. He took up a trowel as his thoughts were upon her.

In an hour of final touches, he stood and admired the beautiful work of his hands with a smile of deep satisfaction. He climbed into the wagon and rolled away to reveal it.

She was alone behind the house hanging the wash to dry on the line.

"Sarah," he called her gently.

She turned and smiled at him.

He held his hand to her. "Come with me."

He led her quietly away from the house, down the lane to the secret path. She had no idea what was the matter.

Her eyes lit up in complete surprise and wonder as she discovered a private sitting bench of smooth stone under a shading arch of sparkling quartz on a hillock that overlooked a vibrant flower garden. She began to weep.

"You did this for me?" she said softly.

He nodded with a smile and put his arm around her waist as they both gazed upon the many variations of oranges, pinks, reds, and blues that emanated from below.

"When did you do this?!" she said, enthralled.

"Whenever I could steal the time for it."

"This is one of the most beautiful things I've ever seen," she said in tears.

"It is for you alone; a secret place away from the children for you to enjoy."

They went together and sat under the shade of the arch and she laid her head on his shoulder.

"Whenever I sit here," she said, "I'll think of you."

𝕴n the afternoon of another day, Cecil and Burney worked alone together in the expansive loft of Mister Breggins' hay barn. Men down below were raising large bales up to them by a block and pulley system that was mounted high at the center of the barn ceiling. Burney stood at the ledge with two large bale hooks and pulled them to him. Cecil, who stood twenty feet away, took them from Burney and stacked them in the spaces for rotation. Both men worked hard and quietly together and only the sounds of the many workmen outside the barn were with them in the loft.

In an instant, the block and pulley system, which was housed in a large metal box above, broke away from the beams it was bolted to and immediately swung down on the ropes towards Burney. The thing was enormous and made of solid iron. Almost quicker than Burney could see with his eyes, Cecil ran in, pushed him out of the way, and turned to his side, bracing for the impact. Burney flew backwards and landed on his back on top of the hay against the barn wall. As he did, Cecil used his shoulder and rammed into the massive iron box as it swung down and broke it into a dozen pieces with an awesome boom. Burney raised his arms up over his face and cried out.

Cecil turned to Burney in fear, breathing heavily and trembling with wide eyes as he stood within the rubble and a huge cloud of smoke-like dust, unharmed and fixed. Burney looked to him, amazed and shuddering.

"Oi!" the men yelled to them in dismay from below. "Hey now! Are you men alright?! Is anyone harmed?!!"

They scrambled up the ladders on all sides into the loft and found Cecil pulling Burney up by the hand. All were astonished.

"This could have crushed the both of you!!"

Cecil remained looking into Burney's eyes as he lifted him to his feet and spoke. "We were fortunate to have rolled clear of it...out of the way," he said.

Burney kept hold of Cecil's hand and stared into his eyes in awe. Cecil pulled his hand free, descended a ladder, and went out of the barn. Burney watched him as the men went over what happened. He followed and found Cecil standing alone outside against the side of the barn and approached him.

"Our God has saved us to day," Burney said, strongly and shaken. The two men stared at each other eye to eye, face to face. "See the good in that."

Burney continued to look into Cecil's face for a moment more, deeply longing for him not to fall and then turned, keeping his caring gaze upon him to reach his soul, and walked away into the barn with sorrow.

Cecil's face at that moment reflected the fathomless discouragement and sadness that had been there since the death of his innocent youth. Effective hope for his life and for all had faded within his heart.

Near dusk, Cecil was alone in the goat fields of Mister Breggins' property, rounding up the last of them into their sheds to be safely locked away for the night. From somewhere within, he felt a deviating desire to kill one and eat its raw flesh as he walked among them while no one was around. He was confounded by the momentary thought and his human nature forced him to ignore it.

As he settled all but thirty, a strange sensation overcame him and he stopped what he was doing. He walked out from among the animals and turned, casting his eyes towards the tree line that encroached upon the land beyond the fences. He spun around slowly as he searched and there, standing only fifty feet away, was a lone gray wolf, crouched and growling, showing its teeth. The beast had come from afar, searching for what had turned out to be a man.

Cecil returned a threatening glare and breathed out slowly with something of a growl and a hiss under his breath. He quickly lowered his head, keeping eye contact with the wolf and the animal growled even louder.

The wolf was confused and then immediately felt fear of Cecil and backed away, turned and ran, jumping the distant fences into the forest.

Cecil stared on with his head tilted downwards with a low growl and a huff on his breath. His face reflected a formidable hatred and his glaring eyes flashed with memories locked within a blazing, unforgiving, and unquenchable rage.

Chapter 6

$\mathfrak{T}$he sky was darkening just moments before an evening storm. Seven boys stood upon the backside of a hill near the forest on the opposite side of their house which was some distance away. Alphonse, the oldest, who was seventeen years of age, shouted to three of the others.

"Hunter! Ramsey! Washington! Grab him and strip him down!!"

Five of the eldest took hold of one boy, who was age ten, before he could run and tore his clothes from him.

"No! ...No! Stop!" he screamed in horror.

Simon, who was nine years old and the youngest of them, watched on and said nothing in great fear.

Alphonse took some thin cord that he kept in his hand and they began to tie the boy to a tree trunk at the lower edge of the hillside. Hunter and Ramsey pulled the boy's arms and forced him to hug the tree with his chest held against it along with Morris' help. Alphonse and Washington wrapped him round with cord across his back and legs and tied him standing upright with his buttocks exposed. His back was not turned to them, but he stood sideways and was able to look upon his tormentors.

"Let me go!" he pleaded as he struggled to free himself and run away.

All of them, except for Simon, made a commotion.

"Teach him a lesson!" they shouted. "Whip him! Put lashes on the little maggot!"

"You regretful worm!" cried Alphonse. "You burden your mother with your life!" He took up a thin wood rod, a long switch he had kept aside from the forest. He stood at the boy's side and struck him across the buttocks as hard as he could. The boy cried out in pain as the others yelled and cheered.

"Yes! It is time for your lashes! Ha! Ha! Ha!"

Alphonse whipped him again and he wailed in pain, struggling frantically to get free. "It is one you're not soon to forget! The Birch rod straightens the crooked roads of a vagrant beggar! Or maybe you would rather take it like a man?!! Ha! Ha!" Alphonse cried with laughter. "We could find something more for you to enjoy in your twisted pleasure!"

"Alphonse! Let me do it! Let me do it, Alphonse!" Ramsey shouted, brimming with disturbed anxiety.

Alphonse gave the stick to Ramsey and he swung as hard as he could across the boy's legs with an evil smile. The boys yelled, made noises, and jumped up and down with heightened madness.

"How do you like that?!!...you little abomination!" Hunter shouted while laughing.

Alphonse took the rod back into his hands again and pushed Ramsey aside as they were all shrieking injuring remarks. Simon looked on petrified and his face was white.

"Beat him! Slash him! Make him bleed! This is what you deserve for being a worthless pig!"

Washington screamed, angered, and then began to squeal like one.

"The disgrace of the Harrow family!" said Hunter.

"This is no Harrow," laughed Ramsey, "This is an orphan!"

Alphonse struck the boy again with a crazed and distant depth in his eyes and his victim screamed out.

"Put one to his buttocks! Lash his legs! Make it sting! Make sure Morris and Hunter have their turn! Ha! Ha!" the boys continued to yell.

Alphonse raised the rod and pointed it at the boy's face. "You'll say nothing of this to father or mother, you putrid filth! Will you?!!" He whipped him again across the buttocks and the boy cried out, weeping in awful agony. Alphonse began to scream his words. "You'll not mention to them anything about your deserved punishments!! Will you?!! You'll take your lashes as they come! Won't you, maggot?!" He swung his arm and whipped the boy again across the back of his legs causing great swollen welts.

As he did, their father quickly walked up over the top of the hill and saw them. He stopped wide-eyed in total disbelief of what he saw.

"Oi!!! What goes on here?!!" he shouted.

The boys stood completely stunned and afraid at the sight of him. Mister Harrow instantly became violently enraged and charged them to deal swift punishment.

He got Alphonse, who was holding the rod, by the hair of his head, punched him on the side of his face, and knocked him to the ground. Hunter gritted his teeth in rage over his brother, jumped onto his father's back, and began to continuously punch him with flying fists. Mister Harrow fell forward to the ground, rolled, and landed on his back. He grabbed Hunter by the throat and stood, throwing him to the side on the ground. Alphonse screamed and charged him, tackling him by the waist and knocking the man again to the ground. All of the other boys, except for Simon, jumped onto their father and beat him.

The boy that had been abused at the tree, in a panic, began to shake and writhe frantically and the cords became loose.

Morris punched his father in the face and his father knocked him in the head. Mister Harrow took a beating and, in the process, elbowed Ramsey in the chest, nearly knocking the breath from him. Some of them got up and kicked him while others landed blows to his face and head.

Alphonse was pushed away and rolled back onto the ground and saw a large rock. He crawled to it on his knees and picked it up in a blind rage. He raised the stone into the air and hit his father on the side of the head with it, killing him instantly. Just as he did, at that very moment, their mother saw it from the hilltop as she came to investigate the puzzling sounds. She screamed in horror and turned to run.

"Stop her!! Stop her!" Washington cried.

"Get her!" screamed Morris to drive in the order.

The boys quickly got to their feet and ran after her as complex lines of lightning struck the fields in front of them.

The restrained boy screamed after them from the bottom as they went. "No!...Mother!! No!!!"

The woman tripped and fell to her face. They got her by the legs and dragged her backwards, face down, and she screamed with unimagined fright.

The boy worked himself loose and ran naked to the hilltop as another bolt of lightning struck the field and heavy rain began to pour down upon them. He stood, violently trembling in fear and cold, as they beat and then strangled her to death in front of his eyes.

"Stop it!!! Stop!!!" he screamed with everything in him as he wept aloud in abysmal groaning.

They turned with wild eyes and saw him there against the dark sky. Simon stood beside them as a mute witness, watching in shock.

The boy immediately turned and ran away into the forest and they jumped up after him.

"Kill him!" Alphonse shouted.

The rain beat down and darkness covered the sky as the boys ran in a single file down into the forest and over the paths within. They saw him just ahead among the heavy growth in the jagged threads of light and ran with great speed as their fugitive sprinted for his life.

He cut away from the path and ran hard. He was frantic and tried not to cry out, but grunted in pain, running barefoot blindly through the foliage. His feet were cut and stabbed with poking sticks and sharp stones as he covered ground quickly like a hunted beast in the darkness.

He ran over the side of a hill, deep in the forest, and the others were close behind. He turned and looked behind again, only for a second, and tripped. He quickly caught himself and went feet-first down a long steep slope and was unable to slow his momentum. In the rain that flowed, he slid down over a concentrated patch of slick ivy leaves that hid the mouth of a deep well at the bottom. He fell through the ivy cover into the hole below and caught hold of the wall, six feet down from the top. He cried out during a blast of thunder and was not detected.

At that moment, the boys ran past the opening of the well above from another direction. One side of the rock well was pressed against the hill and the opposite side was exposed. It rose three feet above ground, but was densely covered and nearly completely hidden in ivy.

Alphonse stopped running, alone and not far from the well, as the other boys kept going in the downpour and disappeared. He leaned forward and put his hands on his knees, trying to catch his breath. He looked side to side, scanning the dark shapes in the trees for movement, and the rain beat loudly upon every leaf of the foliage around him. Lightning lit up the top of the rock well and he noticed it.

Alphonse turned and quietly went and looked upon the ivy that covered the mouth. He put his hand out and quickly yanked it to the side. Thunder cracked over his head and lightning flashed as he and his younger brother, who was clinging to the inside wall, stared at each other face to face just six feet apart. The boy had a look of utter terror on his face as his bare legs dangled down into the cold darkness beneath him.

A new look of calculating madness migrated into Alphonse's eyes and he immediately dove for the boy's hand.

The boy let go and fell into the deep dark with a cry. He went all the way down and hit the bottom and plunged to his stomach in a cold viscous black muck of mud and grime which broke his fall. Rain poured down the walls and he could see Alphonse thirty feet above in the multiple bursts of light.

The other boys came running and looked in beside their oldest brother, panting. Lightning scattered around them and they could dimly see the boy up to his waist in the mire far below.

"There's no way out'ta there," Ramsey said, staring down with no emotion. Water poured over the boys' faces and ran from their eyelashes in continuous streams.

"He's stuck," said Hunter in the elevated noise of the beating drops of the forest.

Alphonse took hold of a heavy stone lid that lay up against the wall and tried to lift it. The other boys knelt down and helped him get it up over the rim as Simon watched them and was afraid.

"Simon!" Morris shouted. "Push!"

The young boy stepped in on Morris' end and helped him slide the stone lid into place as if he were in a dream.

Their brother watched from below in the darkness, the lid moving over top of the hole, sealing him inside.

The boys backed away twenty feet from the well and Alphonse stopped in the downpour, breathing heavily. "We'll have to change our names...and we cannot see each other again." He looked each one of them in the eye. "Take what you can from the house. After tonight, we do not return."

The boys turned and each one of them ran, up and through the fatal paths of consequence that led them away.

Lightning revealed a small crack in the upper wall of the well beneath the ivy. Below, the boy reached up and tried to take hold of the rough stone edges of the wall around him and pull himself out, but could not. Panicked, he tried desperately to get his legs free. Water flowed down the walls on all sides and started to rise on top of the muck around his waist. Faint light flashed down to him from the tiny crack in the wall above ground and he saw a large hole in the side of the wall where water began to flow in quickly. He sank his arms down into the mire and pulled on his legs to get them out. As he struggled, he cried out, but could not get free. The water quickly rose up his chest to his neck and then over his head. He stretched his face upwards to breathe until the level closed over his nose. He inhaled a final breath and went under.

The water climbed two, three, four, six feet over his head rapidly and his writhing and twisting worked his legs free in the dissolving grime. He kicked in the black sludge and swam upwards to the flashes above. His face broke the surface, still very deep in the well, and he gasped for air. It was not possible to cling to the rock wall no matter how hard he tried and he treaded the water as it rose.

Slowly, he was elevated to the crown, the water pouring in all around him. Gasping, he repeatedly tried to get a hold of the slippery ledges that had been coated in slimy mud over time.

The water took him to the very top and his head touched the stone lid. It continued to rise and his face was pressed against the bottom of it.

Finally, the water level topped off, leaving him with no more air to breathe. He drew his last breath and slipped down deep into the darkness that claimed his soul.

Chapter 7

The moon finally became full in a clear July night sky on the edge of a small town outside of London city. HUGO FAULKNER~BLACKSMITH was written on a metal business sign that hung out from the roof and swung lightly in a soft wind.

In a barn, near a forest on the backside of the property, Hugo's wife walked the center aisle. A lantern lit her final chores at the opposite end from the doors as she put things away for the night. An unkempt and thin woman, she had disregarded the duties of adornment for herself, being scraggly and rough. She had been with her husband for many years and he, in the line of work that he was, rubbed off on her in neglectful appearance. She had given him a son and the lad was an obedient child; the singular fruition of worth.

Inside were four horses, but two of them were put in the last stall at the end of the barn near the hanging light. She went to the post, took the lantern into her hands, and raised it to the pair that was boarded together.

"What am I gonna name you two?"

She had a malevolent look on her face as she turned upon the doors to leave. After she had traveled halfway through the barn, she heard a creaking of wood under pressure. She stopped in her tracks and slowly pivoted to look around. She saw nothing in the light or in the shadows and raised the lantern high to look up into the hay loft on one side.

Dimly, in the darkness above her, a black werewolf's angry face appeared. His eyes only slightly glowed orange in the lantern's light.

Hugo's wife had her back turned to him below, then spun and looked again upwards, but saw nothing in the dark around her. She lowered her light, thinking no more of it, and went out of the barn, latching the doors behind her.

Hugo hammered away on a piece of hot iron in his smithy. The clank of metal to metal sparked fire against his soot covered apron and the harsh sound bounced off the ceiling overhead. The iron tip bent around the end of the anvil to a precise curved point and he dropped the hammer to his bench.

The boy ran in to him, distressed and shouting.

"Father! The dogs are gone!"

"Gone?! What you mean?!" he answered, severe and angered. "Not on their chains?!"

"Their chains too!" he cried.

Hugo stopped and stared at him for a moment as he sank into determining thought. He immediately removed his apron and threw it down, got into a shelf at the wall, and took his musket gun.

"Wait here!" He turned and went through the door in the back.

Outside, in the yard beside the forest, he walked to the area near his house where the dogs were kept. Their shed was empty beside two iron posts in the ground connected to short links of broken chains. He stepped out from them into the middle of the yard, looking toward the trees and listened. In the quiet of the night, he heard whimpering far off in the forest. He brought his gun to his shoulder, entered in, and then heard it again.

He went quickly toward the sound, but it became quiet in the trees and nothing else moved to signal him. He continued straight in as he searched and came upon his pair of Rottweil butcher's dogs hanging by their necks from neighboring trees – their chains wrapped over the broad lower limbs. In shock, his eyes widened and he pulled his gun to his shoulder and spun around, ready to fire. He took only a split-second moment to scan the area and saw nothing. He quickly lifted each one, unraveled them from their chain nooses, and dropped them to the ground. Both animals were dead. He stared upon them, afraid, and then immediately looked up in the direction of his house.

He ran back, leaping over the fallen timber and debris of his winding path. Into the smithy he went with shouts to his son.

"Get to Master Taft's place!" he said as he opened the door to the yard and pointed. "Run! Stay there until I come! Go!"

The boy looked at him, afraid, and ran off as fast as he could into the night.

As soon as he disappeared into the dark, Hugo turned to his house in the instant thought of his wife. In the moonlight above, he saw the black werewolf crouched on the roof of the porch, staring at him. He drew his gun to his shoulder with severe trembling and fired as the wolf turned and smashed through an upstairs bedroom window. Hugo's wife let out a blood curdling scream from within.

"Helena!!" he cried.

He dropped the spent musket to the ground and reached for a large sickle just inside the door on the wall. He sprinted over the yard to the front door of the house and busted in, splintering the frame. In the dim light of the front room, he ran forward, clenching the curved blade in a tight grip. As he flew, he heard his wife scream beneath heavy thuds against the floors and walls upstairs with the reverberation of wood being smashed and broken. He dashed up the stairs while everything was being destroyed in the bedroom ahead of him. Helena screamed out again as he kicked the bedroom door twice and broke it in.

As he charged into the room, his wife flew past him sideways through the air and smashed into the vanity mirror against the wall to his right. Everything on top of it was shattered and her legs missed knocking over an oil lamp by inches. She was killed on impact, breaking her back and neck. Her body dropped to the floor in the broken fragments on the vanity's left side, away from him.

In the Full Moonlight and two kerosene lamps that remained undamaged, Hugo saw the black wolf creature standing at the other end of the room. He threw the sickle at it over-handed and it flew, spinning through the air. The large curved blade stuck into the wolf's neck and shoulder and the beast roared out. As he did, Hugo dove for the vanity drawer, pulled it open, and with his left hand, grabbed hold of a pistol, backwards, with the barrel facing him. With his right hand he took hold of the kerosene lamp and slung it at the wolf.

The wolf deflected it with his left arm and the lamp shattered on the wall beside him, lighting the wall and drapes on fire. As he did, he swung his right arm across the other oil lamp on the night stand at his knees. It flew across the room and smashed on Hugo's arm and body, lighting his shirt on fire.

In an instant, before Hugo even had a chance to turn the pistol around in his hand, the flames ignited the powder and caused the flintlock gun to misfire and shoot him in the hip.

Hugo cried out as the gunpowder burned around the hole in his flesh and bright flames rose up into his face. He turned in pain and fright to run away. The enormous wolf jumped against the side of the wall by the door and pushed off it, caving it in. He landed directly in Hugo's path and caught him.

The wolf threw Hugo with such tremendous force that he flew over the room, smashed out of the second bedroom window, and landed in the yard below, taking glass and window framing with him.

The wolf took hold of the sickle by the handle that stuck out of his shoulder and pulled it out. Blood squirted from him in a wide spurt over the ceiling and floor.

Hugo rolled in the grass and got to his feet quickly. He limped along as his hip poured blood and tore off his burning shirt. He dropped it to the grass behind him, running for the door of his smithy as fast as he could go. His face and arms were sliced and bleeding from the razor shards of broken glass and he could feel the sizzling shot burning inside his body.

He slammed the back door of the smithy and locked it. He pulled long iron bars across the top and bottom that acted as dead bolts, quaking with cold terror. Just as the last bar penetrated its mark, the door was punched with incredible force from outside and violently shook with a deafening sound. The chains and iron tools on the walls and around the door rattled with tremors. He fell backwards to the floor in surprise and turned to the big hearth of hot coals burning in the center of the room while the wolf continued to beat upon the door outside.

Hugo took up a long sword-like shape of iron from

the coals with a red-hot tip and ran to the door. He held it out in front of him and it shook in his fear. He stood, breathing with rapid succession and the assault upon the door stopped. All went silent and there were no other sounds except the crackling of coals and wood in the fire behind him. He stood and waited, hoping the thing was gone. He looked side to side and then to the door, backed away and turned around to discover the front door of the smithy was slightly cracked open. His heart dropped in despair and nearly melted inside him as he ran to it and slammed it closed. With short quick strained breaths, he worked every latch and lock all the way down, expecting an immediate blow upon it to jar his hands.

He backed away, looked to the other door, and limped around the room, staring at the walls and listening for sounds outside. At the hearth of fire in the center, he attempted to quickly examine his gunshot wound. He pulled out his trousers and saw blood running down his leg from a hole in his flesh. He pressed his hand against it. The blood flowed through his fingers and he gritted his teeth in pain.

The wolf stood up behind him, beside the hearth, and roared out with terrifying intensity. Hugo spun around and nearly fell, stunned, and saw the eight foot tall black-haired werewolf creature illuminated in the bright fires of the smithy. Hugo trembled and backed away, raising the sword-like shaft of iron. He swung it side to side in a defensive manner and the wolf stood still, looking down on him. The beast turned his head away and glanced to the hearth. Another piece of red-hot iron lay in the fires and he looked again to Hugo. The wolf growled low, took hold of it, and showed his teeth in a snarl, humoring him.

The wolf held the red-hot tip out and slowly and deliberately pushed it towards Hugo and watched him.

Hugo swung his blade and knocked it away from him in fear. The wolf did it again, but this time as Hugo swung to knock it away, he raised it high and the man missed, swinging at the air. Hugo moved his feet and put the hearth between him and his terror.

The wolf looked down onto the coals and then again to Hugo. He stepped on a bellows at the base of the forge and the flames rose up between them. He kept his eyes upon Hugo and did it again. As the fire rose up, he stuck his blade into the coals and slung them at Hugo who was shirtless.

Hugo flinched and jumped as some of the burning ambers landed on his bare skin. With intense fear, he kept his trembling weapon raised.

The wolf did it again, toying with him, and slung hot coals at his face.

Hugo ducked to the side and backed to keep from being burned. When he looked up again, the wolf was in front of him, out from behind the fire and struck down onto him, repeatedly, with the blade. He took the blows on his iron, which he held over his head with arduous exertion. As the metal clashed together, hot sparks exploded from them in all directions.

The wolf beat down again and again, pushing Hugo backwards as he hunched over him. Hugo screamed in agony as his arms were nearly broken under the jarring strains. The wolf roared in anger, his long legs shifting and moving as he swung the iron and bent downwards, wearing the man out.

The blade in the wolf's hand snapped in half from the force and immediately Hugo was pressed to the floor against the wall. He stabbed forward with the hot iron as the wolf was hunched over him at arm's length, ready to reach for him. The blade penetrated the wolf's left shoulder and sliced through and out his back under the shoulder blade like butter. It instantly seared the wolf's flesh and burned off the hair that touched it. The beast roared in pain with such ferociousness that it shook the walls and rattled the tools that were strung upon them. The wolf backed away and the blade slid out of his shoulder as he stood.

Finally in his wrath, the wolf reached to the beam above his head and took down a long rugged set of crucible tongs with four-foot handles. He looked down onto Hugo one final time and showed his teeth in hatred. With the wide-mouthed scissoring tool, the wolf clamped Hugo around the waist and threw him onto the hot burning coals of the hearth behind him.

Hugo landed across it and the wolf roared as he held him there with the tongs and stepped on the bellows. Hugo screamed as the wolf's angry eyes were glazed with spinning tongues of fire.

Cecil laid face-down at the foot of his bed. The shutters on his window were opened at the other end of his room and the white, five-thirty AM sunlight shone on him. He woke and sat up, getting his feet over the side. He stood on the hardwood floor and slowly walked to the ceramic basin that sat on top of his dresser chest of drawers. He placed his hands into the water and leaned forward to it. His face was hot and he gently splashed the cool drink onto his skin and placed his hands on each side of the chest at his waist. He leaned forward and looked at his reflection in the tall mirror that rose from it whose opening was in the shape of a headstone. There was a burn scar on his left shoulder and another going around the lower part of his neck, around to his back. As he turned in the mirror, he discovered another burn scar on his back, under his shoulder blade. He leaned in closer and stared with a cold penetrating look into his own face and could see the wolf staring at him, drawing deep breaths with a sneer in his golden eyes.

Thirty minutes later, Cecil rode the farm wagon over the fields and lanes with seven other men to work. All of them were quiet so early and kept to themselves. He stared at the backrest that ran along the other side of the cart where no one sat. His mouth was partially open, his lips were tightened in a small circle, and he licked the inside corner of his mouth. A slightly happy and sly look sat upon his face as the wagon rocked on the lane.

The front door of Hugo's smithy was open and several London police detectives searched the entire area for answers. Commissioner Howe stepped in as the burned body lay upon the hearth, away from him, in the middle of the room. Howe's face was staunch and stone as he was sickened and dreadfully angered by what he saw.

"Hugo Faulkner, the blacksmith," Detective Halsey said to him.

Officer Lanstrom entered the doorway in the back, facing the house. "Sir…" he said.

Commissioner Howe followed him into the yard toward the half-consumed house. He discovered the upper portion was burned and the roof was mostly gone. The upstairs floor was still intact as some of the side walls were partially burnt away. He and his officer climbed the charred and blackened staircase.

The bedroom was badly incinerated. The roof over it was gone and one wall facing the smithy was partially burned down. Lying on the blackened floor was Hugo's wife's body in a puddle of water. There were a few officers looking on, watching the commissioner enter.

Commissioner Howe was greatly distressed as he looked upon the expression of horror on her blackened face. Her hair was burnt off to her scalp.

"Is this everyone? Are these the only victims? Was there anyone else?" the commissioner said in subtle dismay.

"The man had one son," Officer Lanstrom replied.

"What of him?! Is he dead?" Commissioner Howe said, worried and nervous.

"No, sir," Lanstrom answered. "He was away at a neighboring homestead."

Detective Shipley spoke up. "He is outside, sir."

Commissioner Howe quickly left the burned out room and descended the crumbling staircase.

In the yard beside the house, near the forest, he came upon Hugo's son, who was surrounded by officers, neighbors, and townspeople. The men were speaking, ignoring the boy, and one constable had his hands on his shoulders as he stood behind him. Commissioner Howe extended his hand to the lad who was looking to him and afraid. The boy walked away from the crowd and came to him as the people were debating. Morton placed his hand on the lad's shoulder as he knelt.

"I am sorry for your calamity, son," Commissioner Howe said softly with a heavy heart. "I truly am. Don't be afraid now. We'll take care of you. Can you tell anything of this night?"

The lad spoke softly and sadly. "The dogs went missing and my father told me to run quickly to the Taft Farm...and to not look back, sir. I heard gunshot not long after."

Morton stared at him and took a deep breath with a look of sadness.

"When I came home again with Master Taft, sir, the house was burning."

"You saw and heard nothing more before or after this, child?" Morton asked.

"I did not, sir." The lad looked down with anguish. His lips quivered with sorrow and he fought the urge to cry.

Morton put his other hand on the lad's shoulder and looked him in the face. "Have no fear. I will find out who has done this."

The boy looked him straight in the eye, most intently, and gently nodded, but did not understand what it would mean.

Commissioner Howe stood and sent the lad on to the neighbors who gathered nearby. He approached an officer that he knew personally with an order. "See to it the lad is cared for properly."

"Aye, sir," Officer Branthrop responded.

The commissioner turned away from him and entered the door of the smithy again, past the guard of an officer. He walked alone to the stone hearth and gazed upon the body. Hugo was completely burnt except for his face, which like his wife, held an expression of complete horror. His eyelids were burned off, giving him a frighteningly grisly appearance.

Commissioner Howe stared on with a sober look. He took in a deep shaking breath and slowly let it out.

Chapter 8

The dustman traveled upon horse and cart through the streets of the city. His passage was not like the daughters of kings in gilded carriages of imperial luster, but reigned in the rotted stenches of necessity as a pallbearer of the dead. He could be sensed in his threat by smell if the wind were not favorable, collecting domestic refuse and ash, travelling the straight lines of the London trenches as an Old World dung beetle stealing his acquisition, navigating by the stars of the Milky Way. It was day by day, his routes of repulsion, tracing the unseen detestable underbelly of a giant awe inspiring and magnificent dragon. In his treasure troves were discoveries of poultry heads and feces-lined hog intestines, molding fruit rinds turned hairy gray with old age with pungent gristle steeped in rancid blood marinade, decomposing fish skeletons with offensive brain matter and eyeballs, curdled goat's milk and jellied lard, putrescent egg shells in a coagulate of unknown fatty fluids, and fragments of contaminated bone. But on this day it was a man.

"Saint Lucius of Cyrene," he said to himself, dumbstruck, "what is this?"

The hunchback climbed down from his cart, bent over in his way and went to the heaps of rubbish that corrupted the walls of the alley. It was early morning and the body seemed relatively fresh and unblemished, escaping a night of carnivorous dogs and egg laying flies.

"My my," he stated. "What has brought ye to me diocese I wonders?"

He rubbed his hands together as he paced side to side, examining it from directly overhead and only inches away. He sniffed it and put his face down close to the face and looked it over thoroughly with one good eye and one bad, which was partially closed at all times with an unworkable lid. He stuck his hands into the pockets and sifted them for any prizes and roamed to the inside where there was sure to be something. To his exceeding delight, he had fetched a purse of leather that had not been recovered and he quickly opened it to find three folds of paper money.

"What?" the body spoke softly.

The hunchback's eyes got as wide as ever and he looked upon the living dead, frozen only for a moment. "You're not a body atall," he whispered to himself in wonderment.

"What 'ave you gone about doin'?" said the body and he stared up at a repulsively unattractive man with long greasy black hair, bent at the waist and kneeling over him on one crooked knee.

"Am I dead?" the man in the leavings asked.

"Nay, sir. Nay indeed. Ye are not dead. No sir, indeed, not dead atall I should say," the hunchback answered very factually with a pragmatic look. "If ye *were* dead, you're not now, not by my watch, sir," he answered quickly, revealing that he kept only few remaining teeth. "You're still in the Queen's London, unmistakably. The Kingdom Come it is not, although some would consider it to be and some would not. I am still yet to make a decision," he said with a maimed smile.

The man below blinked slowly and had not yet fully come back from where he was to reality.

"I've almost taken ye purse, thinkin' that ye be a dead one and all."

The filthy man raised the small leather pouch and handed it back to his unusual find.

"How would the sir like a bit of food, yes, a bit of food for the stomach...get his health restored indeed, make him at evens again?"

"I *am* hungry," said he.

"Here in my cart I have a bite enough for ye, sir. Please. And I will share it with you, my friend."

The hunchback quickly went away and got into his foul gurney for the expired. In its idleness, it had gathered together many armies of the lord's flies. He returned with a tear of hard bread and a sliver of dried meat that he took from the bottom of a rolled sackcloth bag. His disabled patient accepted with a dazed gladness from the solid black and polluted hands that delivered it to him.

"Now, see, sir? I have a bit of bread and meat that will take care of you right now. Grindle is my name and happy am I to 'ave been one to find ye now 'afore some other unfortunate thing, yes indeed, sir."

The bemused man sat up from his back and leaned against the wall behind him, agreeably eating to his necessity.

"What put you here in the refuse?" said the hunchback with a good measure of heart.

"I was about, walking in the night to return home at late...and then remember no more, but this here," he answered after he swallowed his sustenance. He paused and then became inclined to admit what he knew was the honest truth and conclusion. "None other than I."

"A man should not stay out so late in the night, nay, sir. It is not good," said Grindle. "There is much lurking for a man's soul in the night. It is not good that a man should go so far to the very edges of death and look in. He should stay back and not step near the outer darkness. He should remember that he could slip and fall unexpectedly...even when he knows that he will not. Indeed, he should linger in the light and when the darkness passes by he should step back from it and let it pass by him unseen....for it may be that as it is unseen to him he may be hidden and it may not be able to find him."

The dustman was most sincere and nodded in hopes that his words were regarded by the stranger who gave him a rare opportunity to speak with another person for so long.

"A man has to keep oil in his lamp. The Bridegroom is coming soon," Grindle said with affection.

The man kept his eyes downwards and was silent as he ate and as he finished, glanced to Grindle.

"I thank you, sir, for your goodwill," he said. "I am better for it."

The living dead finally rose to his feet and seemed to tower over the hunchback, who could only stand to a little over four feet in height in his condition.

Grindle raised his arm and put his reeking hand upon the man's shoulder and turned to the side to look up to him, unable to move or bend his head and neck.

"What be ye name, sir...that I may know it."

"Jack Todd."

"I pray a blessing on ye, sir."

With a smile and a nod in the wearing of the

destructive cloud, Jack replied, "And one on you as well."

He turned and went his way and the old hunchback looked on for him in hope.

Miss Raddeford, a feme sole in her late twenties who had not yet married, taught world history in the Saint Mary's Church of England Schoolhouse as Davey sat at his wood writing desk, but his thoughts were elsewhere. He was sullen and stared into the blank parchment in front of him with conflicting emotions. He knew what he saw and he knew what he felt, but did not know what to do with them and was near to yielding to the inner struggle. There still had been no news of an arrest or trial of a killer and he did not want to be the one to report his very friend when encompassed in so much doubt. He was overwhelmed with dismay and it weighed on him constantly to the point of fighting tears. He wanted to believe in Cecil. He wanted to know that his friend was everything he imagined him to be. His thought dwelt upon him much and he was sad in the face of losing all hope in something that he loved – like a smoldering dream.

His teacher's voice echoed against the walls and traveled down into a foyer hall in the stone interior braced with dark oak beams. He was lost in their monotone color as a Saint Andrew's Cross Argiope lulled by the rhythmic plucks to its web by a preying Portia spider.

Ralph sat beside him and tapped his arm when the teacher turned her back to write the names of notable sixteenth century Spanish Conquistadors on the board.

"It wasn't a man…it was something else," he said in a whisper, leaning closer.

"What you mean, 'something'?" Davey said in surprised confusion with an immediate lifted disposition.

"Like an animal…a lion or something. Like a wolf."

The teacher turned to face her class as she was speaking and the other boy quickly returned upright, pretending to be listening.

Davey stared to the windows as he struggled with the meaning of the news and an ambiguous look, like his thoughts, both happy and troubled, moved over his face.

Cecil worked the fields in the summer heat a great distance from most of the other men. He stood, breathing hard from swinging a scythe and stared off. He wiped his mouth with the back of his gloved hand, deep in thought as the others pressed forward in a long row, harvesting the other fields of Spring Wheat. The wolf beast and the Windham family were not the only things that crowded his mind.

Everard Abraham, the only other man that worked nearby, had long since removed his upper garment in the oppressive humidity. He turned to a sweating Cecil and quickly looked him up and down.

"Cecil. Why don't you make your life bearable? Tie that smock frock around your head!" he said in observation. Everard had done the same and it had greatly helped. "It'll keep that scorching demon from sticking the hot pokers into your eyes!" he said, smiling with a nudge toward the overhead sun.

Cecil, with all of his numerous and intricate recent scars to where no realistic lie or valid explanation would appease a normal inquisitor who had seen him shirtless before, knew what he was doing.

"I'm comfortable as I am, Everard," replied Cecil with a nod and continued to work.

At lunch hour, the excited men sat lined up on the long wooden tables with their employer and scooped boiled red potatoes covered in herbs to their plates. Burney looked around for his friend at the table and afar off. He began to eat, but was sorry that Cecil had not joined him.

The detectives who had been working the Faulkner deaths for the past several days were scrambling in their case working office at the West London Police building. Boards with posted papers were along many of the walls to assist the men in organizing their pursuits. Desks were in rows front to back to allow for impromptu meetings. There was an open hall that ran along one side where Commissioner Howe entered and met with his men. They gathered around at the sight of him and sat upon the nearby desktops.

"Yes, Mister Shipley?" the commissioner asked upon being summoned.

"Sir," he responded quickly, "we believe we've uncovered a plot as to Mister Faulkner's treachery concerning the heretical Mallory and Barnes Sect. He was in league with them. A co-conspirator to the anti-establishment group, he was a stipendiary to smuggle small arms into London...not so innocent a victim. He then became a turncoat for an yet unknown beneficiary and was discovered...consequently sprouting a plot of murder."

"But why his wife?" Howe questioned.

"Perhaps revenge, sir...perhaps she was witness to her husband's affairs...and perhaps she condoned them," Shipley answered. "We could never be certain. And another odd thing... her back was broken as well as her neck...a bit excessive by anyone's measure."

Commissioner Howe appeared distressed and angry – not so much for the allegations, but for the violence of execution. He looked to the floor, scrunching his brow in frustration. Detective Shipley continued.

"We have not yet pinned down the conspirators to a location, but I am pleased to say that a segment of our beloved constables in North London have eliminated a bit of the tedious footwork for us. They have a man in their custody that was captured on unrelated charges who was accidently conferring, by a chance encounter, with a bedfellow, previously imprisoned, within earshot of a quietly passing guard...which has revealed the information that we now possess."

Commissioner Howe looked at him and clenched his jaw in eagerness to grind the prisoner into powder.

"But there is one small problem. He refuses to further disclose any more information and denies any such accusations of involvement by the meager attempts of our friendly and somewhat over-hospitable North London officers," Detective Shipley noted with a smile and he raised his eyebrows.

Morton Howe became angry. "We will route out these heretics and murderers and show them no mercy, Detective," he said and then turned and looked upon the faces of all men. "Dismissed, gentlemen!"

The officers got up and filed from the room.

"They just need a little coercion," Morton said with a decisive look to Robert Shipley and Brannigan Allcott who stood beside him.

With an amused smile, Detective Shipley responded with his own small investigation. "You say that as if it were personal, Commissioner."

Howe said no word.

"At what point should any fool heretic with sights imposed on the monarchy be able to go without punishment?" Detective Allcott said with a sly grin to Robert in Howe's defense. It was a seemingly innocent and well-meaning question, but for the hugely barbaric undertone.

In the cool shades of the hillside where Cecil made a familiar path, he was startled by a tiny blue-gray bird who lay against the base of a passing tree. He drew near and discovered her alive and apparently injured to the point of remaining still rather than attempting to fly. She breathed fast and afraid and he could see her pain although she was calm and held her head still.

"Have you hurt yourself little bird?" he asked softly with an upset face.

The thought came over him to kill her for mercy's sake to end her suffering.

Her face was a light gray, like silver, and she looked to him with quiet sadness and slowly blinked her full and round black eyes a few times. She had strikingly beautiful black eyelids that were in stark contrast against her light color with long black eyelashes; like those of the gypsy dancers of Persia. It was something he had never seen before and it made him very sad. His heart was instantly pierced and he could not harm her; not even to quickly end her misery out of love.

"You're a beautiful little lady," he said in a calming voice. "Do not fear. I will care for you."

He could not get over the way she softly blinked her eyelids as if she were a small mute damsel filled with an unknown sorrow for things past. He did not know why, but he purposed to keep her safe.

He searched nearby and found a fallen limb whose bark was dry enough to be easily pulled away. He split it from the dead wood in a small chunk that was rounded like a basket and opened on each end. Cecil broke pieces shaped to fit into the end gaps and then tore green grass in handfuls to build up a soft bed inside. He went away seeking a rock that was submerged into the soil and immediately found one. He lifted it to discover several small redworms wriggling. Cecil collected them and placed them within the fragile nursery.

He drew near to her with gentleness and slowly slid her into the cradle of grass.

"You'll be safe in here and when you're on the mend there's a few redworms I put in to sustain you. I hope you like them," he said with a tender smile.

He raised it over his head and placed her into the crook of the lowest branch against the trunk, hidden above passing danger.

"I shall soon come back to see to you, Lady Bird."

He stepped away with the warmth that one feels when something lovely has been saved.

In the cover of night, two shackled men were thrown into the back of a prisoner transport carriage in an alley behind the North London jail and the cage was locked behind them. Their mouths were gagged with bindings of canvas tied around their necks and they were blinded by bags placed over their heads. Morton Howe sat upon his horse alongside Detective Allcott who held the reigns of the prisoner carriage and Detectives Shipley, Graneere, and Lanstrom who were also mounted. None of the men knew what Morton planned to do and they did not question his authority or motive.

"To the Tower, Detective," the commissioner said in a dead stare to Brannigan.

"The Tower of London, Commissioner?!" he said in amazement. "But tha...." He was cut short with Morton's stern penetrating gaze and got the idea. "Yes, sir," he responded quickly.

Detective Allcott whipped the reigns onto the backs of the team and the riders followed after him.

The prisoners were dragged under their arms down echoing halls. The boots of the officers emitted a cold sound on the hard floors of cavernous spaces. They were thrown to the floor of a room that was secured by the hollow moan of a five hundred year old door. To the blinded men, it was the sound of an ancient ghost calling from the dead corridors of the past. One particularly chosen conspirator was lifted by the irons on his wrists and ankles and thrown down onto his back on an uncomfortable odd shaped table. He cried out through his gag under his mask as the iron was removed and then replaced by tight loops of heavy rope. His hands were raised up above his head and then held there by tension and he began to cry out into the darkness.

The other prisoner writhed on the floor, bound hand and foot, at the panicked screams of the man he knew. He was stood up and tied to a short post that was positioned in front and the masks on both men were yanked from their faces.

In the light of multiple flaming torches they

discovered they were in the rack room within the Tower of London. Both men began to cry out with muffled screams and tried to wiggle free. Morton Howe stood beside the detectives, facing the man who was to watch from the post. They removed the gag from the tormented soul on the rack and he began to beg for mercy. Morton looked to Detective Allcott with a glance in his signal to commence.

Brannigan took hold of a long wood pole which acted as a lever to turn the rollers at both ends. He leaned down onto it and the man, who was propped with his head end upwards, partially lying back, began to scream.

The spectator on the post ten feet away trembled and his eyes were wide. His words were muffled and the scourge that bound him had no interest in hearing him as of yet.

Detective Allcott again raised the handle and with Detective Graneere's assistance of weight, forced down onto it again. The ratchet attached to the rollers beneath increased tension on the ropes by means of pulleys. The man's arms and legs were stretched away from one another and the ropes strained without return or give.

The man screamed as his joints threatened to snap and begged for his life and for mercy.

Allcott and Graneere raised the handle again and paused to look to the commissioner. Morton gave only the slightest nod as he kept his stare fixed upon the terror of the forced witness. They slowly clacked the pawls of the ratchet and amidst the wails of the tormented man, heard the loud popping of cartilage and ligaments upon his bone.

The sufferer fainted with the pain of all four limbs being dislocated at once and the room went silent. The man strapped to the post breathed heavily with great drops of sweat and trembled in excruciating horror.

The officers loosened the pull of the machine and raised the helpless prisoner from the rack. They untied him and laid him to the floor without further regard because he would be unable to simply crawl for months.

The gag was left on the second man and Detective Lanstrom went around behind him. He ripped the prisoner's shirt from his back and took up the leather cat as Commissioner Howe and the others stood facing him and watched.

Lanstrom rolled up his sleeves and set his hat aside. In the wavering orange light, he flogged the man across the meat of his back. The first strike slashed him deep with pitiless steel barbs and the man cried out with it. Again, Detective Lanstrom dealt him hateful blows and there was no mercy. Tears of unrelenting pain streamed down the heretic's cheek into the absorption of the cloth that resisted his screams.

The butcher began to tire and leaned upon his knee with heavy panting. At that, Morton nodded to the others and they took him from the post and dragged him backwards to the rack.

He shouted in terror as they threw his shredded back to it and raised his arms above his head. They wrestled his hands and feet into the stirrups and he went hysterical. Again, Morton nodded to the officers.

Detective Shipley cut the gag from their prisoner's mouth with a blade, held his head down to the rack by a handful of hair on the top of his head, and screamed into his face.

"Where's the meeting place of the Mallory and Barnes Sect!!"

On a day where the rain fell from a dreary gray sky, the heretic's detailed response was clearly recalled by the men in the rack room. A horse hoof stepped into a large puddle on the edge of the street and was followed by a wagon wheel. Fifty London officers arrived at a street corner by means of horseback, carriages, and a large multi-horse drawn open wagon in the pouring rain. Commissioner Howe was among them on horseback. They quickly coalesced together and ran in a single file down the avenue to the next block with guns in hand. Some officers carried muskets tightly in their grip with bayonets affixed to the ends.

Inside the meeting place of the Mallory and Barnes Sect, a large two-story house in the middle of London city, the ten men the tortured prisoner had described were at work and play. The building was relatively new and was in prime condition, provided with fine furniture of Georgian flavor to the occupants' luxury. Four of the men carried in wood crates through the back door. They loaded them into a secret room of the house, upstairs, climbing the staircase which faced the back of the house and also could be seen from the front door.

Bertram, Bob, and Jasper played a game of Whist with a dummy hand around a table in the sitting room at the foot of the staircase. The players were wily foxes of sorts, devious and artful in their goings; all of whom were drawn in league early in life and now exploited the weaknesses of humankind in their twenties and thirties.

"Now my fellow tricksters, I will teach you why you put on your pants to day!" Bertram said with taunting derogation. His face was always an indicator of

Machiavellian sarcasm and beneath the rugged attire of a tatterdemalion he did not fit in with the delicate authoritative armchairs that he was always found in.

Bob held the remaining nine cards of his original thirteen and played the Ten of Hearts on the trick.

Bertram sat to Bob's left and looked upon the play with a subtle smile. Being in the next position, he dropped the matching Queen to the table and beat his opponent's play.

"She *is* a lovely woman and one to take the very *heart* of...or should I say the very last penny of a cold and stringent moneygrubber with his wholehearted concurrence! Ha! Ha!" laughed Bertram. "At this gait, yours truly will be holding all Honors!"

"It ain't over, Bertram. Keep your bite in the muzzle 'fore the master's boot is kicked down your throat," Bob said with his continued unrelenting game threats. He played another for the seventh trick upon the same suit and Bertram lay in wait.

The dummy hand played cold after Jasper had none to contend and as Bertram suspected, Bob turned over his King.

The slippery fox then presented his Ace of Hearts.

"Now, Bob, that's how you finesse the Queen!" Bertram cried with a jagged smile.

As the words left his mouth, the front door caved in and fell to the floor with a crunching bang and a line of police officers surged over it.

"Surrender! Police!" Officer Lanstrom shouted as they smashed into the room.

Bertram and Jasper immediately turned from their chairs at the table and busted through the window. Bob fired his pistol as the words were coming from Lanstrom's mouth and struck him in the forehead. Three officers behind the slain detective fired at once and blew Bob's head off as bayonet wielders charged forward to the back of the house.

A man on the staircase was caught off guard as he was ascending, carrying a crate. He threw it aside, dashed for the cover of the top of the stairs, and was shot in the back. He fell backwards onto his head and plummeted to the ground floor.

Outside, Jasper and Bertram fled from the broken window on foot, running in the narrow space between the houses towards the back. Five constables of ample competence ran after them into the wet streets of London.

In a barrage of gunfire and smoke, several officers jumped up the staircase. One man, standing at the back of the house, was killed instantly, shot in the throat. He fell back against an ivory inlaid cabinet, breaking its glass, to the floor.

A man behind him tried to turn out, but was impaled by an officer's bayonet. As he was being bored into the organs in his chest and lifted upwards and back, he pulled a pistol and shot the officer in the face, killing him.

The police arrived on the second floor with guns pointed. There were no sounds up there, only the shooting, shouting, and banging on the first floor below. They walked carefully and quietly and spread out as they searched. They saw nothing and only heard the floor boards creaking under their steps.

Commissioner Howe sat on horseback, watching the house from a distance in the rain. A man darted from the back door, unseen, and ran down the alleyways. Morton kicked his horse with his boot heels and quickly charged off after him, alone. He rode hard and the man shot off into corridors and alleys on foot, running and jumping like a gazelle. Morton's horse ran hard, slipped, and nearly fell a few times on the wet cobblestone and patches of greasy mud. The commissioner turned his horse, got over a block parallel to the fleeing suspect, and saw him turn away, down another street. He drove his horse inwards to the right and pursued him at great speed.

The five officers chased the men at full sprint. Jasper and Bertram split and went different directions through the city. Three officers followed after Bertram while two continued after the other. All men following ran hard and swift.

Bertram manipulated corners and leapt over stairs between buildings. He came up against a high block wall that hedged him in on three sides in an open air fountain. He ran up the side and reached for the top edge, but could not. He fell back down and turned to another side, attempting the same thing again, but failed to surmount it. As he went to the ground, the officers came in on him and stopped, covering his only exit. They looked at him, smiling as they panted for breath with the intention to make him pay for it. They inched closer and closer. Bertram attempted in desperation to thrust between them, twisting and swinging as he was quickly beaten with clubs. He fell to the ground and screamed as the officers bludgeoned him without restraint.

The two officers chased the other window escape artist at a much faster pace. Jasper was very fit and wild and ran with a long stride. He began to leave the officers behind and leapt full into the air over a four-foot wrought iron fence. As he did, the officer in the lead threw his hickory truncheon and struck him in the back of the head, knocking him face first into the ground. His nose was broken and he was immediately debilitated by the blow to the head. The officers quickly assisted each other over the fencing and began to brutally beat him as women and children rushed to the nearby windows.

The children were pulled away and the women

looked on in horror as Jasper was nearly kicked to death below.

In the meeting house, several officers crept slowly through the space of the second floor, pointing their muskets and pistols. There were now no sounds anywhere inside the house and the still was unnerving. Their footsteps occasionally creaked upon the wooden floor as a narrow closet door in the middle of a hall soon appeared before them. The officers gathered around, filling the hall, as two men readied themselves at the front. One stretched forth his hand and gently touched the doorknob, barely making even the slightest sound.

Two shots ripped through the door and instantly killed them both. They fell backwards as the remaining officers fired into the door. Immediately, after their guns were emptied, the door was kicked open from within. From a long and narrow stockroom filled with crates upon racks, two men jumped out swinging very big knives. The metal clashed together, knives against bayonets, in a hand-to-hand battle of death. Standing over top the dead officers, the two men took on everyone at once as they pushed a way to their escape.

One officer was quickly stabbed by the champion of the blade and the guru turned and slashed another. An officer was caught off guard by the close action and wrestled with the other suspect who was stabbing and strangling with the madness of a blind animal. Blood squirted across the men's faces as the blunt fighting was executed. The weaker suspect's face was slashed across by a bayonet as another officer fired a pistol into his chest. The champion gritted his teeth and stabbed downwards into the officer in his strangling grip, but was overtaken and stabbed under his jaw, up into his head, as another officer pointed a pistol to his brain and fired.

At that moment, shouting came from within the secret room and surprised them. "Mercy! Mercy, I beg you! Do not kill me! I beg you for mercy!"

A man lied face down on the ground covering his head with his hands and more officers busted in, pointing guns at him. An officer in the front with blood all over his face came in and swung down onto the man's head with his pistol, knocking him out.

Commissioner Howe was in full pursuit. His horse was swift and effective over the streets. The fleeing man saw that he was being hunted and slipped into a thin gap between two buildings, cutting off the commissioner's horse. Morton turned quickly and ran his mare along the street to the next corner at the edge of the city. He pulled away from the building and stopped, quickly scanning the gray fields, trees, and hedges that led into open country under the dull sky. The horse breathed hard and steam was expelled from her nostrils in the cold rain.

Howe looked beyond the hills into long grasses and saw the tiny figure of a man running away from the city. He kicked his horse and rode after him. He pulled a pistol from a leather pouch attached to his saddle and took aim as he came upon him. As he did, they neared an apple orchard. The man saw him in a glance and disappeared within.

Howe rode up against the outer lines of apple trees in the rain. There was not a sound out there beyond the city but the uninterrupted drops upon the leaves. He scanned the area and backed his horse a few times, searching. He quickly climbed down and tied the reins to a low limb.

Morton stepped carefully, edging quietly within, deeper into the lines. They were silent and still in their perfection and within, not even the wind dared breathe a sound. He waited as he listened, sometimes moving forward, sometimes crouching against a trunk. He stopped and peered through the orchard from the ground. The place was as lively as a graveyard.

After a moment of unresponsive observation, his prey darted full force from behind a far tree as a prize fox and raced away toward the distant country. Howe jumped from his place and sprinted after him without a sound in the long wet grass.

The man veered to his left, dodging between trees, and then found his pursuer just behind him in full force. Morton cut him off from an angle and tackled him to a slump of ground that had retained a few inches of water. They hydroplaned over the surface and slung it out in a wide spray as they came to rest. In the mud, Morton got on top of him and put his knee into his objective's chest. The man tried to break free and run, maybe even surrender, but Commissioner Howe had him with superior strength. Morton beat down on him from above with his full body weight pressed into his ribs.

The man could barely inhale and reached up to defend his face from the blows. He spoke softly, unable to breathe with terrified eyes. "Please…I surrender…no…"

Morton's look was crazed and he got his hands on the jaw and head of his foe.

"Sir…please…" the man pleaded, almost inaudibly.

Commissioner Howe pushed upwards with one hand gripping his jaw and downwards with the other on his head, breaking his neck and killing him.

After the sound of cracking bone, the landscape returned quiet in the drops of rain. The commissioner stared on with wild eyes and breathed hard in anger. He looked around behind to be sure no one had seen them – far out in the middle of the orchard.

Chapter 9

A laughing woman sat in Jack Todd's lap on an elaborately sculpted couch; one that was fitting to die in. Together, they both had the appearance of royalty with their plush amenities, but for the glazed red eyes of fiends and the dark rings that accompanied them like the markings of another type of royalty - the poisonous Monarch butterfly - that identified them. The pleasure room of Le Club Des Haschischins was dimly lit in the night with beeswax candles, but it was the glowing ladies of the night that kept it shining. The wicked harlot mixed him Absinthe and after the water trickled over the sugar cube and blossomed the essences, he took the glass to his mouth and drank. It was for him. It was all for him and he swam in the rivers that really took him places.

The door of the pleasure room opened to the red and gold hall and Jack quietly stepped out while blinking his eyes slowly. In his waking slumber, the door seemed to close by itself behind him as he walked down the stairs and into the attractive clamor of the brothel.

"Now where do you think you're goin', Jack?!" laughed a prostitute who joyously wiggled on another man's lap.

"Let's have another, Jack!" a large happy drunk man called to him from a stool at the bar. "My treat! Hoy! Where you off to now?!"

Jack had a very slight smile and paid none of the patrons or prostitutes calling on him any mind as he walked straight to the front door and floated through it.

He stepped into the street of London city and turned into a dark cobblestone alley near the brothel. He was drunken and imbued with opium as he shuffled his feet, going along in the moonlight. He traveled a ways from the main street and stumbled to the ground. He laughed out as he rolled over onto his back and looked up to the sky between the buildings. He pointed his finger to the Full Moon with a laugh.

"It's all your fault!!" Jack said with slowed speech.

The moon transformed from a real moon to a scary smiling face in the craters as if it had been drawn on with a pen.

"The months of moon are a curse upon the sons of men!! You take the innocent from their mother's breast and make them into monsters!!" He became serious. "You look upon me...here...in what has become...and do you laugh?!! Are you filled with remorse?!!" he shouted.

He became yet more serious with a sad anger. He paused in sorrow and puffed through his nostrils in two long snorts as he felt wanting to weep.

"Will you go on?!! Will you last forever?!! ...Will I?! Curse you! Your light is darkness!!" He rolled over and staggered slowly to his feet. He was close to tears. His lips trembled and his eyes were watery. "...as is mine," he said softly as he stared onto the rocky ground.

He walked along through the city streets alone. There were only few other people in his distant company in the dark and the city was quiet. Stumbling along, he turned corners of buildings along the alleyways toward a miserable lonely place that he called home.

On his path ahead, there were dozens of tiny yellow lights traveling from the nooks and crannies of the avenues and architecture. They ran along the ground and jumped into a puddle in the middle of the street. Jack drew near, nervous at the odd thing, as the little glowing ambers, like stars, passed between his feet and dropped into the two inches of water in front of him. The ambers ceased coming as he stopped and looked down.

In the dark water, the face of an ugly green grotesque and evil goblin fairy appeared, looking back at him with contempt. In a long and slow deep echoing whisper it spoke to him from among distant mingled voices.

"Raaaaamseeeey!..."

Jack Todd was horrified and began to shake. "I told you to leave me be!"

"It is time you paid for your sins, Ramsey Harrow..." it said in a long hair-raising hiss as if from caverns in the depths.

"I owe you nothing! Do you hear?!"

The fairy smiled and spoke slowly. "Come and dine with me, Ramsey...Our table is ready. Your place is set."

Jack Todd stood looking down into a dark empty puddle in the middle of the street and shouted. "Leave me alone!!"

Trembling, he backed away from it and walked quickly. He turned and looked behind in fear as he got further from the place. Movement above him caught his attention in the dark shadows of the high terraces. He stopped, wide-eyed, as the large shape of the werewolf moved just slightly in the darkness, watching him.

Jack, in a panic, turned away and dashed down another street. He tripped on his own feet and fell to the ground. He got up again and ran, looking back. In a tiny passage, between two buildings at Jack's side, he saw the wolf beast again, standing still in the gloom.

He cried out and turned a corner that brought him to a construction site in the open with a wide dark hole hidden on the ground. A growl came from behind and he turned to see. The wolf, barely visible in the shadows, walked toward him in the alley. Jack backed up quickly, almost running, through the debris of the site and tripped on a wooden plank ramp that descended into the underground sewer system. He fell head first down it, rolling over himself and completely submerged into the knee-deep water below.

He stood and quickly wiped the cold sewage from his eyes, being some twenty-five feet in from the opening overhead, watching. He blinked hard and stared long from the blackness as the sound of his splashes echoed deep in the darkness of the newly built brick catacombs. He stood silent, fearing the thing with violent trembling. Above him, in the broad opening to the street, the wolf rose, ferocious, in the moonlight at the top of the plank and moved his head and neck down into a pounce position. Jack turned and ran away deeper into the tunnels, fighting the repressive water as he went.

In the failing light, he turned this way and that, going deeper into the cold labyrinth. He ran in complete darkness with his hands stretched in front of him. He fell into the water and the troubled current flowed over his head. He stood with a gasp and continued until his hands touched a wall. He felt along it and stood still for a moment, trying to listen and not make another sound. There was nothing – only his own breathing and far away drips echoing in the dark. Shaking in fear, he was frozen with his hands against the wall. In the hush of the water's disruption, he could hear the commotion of rats in the darkness; their scraping and gnawing and running along shallow ledges. In his mind, their sounds were of tiny souls of people forced to forever move upon miniature ineffective machinery with the sole purpose of continually wearing down their bodies in meaningless cycles.

Soft, very slow movement troubled the water some distance away from him. His breath shook as his heart pounded emphatically like the coal driven pistons of a steam engine. The agitation in the water became slightly closer. A stone or a brick smacked against the bare walls somewhere in the tunnels around him and the echo was long and deep. Jack did not intentionally move, but his quaking stirred the river around him.

After a long threatening silence that was thick enough for Jack to feel on his skin, a large object plunged into the water less than ten feet from him. Jack tried to run, but the sewage became deeper in the dark. It rose to his hips and he was useless as it slowed him down. He dove forward, prostrate, to try and swim in the muck and putrid water.

The wolf got him by the ankle and pulled him extremely fast through the water in the opposite direction, dragging him behind and further into the darkness. The beast turned him loose and Jack then saw a long streaming spark scrape along the walls above. A torch flared up in the wolf's hand as he hunched down over him. The beast with long black hair roared in the light of the fire and the rats cowered in fear.

Jack, not yet to his feet, screamed out when he saw him. He rolled over and began to run away from the light. The wolf quickly slid the torch into an iron sconce that was made into the wall with its lighting kit and went after him. He ran along a tiny edge above the water over the retreating rats at great speed and leapt from it. Jack was captured from behind by his clothing and the wolf pushed him back to the light.

The wolf stood behind and gripped him by the back of the head with his large hands and long claws. He forced Jack's head into the water and held him there.

Jack reached up with both hands, grabbed hold of the wolf's wrists behind his head, and frantically tried to get loose. He kicked and flailed violently, but was powerless to stand upright.

The wolf pulled him out and allowed him to catch his breath just a few inches above the waterline. Jack screamed in the cavernous tunnels and it echoed for what seemed like forever. He tried to pry the wolf's fingers from his forehead as the wolf hunched down beside him and put his face beside his at the waterline.

Again, the wolf slowly pressed Jack into the filthy sewage while closely watching his face. Jack put his hands on the ground and tried to push himself up in the shallow water. The wolf pushed him down more, bending his elbows. Jack raised his hands behind his head, out of the water, and grabbed hold of the wolf's hands again to pull them off.

The ugly fairy swam up from the darkness below Jack in a translucent green glow with a terrifying smile on his face. As he came, it appeared that the water Jack was in was deep enough to go to the center of the earth. Jack's eyes grew as wide as dinner plates in an almost paralyzed horror. The ugly fairy grabbed Jack by the shirt collar around his neck and yanked on him with a violent thrust. Jack let go of the wolf with both hands and tried to pull the fairy's knotted and deformed hand from his collar.

With a twisted face and a ghostly scream, the ugly fairy cried, "Ramsey!!!!!!!"

Jack screamed underwater and the bubbles rose to the surface from both sides of his mouth.

The wolf lifted him completely out into the air near the domed ceiling of the sewer tunnel. Jack gasped for breath, gurgling water as he tried to scream. The wolf dropped him on his head in the shallow rivulet and broke his neck on the brick passage.

In the slow current, Jack's body floated away face down from the dancing torchlight into the silent and eternal darkness.

The white morning sunlight very subtly illuminated the dark wooden floor at the foot of the bed. The harmonica lay in the same place it had for weeks against the bedpost and had not been moved. An old tattered handkerchief was thrown over it and it was quickly taken up.

Davey walked home alone in the afternoon, carrying his books on his back. He looked side to side, searching the fields and lanes as he went. He remained uneasy, travelling alone from school, and always watched for Cecil for an assurance that he gained from him.

Davey's fondness for his friend kept his hopes up and he admired him.

As Cecil traveled a path that only he had known, he

kept his eyes lifted toward his tiny friend. As he came to her tree, he stood at a distance and called to her.

"Lady Bird, it's me. Are you well?" he said lightly.

He came with caution to see and slowly raised his hand to take hold of her makeshift home.

In an instant, she flew from the cradle above him and sailed away on a breeze. It was a sight that he deeply cherished.

Within view of the old yew tree, Davey saw him sitting there later in the day, looking up into its branches. Cecil soon noticed him and smiled as he drew near.

"Hullo Cecil! What 'ave you been doing?"

Cecil was distantly unsettled and his smile was slightly put on, but he was happy to see him. "Nothing and much at the same time…without exception," he responded with humor.

Davey sat and put his books down and seemed anxious to speak.

"I can see that you've something on your mind. What news have you? How do your fellows get on? Or what about a girl? Have you met one of those?" Cecil gave Davey a wink with a smile.

"I suppose there's not enough time for a girl," Davey said somewhat flushed. "…and they're trouble."

Cecil snorted a short laugh and looked at him with an inspecting eye. "Now you *have* stumbled onto something," he said. "But I tell you…they tend to grow on you when you get older." Cecil smiled, but truly the subject filled him with perpetual pain.

Davey chuckled and then turned to a solemn mood before Cecil could say more. "Do you think there's a wolf that lives in these forests?" Davey asked.

Cecil turned to him with alarm, not anticipating the

lad's acquaintance of the things that were at hand. "What makes you say that?"

"I've heard that it was some wild beast that struck at the Windham Family farmstead."

Cecil got very somber and wondered how this word or this rumor was issued, but did not question his sources in a hopeful pursuit to divert the conversation's new subject. "Oh?"

"That it was not a man who killed them, but something other...perhaps a wolf. Did you hear?"

Cecil shook his head with some small measure of relief but it was only remote. "I did not." He looked down to the ground, sorrowful. "A tragedy nonetheless."

There was a short silence. Davey looked upon him intently, attempting to read inconspicuous behavior and to distinguish his thoughts. He hoped for some kind of evolving comment that would somehow explain his understanding. He said no more and waited.

"Worry not yourself over such things. You're still a boy," Cecil said, flashing a short smile. "Come...happier matters. I have something very special for you to day."

Davey's curiosity was momentarily abated and a tiny smile appeared in anticipation.

Cecil reached into his sack and carefully pulled out an item wrapped in a handkerchief. His hand trembled with sensitivity, which Davey noticed, as he quickly passed it to him.

The boy opened the cloth and found the beloved harmonica. He looked upon it amazed and yet dismayed. He turned his eyes to Cecil, who appeared austere, but held a small devoted smile.

"The harp?!" Davey said softly, very troubled.

"My gift to you. I want it to belong to you now," Cecil said with a deep breath. He was sorrowful, but only because it seemed to him that the time had come so soon. He was not ready and no one who had ever come to that door of an inevitable place ever was. He was no different. Inside, he wept and wanted to go back and hold on to some things again for only a little longer.

"But this was your father's! I shan't take it from you, Cecil!"

"No one can keep a thing forever…I am quite sure."

Davey became sad and shook his head. "But I cannot!" He quickly put it into Cecil's hands, in which Cecil recoiled, trying not to touch it for very long, and dropped it to the ground between his feet.

"There you go now, Davey," Cecil said quickly. "Take it…and do me this honor."

The lad looked upon it and his eyes flashed back to Cecil who smiled at him for only a moment. Davey squinted his eyes in wonder at receiving the gift and at how Cecil was anxious over the thing in a way that was unexpected. He extended his hand and waited again for Cecil to return it.

Cecil reached down, took up the harmonica, and swiftly put it into Davey's hand in one motion. He kept a tiny pleasant smile as if it were nothing as he looked at him.

Davey was troubled, but greatly appreciated what it meant to have it. It was a beautiful prize and would be his most valuable possession. He nodded.

"I thank you, Cecil...and will always remember the story of it for as long as I live."

Cecil looked to the boy with sadness and a great love for him swelled within his heart. He returned a sincere smile and a short nod.

Davey could perceive in Cecil's eyes a different and deeper feeling of fondness his friend held for him inside. He did not understand it, but it was there. He knew that same feeling was also within him.

Chapter 10

everal police constables entered the dungeon jails and sought the men of the Mallory and Barnes Sect. The severely battered Bertram, Jasper, and their other captured accomplice languished in a cold stone pit beneath an iron cage. There was screaming and moaning that echoed from other cells above that were lit by torches that protruded from the walls. Each man was raised out by the officers one by one on a long leather strap and was thrown to the ground above. They were weakened and afraid, being starved, beaten, and deprived of much light.

Along an outer line of musty dark cells in the rock wall, Albern stepped forward to his bars and was partially illuminated in the fire. He was better cared for, as much as could be expected; being that he had not had his slop withheld from him. He shook against the bars like a madman in a violent fit.

"Hoi! Let me out of here! Set me loose!! You pigs! You damned pigs let me out! I'll kill you all!! I'll kill you all!!!!"

His muscles rippled and tensed across his arms and he felt that he could almost break the iron apart, but could not. Amidst the screaming threats of the other lunatics, Albern's words were unheard and ignored. The policemen there to extract the heretics did not turn toward him and dragged the three men away, around a corner, and up a narrow stone stair to the surface.

Sunlight penetrated the Central Criminal Courtroom through high glass window panels with a strong yellow light on the summer morning. The Old Bailey was filled with citizens, police, lawyers, and news reporters. The public was kept at a distance to keep from interfering with the proceedings in high balcony boxes and pews that shadowed from the main entrance. The swift trial of the three men captured by Commissioner Howe and his officers prepared to get underway.

In a high judgment seat behind a beautifully and richly carved podium, the judge sat wearing a black gown and white wig. He was lordly in his discouraging appearance and position and the very sight of him made saints feel guilty for their sins. Along another wall beneath him to his left, a panel of twelve men stood in two rows wearing red robes and white wigs. They also were not the sight an ignorant man would want to see for fear they would expose him to his youth and put him away for being born. There were many lawmakers, recorders, and notable men of judicial influence that sat in boxes beneath the great windows. All four corners of the room housed them as they faced the center with their self righteous and their pure judgment.

A door opened below the judge's seat and constables brought in the three prisoners who were in chains. The men were led up onto a riser on the opposite side of the panel and their hand shackles were tethered to it. The large crowd of people that were seated to watch began speaking and the room was filled with the noise. The Common Serjeant of London, who was an old man and deputy to the Recorder of London, turned to an audience who was as captive as those being tried and spoke.

"The Right Honorable Lord Justice Meadholm presides to deliver Holy judgment concerning the prosecuted heretics of the Mallory and Barnes Sect this fourteenth day of August in the year of our Lord eighteen hundred and forty-one! Long live the Queen!"

The chief panel member who stood on the corner of the judgment row proceeded. "Attorney Roddenfield, your statement."

The gentleman began.

"These men whom I represent, completely and adamantly deny any involvement at all with the tragedy of Mister Hugo Faulkner's death as well as affiliations with the named unorthodox group, Vir Fides Beneficium, and I respectfully appeal from My Lord space for inquiry to be allowed before premature sentencing."

A prosecuting attorney pointed his finger and shouted. "Six of our men, noble men of the law, our Highest Order, were slain in the crusade...for Queen and Country! Six of our beloved men of West London Division! Our fellow men and protectors! These heretics, Godless men who would destroy everything our Lord has put into place, need not burden us any longer with the poisons of anarchy and murder!!"

Commissioner Howe, who sat in the front row among the crowd of people, looked upon the judge as there was uproar among the public citizens.

The Right Honorable Lord Justice Meadholm spoke.

"Over the course of two days I have heard the cases presented to me by this court. I have determined that the evidence clearly points to the truth in this matter and no further space of time will be granted. Therefore, by the Holy power vested in me by God and by Queen, I sentence these offenders to hang by the neck until dead. May God have mercy on your souls."

Several police bailiffs jumped onto the men and pulled them away by their chains. The onlookers began to shout and a great commotion arose as Morton Howe was flashed a look from the judge. As the judge stood and turned away into his chamber, Commissioner Howe returned with a slight nod.

Cecil ran through the London city streets in the darkness of the night. He hid in the black alleys and listened to conversations through windows of those who were ambiguous enough to be restless at so late an hour. In the lamp lights of the streets and the still heat of the baked brick, he came again to the police jail building where he would watch and listen. He drew near to a barred ground window that was covered with thick glass and knelt beside it. Deep within, he could hear the moans and screams of the sleepless prisoners. He focused and could pick out single words among the muted sounds and tortured cries. The blasphemous pollution ascended from the stone walls like the eavesdropping on chambers of demons conspiring against God. It would turn the stomach and corrupt the soul of normal citizens or normal living beings beneath the sun if it had crept into their hearing; a wretched audible river of purest Hell flowing upon waves of sound from earthen pits of darkness. Some were prisoner and some were not. Some were the convicted and some were the soon to be convicted.

Immediately, two officers opened a side door next to him and while speaking, began to step out onto the street. With superhuman speed and strength, Cecil jumped to a second-story ledge of the building and scaled the side of the wall to the third floor windows by swinging from the window ledges. He flipped up onto a wrought iron terrace above him and swung from terraces to terraces like a skilled ape. He back-flipped onto an upper ledge, leapt a great distance to the building across from it, and climbed the wall to the roof. The constables had only just stepped into the alleyway beneath him and began to light cigars.

Cecil walked out upon the ledge of the roof, ten stories above the ground, and looked down on the men, down upon the jail.

Inside the long hay storage barn as September came into place and then progressed, the men were seated to eat with Mister Breggins. Everyone was dressed only slightly warmer with an accompanying vest as the women served the men at the table. In the daytime the temperatures were ideal and the men were comfortable by rolling up their sleeves and dreaming of a rematch.

Mister Breggins took a drink from his simple cup and stood to make a personally anticipated announcement.

"Men, as you may know," he said happily, "this Sunday marks the Harvest Moon of the autumnal equinox. So, in keeping with our annual traditions, all men shall be excused from work this week end, Saturday and Sunday, including the following Monday of Harvest Festival. Those of you who would like to come in for additional wages may, but it will not be required."

"Very good, sir! Thank you, sir!" the men along the table shouted.

"It is in part because of your faithful service and hard work, especially at this time in the year. I hope that you will take time to rest and enjoy the Harvest Supper that our fine parish will hold on the even of the twenty-third of September."

The men began to make a cheerful clamor and fuss with the good news.

Cecil continued to eat at the far end of the table as Mister Breggins held the full attention of the other men. He did not look away from his food.

"Our toil will commence on Tuesday following," said Mister Breggins.

Theodore Tillmire sat near the master and spoke with a great smile.

"Sir, a little lark has brought to my attention his concerns in desiring to know if you'd perhaps be Lord of the Harvest this year?!!"

The men laughed out as Theodore beat around the question, but quickly hushed in the suspense of Mister Breggins' answer.

"I have no doubts that there are certain men and women...and children for that matter," he stated, "who would desire nothing more than to see the one who stands before you dressed so extravagantly and begging for money!"

The men, and women who attended them, let out a hardy laugh together.

"As for the moment, Mister Tillmire," Mister Breggins continued, smiling, "you shall have to wait and see...like the rest of us!"

The men took up their food again as they laughed. Cecil drank slowly from his cup very calmly with a slight smirk as he stared down to the table in his thoughts.

𝕬 town crier, dressed in bright blue, stood on the corner of a very busy London street holding a rolled parchment to his eyes. He rang a hand bell of brass and then shouted the news as people went by on foot and by carriage, listening.

"Strathford University professor of Science, Doctor Moyer Phillips reported missing! Police in exhaustive efforts to recover him! Doctor Phillips declared missing by University!!"

Ten officers stood behind Commissioner Howe on a set of steps that rose up from a walk to the front door of Doctor Phillips' house. As carriages were going by on the street, Commissioner Howe knocked while the men waited silently behind him. There came no answer and Morton stepped away from the door. Two men behind him rammed their bodies against it and broke it in.

The police unit entered the house and began calling for him. Commissioner Howe investigated the rooms as a shout came from the first floor hall.

"Commissioner!" a constable cried.

Morton followed the sound of his voice to the main entry room and turned down a hall. The man had his hand on a locked door that lay hidden behind a curtain.

"Aside..." the commissioner said to him.

The officer stepped over as Howe approached and then broke open the door with his body. Both of them peered in and discovered a rock stairway that led down into a cellar, lit by faint sunlight. The officers followed Commissioner Howe as he immediately descended the stair.

As they landed into a scientist's laboratory they began to search. Along the tables, the men inspected the tubes, flasks, and odd gadgets of electrical conductivity and chemical enhancement.

Commissioner Howe took a glass phial of silver chemical into his hand and pondered it. He then stood still as his eyes adjusted focus, staring upon the black iron cage that sat ominously against the back wall. The door was unfastened and the neck collar hung open from the crude chains that dangled from the center. He slowly turned and looked up to the furthest window which was broken and had been boarded shut. The other officers came near and stared upon it with steadfast curiosity and then turned their eyes to him. Morton's face was intensely focused as he looked into the cage. The wheels of his mind began to turn and no man spoke.

Detective Halsey called down from the door above and broke the silence of the cold stagnant room.

"Commissioner! We've got a body!"

Morton moved nothing but his eyes and looked in the direction of the door above him.

A sewer outlet at the end of a long channel of water on the outskirts of London saw Commissioner Howe's carriage arrive fifteen minutes afterwards. The city's water waste ran at street level in the open at that point where not many people ever went. Morton stepped out and walked along the lowered channel toward a gathering of detectives. The men scoured over the area in front of a ten foot wall that rose up with an opening. Beneath it was an iron bar door that had been unlocked and opened by the city's water authority. On the ground ahead, partially in the water, lay a body.

Detective Allcott met Morton part way and walked with him as he approached the scene.

"Been dead a while. Maybe a month," he stated.

The men approached the bloated pale corpse of Jack Todd. Frozen on his gelatinous gray face was a glimpse into his world of terror. Morton's eyes widened in shock and his breathing quickened because he was unfortunate enough to know him. He was deeply distressed, but kept his feelings hidden.

"I know 'im," Detective Shipley said.

Morton instantly looked to him. His racing heart and nervousness was cloaked with natural concern.

"'Name was Todd," Robert said. "A regular drunk and addict from Worthington Street. The ol' bugger must've fell in and drowned himself."

Detective Allcott put in his conclusion. "No doubts about it."

"'Surprised he didn't do it sooner," said Shipley.

Commissioner Howe stared upon the dead man's face and his breathing became even heavier. His face twitched and he quickly turned away in disgust and sickened fear.

"Get him out'ta here," he said firmly.

Morton went away to his carriage quickly. As he did, he subtly looked side to side to see if anyone was watching him. He immediately climbed into his seat inside and shut the door, staring upon the body from the window, saddened, but with frightened eyes. The carriage pulled away and he remained frozen with his gaze turned to the floor in front of him.

Chapter 11

Large crowds of travelers boarded the London and Birmingham Railway train in Euston Station in North London. Cecil was among them and stepped out onto the platform of the structure that was not unlike an ancient Roman coliseum with its enormous white pillars and looked both ways. In wariness, he quickly climbed aboard the second class passenger car in hopes that no one he knew would see him depart. The time on the large clock face of the station was six o'clock PM as the *Mercury*, the broad gauge steam locomotive engine, gave two short whistle blasts.

The Ramsbury Barlow Harvest Festival was abounding with guests that sat at many long tables of food and drink in a large field. Children ran over it as large fires burned in the center of the celebration as totems to the games. Hundreds of people were in attendance to eat and dance, to laugh and sing, and to socialize. Inspiring music for such things sprouted from an Adufe, Piffero, Crumhorn, Lute, Viola Da Gamba, and others with Timbrels in echoes of medieval Britain from a large group of some twenty hearty musicians. It was a gathering of rejoicing and observance that had been in revolution for centuries to celebrate the harvest foods and the plenteous gifts the earth bestowed and the work of hands. The residents of Ramsbury Barlow always anticipated it throughout the second half of the year. Tonight, the people would be free to relax and eat without their worries for tomorrow.

On the tracks, the Firefly Class engine blew smoke from its stack as it traveled through the English countryside in the dark. Like a nocturnal snake winding through unseen crevices in the shadows, it slithered on its belly for its prey. The yellow light of passenger windows flashed across all of its cars as it curved around the bends of the great hills on a mission of doom.

The Gutendale Hallows Harvest Festival was underway in a remote part of England. Because of the locations inhabited by its participants, the party was more sparsely populated. It was identical in its spirit to the Ramsbury Barlow festival and was the same in every way with the exception being there were fewer people in attendance with fewer fires and fewer musicians playing the same song.

They had their fill of goose stuffed with apples, enough for everyone, pies of pumpkin, apple, and buttermilk raisin. There was plenty more than what the participants could manage and much of it went untouched for the time. Children played 'snap the apple' and jumped beneath trees that dangled the fruit from strings and clumsily attempted to take bites out of them with much practice. Apple bobbing was also a drawing attraction and grown men, without regard to the way they had combed their hair and beards, dunked their heads into tubs of water to the laughter of their wives.

Eaton Barrett, one of the joyous men, his wife, and their many children, danced beside a large fire with spontaneity and unrestraint with the others. He, being buoyant and capable, happily turned a couple of his small daughters by the hand as they laughed and danced around him.

"Come now, Mother!" he called to his love and she, a mild and delightful woman, jumped to him with over enthusiasm and nearly pushed him to the ground. They laughed with one another and the children laughed at them.

Cecil sat alone against a window in a mostly empty car. There were many rows of bench seats with an aisle between them. He sat at the very back, facing forward in the direction of the train, and looked out to the passing landscape trees that watched him through his window with disdain. Ahead twenty feet, a woman sat with two small quiet children and no other passengers were with them.

The door at the end of the aisle that linked the cars together, opened and a man wearing a brown top hat entered with his head down. He came in quickly, holding a brown leather book with a brass latch and sat immediately beside the door, facing Cecil's direction. He pulled down on the brim of his hat which somewhat concealed the conspicuous round scar on his cheekbone with his head tilted forward. As he did, Cecil sensed him and the men's eyes met across the rail car. It was none other than the missing university professor.

They knew each other and Doctor Phillips quickly jumped to his feet, stumbled to his side, and caught himself on the pole as he trembled and backed away. Cecil lowered his head like an animal ready to attack and his eyes glossed over with bloodthirsty ferocity.

Doctor Phillips stared long and hard upon Cecil, maintaining his ground with an evil glare. He slowly lowered his head in the same way and quickly moved his eyes back and forth, scanning each side as a wolf that feels threatened from all angles. He hissed and twitched his lip as he showed his teeth on one side of his mouth in a snarl. The woman sat with her head down and nearly asleep, resting on her children in her lap and did not notice.

Cecil, provoked, constricted his angered face in a scowl and appeared even more wicked than his rival. He spoke softly under his breath to him in a hiss by both telepathy and sound in the rackety noise that rhythmically drummed the floor beneath them.

"I will kill you."

Doctor Phillips heard him clearly and stood only a second longer with the growl on his face. He was frightened by Cecil's warning and knew that in vengeance, might attempt to make good on his words. He held his position of claimed territory to test him in his brazen disregard; both of them understanding the futility of contending.

Cecil jerked forward and took hold of the seat in front of him while making a quick motion to rise. Even if it were a battle that could not have lasting effects, he would disfigure him and tear his throat out.

Doctor Phillips snarled and turned away in uncertain fear, knowing that he had finally met his rival, and a bitter one, and quickly fled Cecil's car and shut the door behind him.

Cecil breathed at a heightened rate while gritting his teeth and reluctantly let him go. He desired to slay the offender but could not risk being hindered, delayed, or prevented from his imperative scheme or schedule; not now or in the grand course. He stared upon the door choosing the greater of two evils with unnatural bloodshot eyes and did not refrain from the intensity of his urge to kill for revenge with hisses and subtle growls.

The fires burned high with awesome brilliance and strength. Costumed dancers jumped and spun around great clusters of corn stalks that had been tied together in decorative fashion. Around a bend in the path behind the people, dancers, and fires, a parade of wood carts began to roll on, pulled by donkeys. They were all ridden by men cloaked as reapers, carrying their scythes. Behind each man, in his cart, were representations of vegetable harvests; some corn, some wheat, some gourds of all colors and shapes. Together, in choreographed movement with the music that seemed to radiate from the fires themselves, their blades were raised high and swung as if chopping the grain.

The great pistons and shafts turned the cast steel wheels of the *Mercury* in the night, stoked to full power.

Something moved through the corn fields at an extremely high speed. The thing was dark and traveled fast so that only the tops of the corn stalks swayed from it in the dark. Nearly a quarter of a mile was covered in a straight line through the corn row in only a swift passing moment.

The people and dancers stopped what they were doing and stared up to the night sky together with smiling expectant faces. The shredded clouds parted like the black curtains of the devil's theatre to reveal the full Harvest Moon in the night sky. The roisterers of the festival began to cheer and applaud for the debut of the immortal champion, the great glowing orb above them; the expert witness to man's immorality.

In the smoke of the train's stack, the moon appeared veiled again as the locomotive engineer sounded the deep whistle from its scorching steam.

The landscape became more illuminated for proper judgment by the full light of the moon. The beast traveled like lightning through the corn and moved too quickly to be seen. Whips of leaves as they were passed and the galloping thuds of some heavy creature coming in the dark were the ghoulish sounds of the fields. The black wolf's head passed near the tops of the corn stalks as he grunted in his speed.

The Lord of the Harvest, Mister Breggins, danced cheerfully upon the final cart of the procession. He was dressed extravagantly, as they had expected, in red, gold, and purple and his audience cheered with great shouts and laughter. He extended his enormous hat, which was covered in colored pheasant feathers, and held out his hand, begging for money as he went. Reapers raised scythes high above their heads, straight up and down, lightly stepping in a march around his cart as it was pulled along. Candlelight flickered like yellow tongues in the mouths of jack-o'-lanterns lined upon stakes in rows like the piked reformers' heads on London Bridge.

The fire in the headlamp burned brightly as the *Mercury* spilled smoke from its stack into the night. It shook and roared as it quickly devoured the miles of track in its boiling heat like an unstoppable monster.

In an instant, the enormous black werewolf tore through the end of the corn rows and flew into an open field of grass like a speeding shot. Stalks of corn whipped in opposite directions behind him in an explosion as he exited with intensified speed and power. He ran on all fours over the grasses toward a dark farmhouse and the earth shook under his feet.

The wolf advanced into the yard from the back of the house and slowed, creeping up alongside it. During the quiet breeze that gently rustled the corn stalks that besieged the property, he slowly sneaked around the side of the house. He walked out and peered into the side family room window. It was black inside with no obscure light. He stepped back and looked up to the second story windows and sniffed the air. There was no one inside.

He returned to the back yard, to the basement stair doors that lay on the ground and leaned at an angle against the bottom of the house. He pulled on the door handle to open it, but it was locked. He raised his fist, pounded on it twice in a way without damaging the wood, and broke the latches inside.

The wolf stopped and perked up an ear. As he moved and turned the tiny inner fragments of the lock, he knew someone was coming. He crept out from the wall into the open and saw a horse-drawn wagon going along the road, preparing to turn in to the right and come to the house. The beast stood still and watched.

A large family with many children entered the front door of the house with a key. It was completely dark and silent. The man carried a lantern light in his hand from the wagon.

"Gloria, Charles…help me fix a light," he said.

The children came with candles and lit them from their father's lantern. They took them throughout the house, lighting others and lamps. The three smallest of them began to whine.

"Father, can we have some jam before bed?" Ella said sweetly.

"Oh please, father, may we?" Patrick begged.

The man laughed. "You haven't had enough feasting for one day?!" he asked, amazed at them.

"No!!" all the children cried together.

"Will it satisfy you enough until morning?!!" he said with a smile.

"Yes!!!" they all shouted.

Their mother embraced her husband with a big smile. "Only the children of Eaton Barrett would be so famished after a feast!!"

He chuckled softly with a smile. "Go on, then!" he said. "Just one before bed!"

"Yay!!" they cheered. "Thank you, father!"

"Gloria, fetch the preserves, my dear," he said as he prepared the oil lamps on the table.

A door creaked open at the top of a wood staircase and a dim lantern engraved the opening. The little girl descended the stairs with her light and drew near the very back of the basement. There were shelves to the ceiling that stored many glass jars of preserves and vegetables. She held her light high and searched them.

Not fifteen feet from her, silent and still in the darkness, was the tall black hairy figure of the wolf. He stood against animal hides and pelts that hung from the ceiling to cure. He breathed softly and she passed by him unawares and his eyes were distinguished among the disguises of fur by the lantern. She carried her jar up the stairs and shut the door behind her without fear. There was no expression in the eyes of the wolf in the dark as he looked to the door, listening to the sounds they made.

When the night had further developed without hindrance, the fireplace in the Barrett home continued to burn brightly. Three of the children slept on the floor beside it near the bottom of a wood staircase. Jack-o'-lanterns along the hearth guarded them with prowling eyes and inaudible screams as the terrible black wolf entered from the kitchen and walked quietly across the wood floor. He watched the children as the one nearest him lay with her face turned away. He carefully stepped onto the stairs in the light of the burning fireplace and slowly began to climb.

The jack-o'-lantern on the corner spat a fizzling spark through its jagged teeth and the wolf was distracted. He turned his head. It seemed to look up at him with mischievous pointed eyes in a spiteful grin as he carelessly pressed onto the crooked fifth step which let out an awful creak. The wolf froze with a scare and looked to the sleeping children. None of them stirred. He held the banister and let his foot up slowly from the step and went over it as the fire crackled softly in the stillness of the room.

He got to the second floor hall, which could also be seen from the floor below with a decorative railing along its edge. The wolf very carefully stepped past the children's bedroom door. It was open and a few of them were just inside in a peaceful sleep with dreams of butter scotch, almond and maple candies, molasses and chocolates, and sugared pop corn. He looked in their direction quickly as he kept moving past on the occasionally creaking floor and the sound of the wood popping in the fireplace below.

The wolf entered Eaton Barrett's bedroom through the open door and stood still at the side of the bed. The man and his wife were asleep beneath the blankets and were quite sound by their faces. The wolf reached in with his long black fingers and long sharp nails. He took hold of the blanket at Eaton's neck and very slowly drew it back, past his knees. The wolf opened his giant hairy hands near Eaton's face just before the man roused from losing his warmth and listened. After Eaton softly exhaled completely, the wolf quickly snapped them around his throat and raised him up out of the bed into the air.

Eaton was stunned awake and kicked his legs wildly while swinging his arms, touching nothing. In horror of the sight that resembled some hideous soul taker from a neoclassical painting, he pulled at the wolf's savage grip around his throat, unable to take in any air to make a single sound. The beast snarled and saliva dripped from his sharp teeth as he brought the man up close to his face and watched his bulging bloodshot eyes.

Eaton's wife barely stirred with her back turned, comfortable in knowing that he was there with her.

The wolf, with heated rising anger exuding from his face, squeezed harder and choked the life out of the man. Eaton's body relaxed and went totally limp and his eyes went cold.

The wolf inhaled a deep breath and quietly growled into the face of the dead in one final angry declaration of sovereignty. He reached down with one hand and took Eaton under the bend of his knees, turned him sideways, and laid him quietly back into his bed; his head on the pillow next to his sleeping wife. He pulled the blanket back up over the body, closed the eyelids with one hand to put him gently to sleep, and turned out.

The wolf went past the children's bedroom on the creaking wood floor in a slow escape. None of them moved as he crept by carefully in his terrifying frame. He took hold of the banister and looked down at the sleeping children on the floor below. In the yellow glow of the fireplace, he quietly descended the staircase, going cautiously - one step at a time.

The wolf put his foot forward and placed it upon the fifth step, but quickly pulled it away, looking to the watching jack-o'-lantern with a low snarl. The little girl on the floor that was closest, turned over and faced him, but her eyes were closed.

The wolf stopped and, in the moonlight from the bedroom windows in the hall behind him, stood still. He moved his head only slightly as he watched her for a moment. With paused study to read her most elusive and ephemeral suggestive distinctions, he knew that she was asleep. He stepped over and continued on, around the banister and across the family room floor in front of the children.

As the little girl laid still, dreaming on her pillow, the distant muffled sounds of the wolf closing the squeaking kitchen basement door, slowly descending the basement stairs, and shutting the cellar doors were not heard.

As the last tiny bang of the hatches sounded outside as the wolf departed, the girl opened her eyes and stared upon the empty staircase. Her eyes became heavy and she went back to her dreams.

Chapter 12

Cecil walked along a lane through the countryside carrying his sack when a farmer's wagon passed by going in the same direction. The fall season had been upon England for a few weeks and it was kind to the comforts of the fields and solitude. Cecil's view was always mixed and he felt like nothing more than a permanent traveler only passing through it; like there would be no real piece of ground that he would call his home until he was finally planted beneath it. It was a thought that was regularly in the forefront and especially at his age. The day was soft and lovely, but recurrently it was hardly noticed and sadly passed without his inherent appreciation.

"Cecil!" Davey shouted from the wagon as it quickly rolled away.

Cecil smiled and waved to say hello and farewell at once, but Davey jumped from the back and ran to him over the long grasses.

"What do you know?! Davey's found wheels that suit him!" he said, cheered from the onslaught of his own mind by the boy.

"Hitchin' a ride home from a passer-by," Davey said.

"Vitality wasted would be sin for one with opportunity to conserve it," responded Cecil with a smile. "No school to day?"

"No work to day?" the boy returned as they both laughed.

"No...I suppose not," answered Cecil. They continued walking the dirt lane and it began to gently ascend upon a low hill along the left side of a thick forest dotted with its display of colors for fall.

"I did not see you at the Ramsbury Barlow Harvest Festival, Cecil," Davey said with a serious concern. He looked up to Cecil who kept his eyes on the ground ahead.

"I did not attend it."

"What for?"

Cecil looked over to him. "For...my own matters," he answered.

"You really missed the finest food, my friend!...and sweets like I've not had since Christmas!"

"I'm sure I did!"

"What are you doing to day?"

Cecil smiled. "You're looking at it."

"I know the fitting thing for us! I want to show you something! Would you like to see?"

"Certainly I would."

"Follow me this way to the Beecher Pond," Davey called as he turned away to his left and led him over another green hill.

The pond suddenly appeared below the lip of the hillside and was calm and quiet. Sunlight glimmered yellow upon its face in a wide circle and Cecil was attracted to it as Narcissus fatefully led to the pool by Nemesis. Cecil had not been there before and the view was very pleasing. Tall reeds stood along the water's edges and the calls of water birds bounded upon its surface. Cecil smiled at the sight of it as Davey brought him to an open place on its edge.

"Here is one of my secret places, Cecil…where I come sometimes to catch fish or even hunt for some insects that I study for school."

"You study insects in school?"

"Yes…among other things. I find them to be fascinating! I got to examine the heart of a tiger worm once! That was an amazing sight!"

"Ha! I cannot imagine!" Cecil said with a laugh. "Now that's something I would've liked as a lad! …Tiger worms have hearts?!"

"Sure they do. They're quite small, but with a proper lens you can see it beating!"

"Now I see why you find it fascinating!" Cecil said with amazement.

The boy took up two cane poles that he had stashed away along the grasses of the shoreline in anticipation. Each one was equipped with a fish hook and a small chunk of cork oak bark to float. Davey held a big smile on his face as he took a pail of moist earth hidden in the shadows of the reeds where he kept a supply of his lively striped worms.

"How is the fishing here?" asked Cecil. "Is there a champion to win in these waters?"

"Sure! Lots of them! Last time I was here I got a bream! Forty centimeters long I know it! On two grains of sweet corn!"

"Impressive! That was a profitable trade! Just be careful not to hook into a pike," Cecil said. "That will be trouble that you do not intend! They won't come easy!"

Davey laughed and they took the tiger worms and fixed them to their hooks. They unraveled the black line that was wrapped at the tips of the poles and cast them out onto the tranquil pond. The breeze rustled the dried blades and stalks of the freshwater plants and it was pacifying.

"It is a very enjoyable place," Cecil said, smiling. He sat on the ground and made himself comfortable while watching the boy. "Here," he called to him. Cecil tossed a golden apple from his sack.

Davey caught it with a smile and came and sat down beside him as Cecil pulled one for himself and took a bite.

"I knew a man that went a long way to see the great pyramids of Egypt at one time," said Cecil.

Davey smiled and was immediately interested in the story.

"For many years he pondered them and figured them to be more glorious than anything that he could have laid eyes on upon the whole earth. He had a strange Greek name: Talaemenes," Cecil said with a smile. "That time eventually came and with much study and preparation he found a way to go. As he traveled far into strange and foreign lands for many weeks, his excitement for fulfilling his dream made it impossible to sleep throughout his journey. He had learned to speak, in some degree over time in the years before, the Arabic language of the people who lived there. He had devoured the books on the great pharaohs and the genius of those mysterious ancient peoples – their gods, and their beliefs in the connection to heaven. He even learned to read Egyptian hieroglyphics and decipher their meanings. The journey ultimately put him packed upon the back of a camel in a caravan that traveled into the desert wildernesses of Libya. After many days of camp, a sudden storm of the Mediterranean Sea overtook them upon the cliffs of Majdul and washed their path to the rocky depths below. Two of the seven men who accompanied him were killed. They were lost and were forced to turn back for another way. After they had endured the storm in the shelter of the rock, their guide led them to the village of Darbal Lihn. The people of that place were hospitable and they were comforted. In that short time there, a band of Arab slave traders lodged as they passed through with a supply of merchandise to be delivered to the western shores.

Right away, he befriended one of them who was surprisingly charismatic and their respect for one another as people, business aside, was mutual. As it happened, he went near the prisoners that evening in his curiosity and concern and was immediately confounded over a young maiden he discovered among them. She was not like most of the others and was an Arab with flawless tan skin. She was the most beautiful woman he had ever seen. He became greatly disturbed over her and immediately fell ill within.

The traders gathered in the night under a great tent, making merry, and his new friend invited his men to join them. They accepted and sat with them upon carpets of silk and floorings of yak hides covered in hair. After Bashir poured the men a measure of clear alcohol, he sat down beside Talaemenes.

Talaemenes spoke to him privately in the native tongue as the others were loud with spirits. 'Sir, there is a maiden slave among your property that I desire to purchase at any cost,' he said.

Bashir turned in surprise and looked into the man's eyes and immediately knew his heart.

'She is one of light skin,' Talaemenes continued, 'unlike the others and I humbly beg that you would sell her to me.'

'I know of whom you speak,' Bashir answered with

a small smile. 'She is not mine to give. You must follow me to Algiers in the North and you shall offer the Pasha, Hassan, what he wants for her.' He smiled at Talaemenes showing his teeth of gold and understood him. 'You shall do well. Have no worries for this creature. I will take special care of her for your sake.' He laughed and tipped back his jar of anise flavored Levantine Arak, but held true to his word.

To him, she was so sad and lovely," Cecil continued. "Her eyes were the mystery that he had been searching for his entire life and he knew it. He could not depart from her. He could not go his way and leave her alone. He realized what the true purpose of his journey was. Without a second thought, he abandoned his mission and followed Bashir to the North. Upon the second day after their arrival, the city was bombarded by Dutch men-of-war which accompanied a British squadron, destroying a corsair fleet in the harbor. In the confusion of destruction, Talaemenes entered the house where she was being held and set her free. They escaped into the night as the cannons burned the city to the ground."

Davey's eyes were wide in amazement.

"He never saw his beloved Egypt, but loved her."

Cecil smiled as he looked upon the rippling water of the pond. "Sometimes you find what you did not expect and a man cannot plan for anything," he said.

Davey also smiled and greatly cherished the things he heard and learned from Cecil. After a moment of quiet, he asked a question.

"Did he marry her?"

"He did…and many years later I met them both."

Cecil paused for a moment. "He was right to turn away and follow after her. She was very beautiful – the jewel of his crown," he said with a small smile.

Davey thought about it for a long while and both of

them watched the birds come and go over the pond.

"Some day, when you are older, you will also find your Egyptian queen and she will steal your heart from the things that you thought you loved," Cecil said to him with a thoughtful expression.

A smile went across Davey's face as he studied it and it was a nice thought.

As luck turned up, the tiny chunk of bark on the boy's line dunked beneath the surface and signaled a hungry fish.

"You've got a bite!" Cecil whispered with excitement. "Get ready!"

Davey's face went severe and he stood with a shaking hand. The bark immediately dove and disappeared from sight.

"Now!" Cecil cried to him and Davey pulled back with all of his might; more than was needed in the thrill of not knowing what was on the other end.

His pole slightly bent at the narrow end of the long tip and Cecil jumped up and took hold of his line for him. Davey threw down his pole as Cecil handed him the line that was taut with pull.

"Get him in!" Cecil shouted with a smile and watched Davey pull on the line, hand over hand with a steady look of intense determination.

A fish jumped from the surface with a strong fight and Davey's eyes were wide with what appeared to be slight anxiety. He dragged him in across the reeds and got him to the safety of the shore.

"Another bream!" Davey shouted.

"It is! What a catch, Davey! They must take a liking to you!" Cecil laughed. He helped him get the fish off the hook and they strung him by the gills to a line of hemp twine that Davey kept stuck in the mud at the waterline. "One more of those and we'll have supper!"

"I will give it a go, Cecil," he said with a proud smile and baited his hook again. Davey cast in his worm and sat again after the excitement had subsided and the two of them enjoyed the quiet of no responsibility for the day. After a while, Davey's thoughts eventually turned again to the things that had troubled him throughout previous days.

"Cecil?"

"Yes, Davey?"

"What do you think about the mad wolf?"

"What do you mean?" Cecil asked, becoming somber.

"The wolf that killed the Windham family," Davey said, pondering the idea with much debate, "how was he able to create so much havoc with so much license?"

"How do you mean?"

"My schoolmates were told by their fathers that he's only a wild wolf and that someday he'll be killed or captured...but there must be something more to him. There must be."

"What men believe is only what they understand," Cecil said as he looked to the ground with some measure of dejection.

"Why didn't Mister Windham protect his family?"

"Why do you say that?" Cecil asked, dismayed.

"Why didn't he shoot the creature?"

"How have you determined that he did not? How have you determined that he did not do everything right?"

The boy looked at him in amazement and wonder as the profound statement engraved deeply into his mind.

"Do you think that men would be so yielding to surrender their lives? Nay, they would fight savagely for them until the bitter end...by whatever means and with whatever reserves they had at their disposal."

Cecil paused for a moment in his thoughts before he

spoke. "And neither would such a beast, if it were, and so capable of such treacherous disregard for innocence, be so easy to stifle or to destroy."

They were both silent there along the water in the retiring grasses of the fall.

"In my lifetime," Cecil continued, "I have found that things are not always what they seem…and the truth of men is not always what they've understood."

Davey meditated upon Cecil's words in wondrous fear as the whirring call of a Kingfisher bird displaced the silence.

Chief Inspector Allcott held a conference for detectives in the West London Police Station. In the great room of meeting, which was rather dull in appearance, twelve men gathered, sitting at tables with their pads of paper to collect notations of significance. The commissioner stood near the door.

"Just a brief word. It has been brought to our attention that our Doctor Phillips is a member of something called the Golden Serpent Society," Brannigan stated, "…a secret club of notable men involved in science, professors of medicine, study, and the like. We have determined that a Doctor Ashcroft of Northamtonshire may be able to shed a little light on the details of our missing professor, being that the two were, on occasion, summoned to give corresponding lectures. With permission from Commissioner Howe we will locate him for questioning."

Commissioner Howe looked to the men. "Robert,

Edgar – you will accompany me."

"Dismissed…and keep your ears open," Detective Allcott ordered.

The men left their seats and began to exit through separate doorways on the right and left sides of the room. The commissioner turned to the Chief Inspector with an additional request.

"I'll take Tindale with me as well, Detective," he added.

"Tindale is on leave for two days, sir," Detective Allcott responded. "His wife's cousin in Belemont has passed away. I believe his name was Eaton Barrett. Said it was peaceful…in his sleep. Can't ask for more can you?...but for the timing. Sad, so young…forty-six or something. He had seven children."

Commissioner Howe became immensely disconcerted and stared at him with disbelief. "Are you certain?!"

"What do you mean, sir?"

"…that it was peaceful?!"

"Well, why wouldn't it be, sir?" the detective asked, puzzled.

Morton shook his head. "Nu…nothing," he stuttered softly.

"Right, sir."

The detective looked on. "Are you alright, Commissioner?"

Morton nodded, staring off in thought and waved his hand for him to go on. Detective Allcott went his way, the last man to leave the room, and closed the door behind him.

Morton Howe trembled and was nearly overcome with despair. His face twitched again as he fought an urge to cry. He quickly rubbed a small tear from his face with his hand and then punched down onto a desktop with his fist in frustrated anger. He cleared his throat and slowly regained his composure as he went to a window and stared out into the street without moving for some time – thinking, speculating, and desperately planning.

The door that stood at the end of the long hall at the Watermill Inn was numbered – 6. Within its void and gloomy contents, Cecil stared upon the words again, handwritten on an empty page in the back of the Bible...

Albern Partridge ~ Alphonse Harrow

Eaton Barrett ~ Hunter Harrow

Hugo Faulkner ~ Washington Harrow

Jack Todd ~ Ramsey Harrow

Morton Howe ~ Morris Harrow

Garrick Winchester ~ Simon Harrow

His face was plain as he took hold of a steel nib pen, dipped it in ink, and crossed out some of the names that were on the list. He laid it to the table and went to the dark window. From the shutter, a calendar of days was suspended by a wire with markings he had made in ink upon it. October the Thirtieth was nearing and had been circled. He lifted the latch, opened the shutters, and gazed upon the crescent moon in the night sky - impatient in his ravenous craving.

On the portion of field left to support sheep on Mister Breggins' estate there had been an opening for escape. In light of the men's fear that the old man himself would come to find out twelve of his ewes were missing, they had set to seek them. It was good that Cecil was one chosen to assist in the humble search. By chance, he had the vacancy in his schedule of duty and Mister Wycliff could not have selected better. With rumor of a killer wolf perpetually on the minds of those who worked the fields in England, especially so close to the now notorious attack at the Windham Farm, the men were pressed to give immediate search, but they did not expect great success.

Three men were allowed to set out from the known property with a ration of food and water in hopes they would be able to return before sunset.

Cecil was given a crook staff on the edge of a far hill and within he could not help but to be so greatly amused. His wagon departed, being the last of the party to be dispatched in his direction of search and he spoke to himself as he went forward on his way into the wild.

"The wolf placed in charge of tending the sheep," he said with a smile.

He set out and followed a buckle in the hilltop that led down like a faint river bed with a skin pouch on his shoulder and the tall staff in his hand. He could not have been happier to be excused to wander the countryside alone on a day that was clear and comfortable. It was certainly good for anyone in mind, body, and sometimes soul. He deviated from his prearranged western course and headed northeast, taking rising and falling hillocks to which at times would overlook vast expansions of scenery. It had been over two hours and he could have gone on all day, continuing beyond what was known, what was expected, and fading into distant horizons - to not come back and let go…never to return. It tempted him to large degree, as it does all mankind, but knew there would inevitably be a time after all was finished, when the course had run, for such things.

They were there, those very simple and defenseless creatures likened unto humankind by God, grazing quietly in a hidden valley of White Campion, Chicory, and Autumn Hawkbit wildflowers. He had detected them very early on from the first hilltop of Mister Breggins' land and with acute smell in tracking, unhurriedly went to them.

With melancholy, he sat beneath a fruited hazelnut tree and took his meal in the breath that blew over the soon to be dormant things from a nearby and unseen November. His thought went to what Burney's would be as he looked upon the staff that lay in his hand, alone on that hill.

As the afternoon drew on, Mister Wycliff was very pleasantly surprised to find Cecil coming over a distant ridge with the lost sheep. Others in the field witnessed his gentle leading them again into the fold and Burney gazed on with a big smile at the image portrayed.

He was met by several men who were nearby with cheer and admirations.

"Very well done, Cecil," Mister Wycliff commended him. "This has lifted a burden from my shoulders I was afraid would not go. I thank you, sir," he said with a handshake.

Burney stood alongside him with a few other men and patted his shoulders.

"It is the good shepherd," he said with a soft smile and a warm face, "who seeks and saves that which was lost." He smiled even more and put his hand on Cecil's shoulder again. "I have found a name for you."

Cecil shook his head at Burney with a smile and his words had secretly filled him with the stinging sorrow of self disappointment.

Cecil found himself in the offices of Mister Breggins soon after, standing at the same door he had so many months before.

"It is a notable thing you have done to day, Mister Griffiths," the old man stated with respect. "I am honored and blessed to have you part of the family here."

He stood from his chair and extended his hand with a smile. "It is appreciated," he said with a nod and a handshake. "Please, feel free to enjoy the rest of the day at your leisure as my thanks. Misses Hartinmoore will have a special preparation of victuals for you to take as you go, in the cookery, if you would honor her."

Cecil, uncomfortable and somewhat humbled by the attention, returned a small smile to his hospitable host and said no more.

Albern Partridge was escorted in chains to the magistrate by two guards. Disheveled, his look was of pure venom and he could hardly refrain from violently attacking all of the men around him and being taken right back to the black hole they dug him out of. His sentence was served in hard time, in length to cool his anger against those whom he had put in his household to protect, and the musts of the cold cellars had seeped into the joints of his bones like a cancer. Forty-seven was too old for such extensive maltreatment and in his mind there was only one cure for the ailment.

He arrived at a high and simple podium to which he was looked down upon by the Justice of the Peace. The room was rather small, low ceilings, and surfaced with rich dark woods throughout that absorbed the mood. Behind the standing authority who dressed conventional in dark blue with silver buttons, were two large windows that cast its overbearing white light into the prisoner's evil eye.

"Albern Partridge, you are to day pardoned... released on your own good recognizance," said the magistrate. "The time being four o'clock post meridiem ...the day being October the Thirtieth." He looked up from his paperwork to the man who seemed bent on killing him with no care on his face.

The guards unlocked the shackles from Albern's wrists and gave him his coat, which was provided a month earlier by his wife, but was withheld. He snatched it from the guard's hand, furious, and put it on as he walked out, leaving the building and stepping into the street.

"I'm gonna kill 'em," he said under his breath and ground his teeth together.

Chapter 13

The office of Doctor Ashcroft was quite spacious. A gentleman of repute in the world of medicine, he was allotted a large area to freely attend to his business in the university that acquired him. He sat behind a very large desk and the detectives who had come to visit stood in a half-circle at the wall in front of him. Curious examples of human anatomy were displayed in glass domes along a shelf that bordered the room's waist. Below these at knee level, many publications of thesis, essay, and periodicals of medicine were stored upright in volumes. Two windows lit his relatively uninviting workspace and the blinds were pulled halfway. He took a look at his callers who had interrupted him with a cordial smile and he remained respectfully seated.

"How may I be of assistance to you, Commissioner?"

"What can you tell us about the man, Moyer Phillips?"

"I can tell you that he is missing," he answered quite seriously.

"Anything else?" asked Morton, unamused.

"Well, I can say that I've known him for approximately five years because of our coinciding professions and that he is a very damned good doctor of medicine, sir."

"And his history, Doctor Ashcroft?"

"From what I understand, he never married, unless you recognize his work, that he hailed from a German father, arriving in London at a young age of fifteen for his formal learning...Studied intensively at Oxford on a prestigious graduate scholarship for what was a celebrated term and had many successes in consequent years of discovery and method. I had not the pleasure of attending university with him as a result of our age difference, he being some six years my junior, and have thoroughly regarded his work with utmost respect. That would about sum him up I should think."

"From London?" Commissioner Howe inquired.

"I should think so, sir."

"...And his family?"

"Possibly a surviving relative or two in France?...but I cannot be certain. I can only say there seemed to be no one of consequence in England that I could imagine."

"What would you know about a live animal cage that he kept in his home, Doctor?"

"He is a doctor of science, Commissioner...I'm sure that they have many of them," he answered sarcastically.

"What about you, sir? Do you keep live animal cages for study in your residence?"

"I do not," Doctor Ashcroft replied as if it were a matter of preference. "I suppose that is his arrangement."

"You would commit your studies to the confines of a more academic establishment?" Howe questioned.

"As I have," the doctor answered snidely.

Commissioner Howe looked at him, considering the changes in his attitude of voice with intense but subtle study.

"What would a man of his experience keep in such a cage, Doctor Ashcroft?"

"I could not possibly say."

"A wolf perhaps?"

"Your guess is as good as mine, Commissioner," he stated with a smile.

There was a pause as Howe stared at him, reading his eyes and face during his responses.

"Did Doctor Phillips at any time mention to you that he had caged a wild animal for experimentation, Doctor Ashcroft?"

"I am not at liberty to say, Commissioner Howe."

Morton frowned in his suspicion of the answer and was prepared for a response.

"You were in league with Doctor Phillips both as members of what is known as the Golden Serpent Society. Isn't that correct?"

"If there were such an institution, I would have no comment," he replied with the duality of a sly and sincere smile. "I'm sure my allegiance would be binding and under no condition could I violate my loyalties to it - those being, in part, the confidence that its members would enjoy," he finished with an antagonistic stare.

"I will take your indisposition for my questions always as a yes, Doctor."

"I am sorry, Commissioner, that I am unable to be of further assistance in these areas," Doctor Ashcroft said earnestly, but was not to Morton's tolerance.

"And the other professors of science that were in some way affiliated with him...are they in the same position?"

He raised his eyebrows and slightly shrugged his shoulders. "You'll have to ask *them*, Commissioner."

There was a short pause as the men stared at one another, unmoving.

"We're finished here," Commissioner Howe told his men. The detectives filed out of the room and Morton turned to the door and put on his hat. "I will most certainly be at arm's reach, Doctor Ashcroft."

"Has a crime been committed?" he asked most seriously, desiring to pry and learn confidential police matters that he could informingly disperse to the curiosities of the Society.

"We're just looking for a missing university professor," he answered with an obvious counterfeit smile and indignation in his voice for the fleeting solutions an unrelenting drive forced him to discover to protect all things that he held most dear and then walked out.

Albern made sure he darkened the door of his favorite public house upon his release before going home to deal with what needed to be done. He stood at the bar, having been there for several hours, and was drunken by the liquor that unlocked the cage door and brought out the vile creature that was subdued within. He knocked back the short glass of colorless Russian vodka and called the enabler that fed his insatiable lust.

"Hoi!...Barkeeper!" he shouted in a tantrum, holding

his empty glass with slurred speech. "Stint not from an patron, weary and scarred, wrung dry in the dungeons of Hell an' near wasted away!! Cried out did I to the lighted angels as they passed and yet went unnoticed but for the devils that held me and savored mine flesh and bone!"

"Alright, now then! Keep it in an ice bucket!" Mister Hettenwood, whose face was frighteningly painted black and white in the image of a skull, shouted back to him from behind the counter.

The front door of the place swung open wide and two large festive men entered the establishment wearing pirate captains' tricornes of beaver fur with accompanying eye patches for a later All Hallows' Eve party. The customers let out a big laugh and raised their glasses in a complementing toast.

"The clear and cunning vodka of the Russian country would so pleasantly decorate my cup!" Albern yelled aloud to the delayed skeleton.

The barkeeper, annoyed at his repugnant drunkenness, pulled the cork on a large ceramic jug and tipped it over Albern's glass. Albern reached into the pocket of his coat for more money and slapped down a plain white folded piece of paper to the table for the barkeeper. Mister Hettenwood put his hand around Albern's glass and pulled it to him.

"You're gonna need more than that for another drink in here, Albern," he said with a mean look.

Albern slightly pitched backward and forward, maintaining his balance, as he brought the note to his face. He opened it, laboriously, with blurred vision, and slowly read the words that were written within.

~Leave the city of London To night ~ Do Not Return Home ~ You are Not safe.

"What is this??..," Albern said softly, angered that it was not money.

"If that is all you have, then it looks like you've finally come to the very end," said the barkeeper.

Albern became enraged, crumpled the tiny parchment into a fist, and reached again for his glass. Mister Hettenwood grabbed his arm by the wrist and held him there.

"You try to steal from *me*?" he said, gritting his teeth in a newly intimidating exaggeration of his costume, now with a good enough reason to beat the nuisance over the head.

Albern's eyes turned red with fury and he pushed the barkeeper backwards against his bottles along the wall. None of them fell or were busted as the ghoul caught himself, easing his way out.

Immediately, the two large pirates, who were chums with the proprietor and sat nearby, jumped on him and tried to get his head locked in the crook of an arm. Albern, with strength that exceeded them both together, twisted round and got them both up at the neck by the collar. He ran them both backwards and slammed them against a wall with both fists clenched, reveling in the brute challenge.

As he did, the white skull raised his head up from under his chin with a stout cudgel as he stood beside him.

"It's a good thing you didn't break my bottles or I would certainly break your head. Get to your home where they tolerate drunken penniless bastards...we don't let 'em in here...before I send you to those dungeons of Hell that you've so acquainted yourself with."

Albern loosed his grip on his two opponents as he fixed his eyes upon the barkeeper's club. He turned his head and spat on the floor and walked out.

On the street, Albern threw the crumpled note that remained clenched in his fist to the ground as he plowed through the avenues towards his flat in a tunnel of revenge. He stomped quickly with determination past the wanting idlers that deteriorated among the buildings in the dark.

Morton Howe and his wife sat in the large open entertaining room of a home of close friends at the lighthearted and engaging party for the observance of Halloween. There were many guests and all were dressed relatively casually; as much as could be expected for a gathering of many friends without overdoing it and to leave enough range of movement to enjoy much of the physical activities that were surely on the itinerary. Everyone, some thirty people and not including children, were in chairs that were lined against the longest walls on two sides, facing each other. This left a generously accessible area between them for playing and dancing. Many candles were lit and three chandeliers burned to allow for visible accuracy in the instance one should need it when in the entanglement of a difficult game.

Their jittery hostess, Misses Edith Sterling, a lively thirty six year old woman, had been preparing for the event for many months and was thrilled to be endued with the planning of the dinner, dancing, music, and most of all, games. Her holiday décor was heavily premeditated and in every nook and cranny was some type of gesture. Images of harvest, crafts made like goblins, and finger cakes formed into white ghosts were in some portion of an empty space and most of her guests had never seen anything like it. It was very suggestive to the creepy mood that would occasionally appear over the party goers and the younger damsels would easily be on edge when the lights went out. After a fine dinner with tea and coffee the games and the ghost stories began.

"Attention everyone! Attention!" Misses Sterling called. "Our next thrill of entertainment will be Blind Man's Buff!" she said with a shrill giggle.

Her company cheered and laughed.

"But! I have a new version! We shall all wear masks and he who is *It* when they grab another, must guess who it is whom they've grabbed by feeling their mask! Those who are not guessed are freed and allowed to remain in the game! When the *It* guesses five names the game is over and we shall have another! If the *It* gets five wrong answers then they're out of all the remaining games!"

"Oh! How very enormously difficult!" a young gentleman, the hostess' first cousin, shouted. "What fun!"

"Don't you agree?!" she exclaimed. "We shall have the most peculiar and difficult game of Blind Man's Buff to date! Ha!" she laughed loudly. "Frederick, my love, pass around the masks so that everyone may play."

Frederick, a young lad about nine years of age, did as his mother told him. He took up a wood crate by the hand holes and went around the room. The happy guests took strange and comical likenesses from a heap and laughingly held them to their faces by the sticks that were attached.

"Now that everyone has one, put your mask on your face and look around the room and try to remember who is who!" the hostess said.

The guests did as they were instructed and it was hard for them not to laugh.

"Now, remove your masks and look at every face and then do it again. Try to remember who is who!"

"Now! Mister and Misses Howe, it is your turn! You must choose which of the two of you shall go first!" she giggled with overflowing excitement.

They both laughed at the choice and were caught off guard. They looked at one another with another laugh.

"I shall make a fool of myself first, my dear," Morton said with a happy reluctance and she could not wait to see what he would do. "I had no doubts that I would be the first to be tested at Misses Sterling's game," he said softly to Julia with a smile as he stood to relocate himself to the middle of the floor.

"Mister Howe, your handkerchief, sir," said Misses Sterling.

Morton took out his silk and blindfolded himself.

"Now, are you certain that you cannot see, Mister Howe?"

With a smile he responded, "I cannot, Misses Sterling. I am as blind as a bat."

Julia secretly laughed to herself because she knew that bats were not all that blind.

"Everyone ready? One, two, three!"

The masked crowd jumped and wiggled, climbing the chairs and leaping from them as Morton Howe held out his hands and quickly went forward at their footsteps and squeals to catch them. Everyone shouted with deceptive calls from all sides and finally a low passerby was nabbed along the floor.

"He's got one! Alright now, listen everyone."

Morton rubbed his hands over the papier-mâché monkey face of a giggling person.

"It is young Selina Goodridge," he said.

Everyone went wild with laughing.

"You're right!" screamed all of the children.

Morton went at it again and got hold of two different arms at the same time with a surprise lunge.

Misses Sterling shouted. "You both must wait and

let him try and guess!"

Morton named both the laughing giraffe and the whiteface clown with accuracy. Again, he revealed the gray witch and the yellow cat with ease and proved his mastery of the game.

Everyone cheered as some playfully accused him of cheating.

"You'll have to excuse the superb powers of memory that my husband possesses," Julia cried, "it comes with the whole!"

Everyone laughed.

"What could we expect from a police commissioner?!" the hostess giggled. "I don't think one of us can follow that performance!"

Everyone at the party laughed and cheered for Morton who stood, removed his blindfold, and took a bow.

Albern stepped to the doorway of his previous home in the dingy golden light of the upstairs hallway. A door of another flat down the hall from him opened and a woman costumed as an imp and carrying a baby stepped out. He turned his head and looked at her with a scowl and she quickly returned in fright, closing and locking the barrier between them.

Albern quietly took hold of the doorknob and tested to see if it was locked, which it was. He drew a deep breath and sighed and then gently knocked.

"It is I, your husband," he said in a calm voice.

"Now as the gentlemen have their respite in the lounge for a drink, the ladies will play a special game of 'looking mirror'!" Misses Sterling said in a voice that suggested it would be a scary endeavor. Some of the young ladies were not so thrilled anymore and did not want to play that one. "Now, it's only a game, ladies! No need for serious alarm!" she laughed. "Although the upstairs bedrooms are haunted to night."

Misses Sterling's face went completely washed with cadaverous depiction and then immediately brightened with a joyous cackle to frighten her guests.

"What we'll do," she said, "is each lady, maidens or married, will take with her an apple alone with one candle into any of the darkened bedrooms. She will close the door behind her and with her light, try to peel it all in one single piece. Then she shall place it in front of a mirror and look in. You will see your true love's face in the reflection."

The nervous girls that gathered around as if listening to a ghost story relaxed and then smiled at the comforting resolution.

"But…," Misses Sterling continued, "if you see a skull it means someone is going to die."

A chill went up everyone's spine as the perfect Halloween hostess softly giggled at their faces.

The ladies took their candles from a basket, lit them from a flame, and gathered at the foot of the great red staircase that twisted away into the dark. Each took an apple on a china plate that was set with a small paring knife, made ready on a table beside them.

"Each one of you go into your own room and close the door behind you," she instructed.

Selina, who was fifteen years old, began to tremble and whine. "I don't wanna go alone into the room. I'm too afraid."

"Don't you want to see the face of your true love?" asked Misses Sterling, tenderly, as she held the arms of the terribly frightened girl. "It will be fun. Go on. You will be quite safe, my dear."

Julia, who stood near her, instilled a bit of security.

"You will be fine, Selina, we shall all only be just a door apart," she said with a warm smile.

Their hostess took a candle and led them quietly up the wide staircase into the dark halls above. She stopped with a final whisper.

"Remember to keep your apple peeled in one piece and to look deep into the mirror."

The ladies went past her, afraid, and took hold of the doorknobs along the halls. One by one they slipped away inside and the lights of the halls were gone.

Julia stood alone, afraid by the warnings and the unfamiliar room. She stood like a statue at the door after it had closed behind her and stared with large eyes at the dark in front of her. For a moment, she thought to retreat and lie, but thought of the other ladies in the other rooms peeling away and nearly finished.

She snorted with nervous laughter at the scare Misses Sterling put into all of them and stepped forward to the vanity mirror that was on her left at the foot of a bed. She sat down into the dark chair and quickly and carefully began to peel the apple in complete silence. Her hands shook and she struggled to keep a firm grip on the knife and had the awful sense that something was in the room with her, watching over her shoulder. She knew it was only her aggravated imagination and tried to complete the task as soon as she could.

Finally, with what seemed like an eternity, she spiraled the apple to completion. She put it to the plate and slowly leaned forward in the dull light of a single flame and her breath was shaking within her nostrils. Julia sat still and peered into the black of the mirror.

A tall skeleton, wrapped in a long hooded cape of mourning, stepped forward from a curtain behind her and looked her in the eye. His face was both agonizing and terrible.

Julia screamed out in heart-stopping fright and all of

the women charged into her room.

"Julia! Julia! What is it dear?! What is it?!!" Misses Sterling cried.

They took hold of Julia's arms and held her as she turned around and saw nothing. She wiped her eyes of tears and quickly tried not to draw any more attention to herself.

"Oh, I am sorry!" she said, trembling with a racing heartbeat, with a cry mixed with a false laugh. "I got so into everything and I scared myself in the mirror," she said, passing it off as naught to them. "I did not mean to scream like so."

"Oh no! No, no, my dear! This was much too frightening a game for us," said her hostess. "We shan't play it again."

One of the young girls, in an attempt to console her, brushed through the curtains behind them. "See, Misses Howe? There is no one here."

"Come," said Misses Sterling, "let's go to the refreshments and get you something pleasant. Let's have no more frights to night."

Julia nodded her head with a small smile and they brought her out with care, but she knew what she saw.

"Albern?!" his wife answered, surprised and afraid from deep within the door. "Is it you?"

"None other," he answered in a normal tone.

"I did not expect you!"

"Well, who *did* you expect?" he said in a way that seemed playfully amused.

"Well, no one, I mean...," she stuttered. "A'..are you well?"

"I feel well enough. Why don't you open the door and see for yourself? What you got me here in the hallway for?"

"I'm afraid, Albern."

"Afraid? What would you be afraid for?" he said sweetly.

"You were so angry....Albern...and we didn't want it this way. We didn't want it this way. You weren't supposed to be taken to the jail. See? I...I delivered your coat for the cold. I do hope it was given to you, Albern. I didn't want you to suffer. We didn't want it this way. I didn't want for you to be gone, Albern."

"Is the boy with you?"

"Yes, Albern. He was just afraid is all. Those men were the only people that he could find to help him. He was just afraid. He's just a young boy."

"What did he need help for?"

"He didn't mean anything to be done, Albern. He was just afraid and didn't know that you didn't mean to hurt me...that's all," she struggled to explain with rising tension. Her jaw began to tremble and it was hard for her to enunciate her words.

Albern took hold of the doorknob and squeezed it in his grip. He began to drip with sweat in the cold air. "There, now. Let's not have it any more between us. You come open this door and things will be back as they were," he said, breathing hard.

"I just want to have a p'...peaceful evenin', Albern. Will you hurt us?"

"No," he said in a way that seemed to make her concerns ridiculous. "I'm not gonna hurt anyone. I just want to come home. I'm tired."

"You just want to come home?" she asked from within with a voice that sounded like she was crying.

"Yes. I just want to lie down in a real bed and sleep. We'll talk more on the morrow," he said, appearing to be sincere. He stared into the wooden door as if he were talking to her face to face with a believable mask. There was a quiet pause and not a sound came from within or from the open hall. The lock on the inside clicked in Albern's hand and he turned the knob.

The door slowly squeaked open and he saw her standing, holding her son beside her, away past the kitchen. He stepped in, closed the door, and locked it behind him. He stood still and his eyes were red as he dragged a smile across his face. He exuded great drops of sweat and it dripped from his chin. She quickly ran to him in nervous fear and wrapped her arms around his waist with her head down.

"Welcome home!!" he shouted like a lunatic and grabbed her by the hair and yanked her head back as hard as he could, pulling some of it out in chunks.

She screamed in horror and the boy nearly fainted with fear. He pulled her forwards by the hair through the kitchen and past the boy. She tried to walk along with him, sliding her feet, as she begged him for mercy. The boy's face went long and white and he completely froze in shock.

Albern beat her in a bedroom that was off of the main living area, then came out and locked her in. She jumped up from the floor after him to get out, but was too late and the door slammed shut in her face.

She screamed with agonizing howls and beat upon the door, pleading with him. "Albern!!! Please!!! Noooo!! Please, Albern!!! Please do not hurt him!!!.... Nicholas!!!! Nicholas!! My darling!!" she wailed, violently.

Albern walked quickly to the boy and snatched him up by the arm, nearly pulling it from the socket and raised him into the air. The boy was petrified and made no sound as he was dragged and shaken like a rag doll into Albern's torture room.

Albern slammed the door behind him with a boom that shook the walls and cracked the framework inside.

The boy's mother nearly went mad as she rammed herself upon the door, but was too weak to get out. "Nicholas!!! Nicholas!!! Nicholas!!!!"

Albern, in his drunken rage, punched the boy on the side of the head and accidentally knocked him unconscious, not inhibiting his strength. As the lad fell over against the wall, Albern got up on a ladder and took down his long leather whip with wood handle he kept high, halfway to the ceiling of the tall room. He went and stood over the boy, switching hands with it.

"I've been saving this for you, you little stain."

He raised it into the air over his head and the window behind him shattered into a thousand pieces.

The black wolf, wild and terrible, jumped onto him from behind and knocked his face into the forward wall. All of Albern's front teeth were broken out of his head and he spun around from the floor to his feet quickly in complete awe and confusion. The wolf slapped him sideways across the head and knocked him down onto the wood floors with an enormous thud. Albern backed away with real terror in his eyes and got to his feet, looking up at the wolf's frightfully intimidating height. With his empty fist, he punched the wolf in the face twice and swiped him over the jaw with the wood handle of the whip in his other hand. Albern backed away, quickly, against the wall and cracked the whip at the wolf to keep him back. The wolf raised his left arm in defense and flinched when the whip sliced through the air, standing still on his feet. The tall beast looked on Albern in amusement, watching his eyes and face.

The wolf stepped forward and Albern cracked his whip in fear. The wolf quickly dodged to one side and then came back, fooling Albern with his position and the whip cracked again and missed. The look in the wolf's golden yellow eyes then became determined and angry as he cornered the terrified man…like a rat.

Albern, shaking with blood trickling and smeared from his mouth, swirled the end of the whip around through the air sideways at the wolf's head and cracked it again down beside his hip. The wolf ducked and was missed as he took another step toward Albern.

Albern crisscrossed the snap of the whip in an X in front of him and in one fast motion sent it at the wolf's head from the side again. The wolf ducked lower, touching his hand to the floor and moved another three feet closer, going slightly side to side as he went.

Albern sent the whip wildly in all directions, slicing down from above on one side and then the other, but could not land a single blow upon the agile beast.

The woman could hear the heavy cracks of leather from her room and screamed, endlessly weeping for her son in madness.

The wolf walked steadily forward and backed his shoulders away or tilted his shoulders forward with both hands on the floor, the whip blowing his long hair only inches away.

Albern, in great fear, panicked as the wolf slowly came at him unharmed and undeterred. As the wolf leaned in, Albern sent a curving tremor through the whip in which it deceitfully appeared to create a loop and then on its finish, released with an upward lash. The wolf jerked his head upwards and away, but the very tip barely sliced open his lip. The wolf paused and put his knuckle to his mouth and looked down upon a tiny droplet of blood in his hair. He looked again to Albern and growled in irritation.

The wolf stood right in front of him as he resumed and whipped the strips of leather up at the creature's face, going underhanded. The wolf darted to the left as the whip came up from the floor towards the ceiling from Albern's right and caught him by the hand while his arm was extended into the air.

The wolf squeezed and crunched every bone in Albern's swinging hand against the wood handle as he clenched the whip. Albern screamed in agony. The wolf took the rawhide from him and raised him up into the air by his hand and he hung from it with his weight. The wolf, keeping Albern hanging by one arm, looked upon the whip and turned it over in his hand. Albern continued to cry out in excruciating pain and was unable to do anything to attack him. The wolf looked to Albern and dropped him three feet to the ground.

The man turned over on his side and rolled up on the floor, cringing, holding his arm. His hand quaked violently and his broken fingers opened and closed involuntarily from intense nerve damage. He screamed continuously.

The wolf stood and stared at the whip in his hand and then looked down to Albern, wallowing on the floor. He growled and flashed his long rows of teeth. His eyes became dark and vengeful.

The wolf raised his arm and whipped Albern repeatedly, roaring down onto him. Albern crawled to a corner, covering his head and face with screams. His right hand was mutilated and deformed.

The fearsome beast did not stop and beat him until the man's blood splattered onto the walls. The whip ripped through the air and shredded Albern's clothes until they started coming away from his body. Albern wailed upon the floor and the heavy wet leather tore away the wallpaper around him. The wolf slashed him with the whip over and over, the blood dripping from the wolf's arms and face, the walls and ceiling. He flogged him so brutally and incessantly that Albern's leg came off and his screams were silenced as he fainted. The woman's screams penetrated the walls from her prison as the cracking of the whip continued without ceasing. The wolf persisted in his blood-soaked execution with the whip until Albern's head was severed from his body and rolled over on its side.

He stopped, drawing great breaths and fatigued. He was wet with patches of sweat and blood in the thick hair that covered his entire body except for two small places on the front and back of his left shoulder. He huffed a low growl in disgust and hatred as he stared upon the mutilated body of Albern. In the light of the burning oil lamps in the room, he raised the bloody whip to his face. His eyes widened in anger at the sight of it and he threw it from him. The handle stuck into the wall and blood flowed to the floor from it.

The wolf held up his hand, watched the blood drip from his fingers, and turned his eyes to the wall. He put his clawed finger to the wallpaper and wrote as the woman continued to beat upon the walls and sob at the other end of the flat. He looked over at the boy, who was saturated with blood and remained unconscious, lying still against the wall near the door. He crouched down low beside him and could see that his chest moved with breathing.

The wolf turned and stood, panting with spurts of saliva in his exhaustion and stared at the door. He took hold of the doorknob and it was locked. He punched it gently at the lock beside the brass knob and broke it open, splintering the wood frame with the dead latch on the other side.

The wolf gently removed the boy's shirt, pulling it up over his head, and carefully wiped away the blood that was over his eyelids. He pressed the cloth to the floor with both hands and pushed it over the entire room, working his way backwards in the blood to the window, smearing away his giant footprints.

The wolf crawled out the window, taking the shirt with him, and down the ledges of the building over a dark alley unseen.

Chapter 14

At Commissioner Howe's police building there was a lot of commotion from the handful of detectives over the missing professor. They had been assigned to teams to track and question each person of science within the limits of London. Commissioner Howe was becoming increasingly desperate for answers and was ready to inflict results, but had hardly anything to go on. He sat in his large office, rubbing his forehead with his hand with his back to the door when there was a knock.

"Yes?!"

Detective Allcott entered and Commissioner Howe did not move.

"Another murder in Zone One last night; a Halloween surprise…one you might want to assimilate…a bloodbath, sir."

"Whereabouts, Allcott?" the commissioner asked, concerned, without turning around.

"Trottenbur Street, sir."

The detective turned and went out.

Morton closed his eyes and bowed his head. He breathed out slowly while very subtly shaking his head, worried, and rose to follow.

The commissioner's carriage stopped at the building that he feared and he stepped out onto the street. He looked side to side and then up to the roof as he let out a very apprehensive sigh. The constable guards watched the entrance that was elevated upon a stair of stone as he very reluctantly went in.

He climbed the staircase to the second floor with the burden of a thousand griefs and followed the constable to the door of Albern's apartment. He stepped inside the flat where he met Detective Shipley near the back.

"Here, sir," the detective motioned for him. The two men entered the room that was filled with police where the mutilated corpse laid.

Commissioner Howe nearly lost his breath and his heart began to race within him as he accidentally looked into the eyes of Albern on a detached head. The scene was shocking and grim and he was not prepared to be seen by the other men around him. He found it hard to breathe and felt that his heart would sink in his chest. To conceal his trembling, he worked his handkerchief over his mouth and fumbled with it.

"I reacted the same way myself, Commissioner, upon first entry," Detective Shipley stated, averting his glance with sensibility. "This is nothing like I've ever seen in my life, sir." There was a pause as they looked upon the red spatters that had dried on the walls and ceiling in abundance. "I am sure there isn't a drop of blood left in his body. Clearly, he was beaten with the whip that is now penetrating the wall behind him."

"I expect no less than two hundred lashes by first impression, Detective," a coroner looking closely at the body stated from the floor.

"I can't imagine someone physically able to do this without limiting exhaustion," Detective Allcott, who stood beside them, remarked. "It would have taken one man hours."

"The *athletic* culprit," Shipley said with a smirk towards Detective Allcott, "obviously entered through the window somehow although there is no terrace or means that would make it straightforward and then exited through the front door by what I perceive from the broken dead latch from within. It is obvious that the footprints were smeared away by some means over the entire room and the shoon were removed at the threshold where the criminal had to have left carrying them.

His wife and her son who lived here with him, who found him, said they were away at her sister's and saw none of this transpire." Detective Shipley looked to the other men with raised eyebrows hinting possible repudiation. "The nearby tenants have nothing to report, claiming to 'ave seen and heard nothing in the night...which was expected in such a lovely...unified colonization," he said sarcastically with anger. "His name was Albern Partridge."

There was a moment of quiet as the coroner carefully picked over the remains and no man spoke.

"This will be a formidable business, Commissioner," Detective Shipley continued. "He had innumerable enemies...a hard man. Just released from prison on domestic charges...turned in by the boy according to a report. Looks like nearly everyone had some measure of animosity towards him."

Commissioner Howe was straight-faced and nodded with his inner stress only showing in his clenching jaw.

Detective Allcott spoke. "Whoever did this certainly wanted him dead...and to suffer first."

Morton prepared to turn away when he was

interrupted.

"And another ghastly thing, Commissioner, to note," Detective Shipley said, pointing. "The wall behind you."

Morton spun around where he stood. Written on the wall in long sharp letters in dried blood was ALPHONSE HARROW. His eyes got wide and he began to shake beneath his coat. A tremor of fear shot down his back and his face twitched with terror. It was a name that he knew very well.

"I wonder what it means?" said Detective Allcott. "Could it be the name of our killer?"

"We shall strive to find out, Detective," Shipley responded.

Commissioner Howe did not speak a word and quickly left the flat and ran down the staircase to his carriage.

Upon the great River Thames in London city, a massive fuse mill sat where ships could import and export its goods. Commissioner Howe's carriage was driven into the alley that separated it from the warehouse building nearby. As it stopped, he got out and studied the size of the place, stepping forward toward the water as his driver waited.

He passed outdoor storage areas packed with empty wood casks that had been stacked in rows. Workers went past him without care as he made his way to the docks upon the river inlet at the back. He stared upon a steamship that sat quietly moored to the shore with a giant cylindrical iron boiler with rivets and a bell-shaped top protruding from the center of its weather deck. He did not move and thought to take it for the Thames flowed into the open sea. He stared long and the feeling inside him was ill-boding.

Mister Hamford of Hertfordshire was in his barn near dark tending to the animals there when he heard a commotion among his sheep in the field. He took up his lantern, ran into his house that was not far away, and came out carrying his musket gun.

As the sun was setting, he quickly lighted out into the field and spotted a gray wolf coming through his wood fence at the far end of his land. The sheep became crazed and bleated wildly, running away from it past him. The wolf quickly dashed into the center of the field and took hold of a young lamb in his teeth by its hind legs. Mister Hamford was at a great distance away, but sprinted towards him with unyielding determination.

The wolf flashed his eyes up and then saw the man coming at great speed.

"Hoi!! Turn her loose, you devil!" he shouted.

The wolf turned with the lamb in his mouth, ran away, and attempted to jump through the fence with it.

The farmer stopped for a steady arm, pulled the gun to his shoulder, and fired.

The mayor of Ramsbury Barlow borough beat his fist upon a pedestal to demand order from the excited attending public. The seats in the town hall of meeting were completely filled in the dark evening and hundreds of onlookers lined all of the walls around them. The place was well lit from above with gas chandeliers as The Worshipful, Godwine Atterberry, presided over the emergency meeting.

"Noble citizens of Ramsbury Barlow, London, and neighboring boroughs! ...let's have order so that our dear Mister Hamford can address you!" he said.

Mister Hamford stood at the front, near him, facing everyone as the ruffled noise of the people began to die down. Commissioner Howe was sure to be in attendance and stood at the very back by the door among them with several of his detectives.

"It was wild and careless!" said the farmer. "I hailed him, but he did not heed my call! I feared for my own small children when I saw the size of it! What if they were in the field unawares of such a beast?! ...and I were not to be found?! I shudder to think of what might have happened here if it had turned out another way! I...thanks be to God...was able to get the gun to my shoulder in time to fire!"

The people began to make their commotion again.

"And killed it I did!" Mister Hamford continued, "'afore some other evil befell us all!"

The people shouted with anxiety mixed with gladness. A man stood up from his seat in the middle of the room.

"Surely, it was this creature! Wolves no longer exist here in England...and to discover this *one* wolf?!!" he cried.

Another man got to his feet and shouted. "Surely, *this* beast was brought upon us by Beelzebub, Prince of demons!"

As he spoke, another cried out. "A plague of evil!...a curse has been lifted!!"

"We've killed the murderer of the Windham family," a man said while weeping and quickly rubbed his eyes with a kerchief. "Our community has been avenged! Graham, Cynthia, and their precious Marie have been avenged!" he said, pointing his finger. "The

248

wild beast is dead…our families are safe!"

The people made a great commotion with shouting and applause.

An Anglican priest stood and raised his arms. "We will hold a dinner of celebration to honor The Lord for this great victory at Christ Church on the Sabbath after the ten o'clock Mass!"

The crowd cheered as Commissioner Howe turned and went out. He went around the side of the building, alone, to a parked horse-drawn cart and threw open a blood-soaked canvas that laid in the back. The gray wolf under it was dead, shot through the heart.

He and he only knew that there was something more and it made him disturbed to his very soul.

$\mathfrak{C}$ecil laid back into his bed. With his cold staring eyes he fixed upon the beams in the ceiling of his room. Another night without sleep, he rose early and went out as the sun was rising. He stood motionless at the door of the Watermill Inn with a vibrant unrest within. The street was silent and still and the red sun of the morning began to make its way over the distant tops of trees. He felt nothing for its beauty or its purpose, but very deep within he wanted to.

As crimson as the Kermes dye of the scale insect crossed over the landscape before him and finally rested upon his face, he both despised its coming and rejoiced for it. He looked long, unflinching, into its power and knew that everything was trivial beneath it.

"There is nothing hidden under you that will not be made known. All is vanity. Men come and go, doing what they will, but you do not remember them," he said with a disappointed spirit.

He stepped away into the cold morning with hardly a covering on his body and was not wanting. November came on with her designs as Cecil had his own.

Before he knew it, he had made his way to the Beecher Pond and waited. The place was still except for the few birds that had not yet departed for winter. He sat along the cattails of the shore thinking about the boy. After some time, the farm wagon which took him to work rolled past on the distant hills and he heard it. He got to his feet and went his way.

Detective Allcott and Detective Shipley rode up on the fuse mill in a carriage where Commissioner Howe stood waiting outside to meet them. He was smoking a pipe and eyeing the rooftops when they stepped out. Another carriage came behind them carrying three more of their party and all five men came together in the alleyway, staring upon their guide. Morton crouched and tapped his pipe onto the ground. When the burning tobacco fell, he snuffed it out with his shoe.

"This way, gentlemen," he said as he quickly stepped away and entered a rugged wooden door at the building's side in front of them. The detectives followed.

Commissioner Howe led his team through a couple of cold halls and entered a large area where dozens of women were seated in many rows along fuse manufacturing assembly lines. They worked together in pairs at rope braiding machines. Along a continuous horizontal cylinder that spun six feet above their heads, dozens of wide belts led down to their equipment and drove them. The men went past with respectful nods and the women watched as Morton met with the floor supervisor and shook his hand.

"This way, Commissioner." The man took them through another door and into a massive open warehousing space and stopped. "If you should require anything further, sir," he said as he courteously nodded and went out, closing the door behind him. The sound of his voice and the door echoed in the empty expanse. The men were alone.

The detectives carefully unwound an enormous roll of heavy chain on a spindle against the wall and dragged it across the room, going some one hundred feet to the center. Commissioner Howe called out to them from the front to signify its placement. Along another opposite wall, Detective Shipley cranked a large iron handle, winding a massive chain upon a reel. As Detective Graneere uncoiled a long line of cord from a wood box, Brannigan flipped a tiny metal switch back and forth upon the great roll of chain. Commissioner Howe stood back and looked over the space to the ceiling that was fifty feet in the air and then drew near to his men.

"Remember your orders. Tell no one of this," he said as he turned away and exited through a door.

"What is all this about?" Detective Cornwall asked.

"You're a detective, Cornwall. Why don't you figure it out," Shipley said with only a very subtle gleam in his eye. The other detectives looked at one another in wonder with slight smiles, but said nothing.

Mister Breggins, in his usual custom to deliver important news to his employed, stood at the tables with his early November report. The food was served in the comfortable environment of the hay barn and the men gave him their attention as they ate.

"Well, another is again upon us," the master stated. "Three days is the fifth. The Gunpowder Plot of 1605 has given us reason to light fire and make merry in excesses."

The men laughed.

"I want to make known that the Ramsbury Barlow organizers have devised a special observance that I understand to be safe and memorable for all; a simple and enjoyable celebration including grand fireworks, bereft of religious infractions or parliamentary exploitations."

The men then looked on Mister Breggins with smiles and partially serious faces; faces which reflected inner feelings of mild anarchy and moderate apathy for portions of England's leadership that were common in some realistic measure.

Mister Breggins looked at them with a snort, unable to ignore it and paused, taken aback by the subtle expression that resounded from them all.

"A time when we all get to relieve a bit of angst," he said with another snort.

The men lightened and snorted themselves as they looked to one another over the tables.

"What will your effigy be?" the master said with a smile. The men laughed again and several of them were forced to bite their tongues. "Shouldn't it only be the devil we're all at odds with?!"

Cecil looked on with raised eyebrows as the others

poked at each other with whooping.

"Everybody secretly wants someone to burn," Mister Breggins cracked with a hardy chuckle and an eye under an insinuating brow and the men pounded on the table in their laughter.

Cecil looked upon Mister Breggins and his fellows from the end of the table with an agreeing and entertained smile.

Working class children solicited door to door on Guy Fawkes Day begging for money or means to build the fires that would accentuate the outer edges of Queen Victoria's London. The city streets of the afternoon was swarming with great numbers of them after their day of school had been dismissed.

Commissioner Howe exited his police building to take his carriage and stopped to look at them as they stole his attention and his thoughts. He left his path to the curb and walked along the buildings of the block away from his transport. He put his hands into his coat pockets and followed two of them up the street. As they climbed the stair to a house and knocked on the door, he stopped and watched them from afar.

The door opened to them and the young boy and girl held out burlap sacks and began to sing.

> *"Don't you remember,*
> *the Fifth of November,*
> *'twas Gunpowder Treason Day.*
> *I let off my gun,*
> *and made 'em all run,*
> *and stole all their bonfire away!"*

"Ah! Wonderful, dear ones!" the elderly couple within remarked. "We've got a bit of goods and chattels for your sacks!"

The woman placed combustible strips of worn clothing into the mouths of burlap and turned with another gift.

"You've won a pleasant surprise, poppets. Treacle sweetmeat for the delight of your bellies!"

"Oh!" the children said in elation. They held out their hands and each one got a break of bonfire toffee.

"A pittance goes a long way!" the woman said with an affectionate smile.

Morton Howe stood still and watched the children depart. He turned and headed back to his carriage as a curiosity took form in his head.

He passed near the outskirts of the city en route to a private and voluntary cross-examination of Doctor Bentridge at his offices. From the window of the door he saw children gathering wood from the brambles and hedges. They threw them in heaps for the festivities that would soon transpire.

As he arrived at his destination, Detective Shipley met him at the doctor's door as he was exiting.

"Nothing," he said, disgusted.

Commissioner Howe looked at him with a bitter expression and did not speak.

"I just spent an hour with him and learned nothing of any significance at all. We're dead in the water, Commissioner."

Morton turned around on the step and gazed out to people who were stacking long scraps of wood into tall cones and carrying boxes of entertainment supplies from the carts nearby.

"There's something more to Ramsbury Barlow," the commissioner stated to Robert, who stood behind him on the step, in a soft whisper while keeping his eyes on them.

The detective lowered his head and looked upon Morton with intense concentration and curiosity for his manner. His declaration came out of nowhere.

"When the fire draws out the rats, we shall have a peek," Morton said, facing away, yet with a continual distant look in his eyes.

The teenage boy that did Mister Holling's bidding at the Watermill Inn softly knocked on Cecil's door in the silence of the hall. The door opened a small amount and the boarder leaned against the wall in the gap.

"Evenin', sir," said the boy. "There be a cart to carry residents to Potterbur Field for tonight's party if you'd be wanting, sir...to leave in an hour. Should we expect you?"

Cecil looked at him in odd quiet. In his delayed response, the boy could see that he was in some exigent debate about the option. He said no more and waited.

Without so much as a minute detail of character, Cecil answered him slowly as his eyes looked past, down the hall and back. "Very well."

The bonfires raged across England and the night sky was decorated with immeasurable towers of smoke embodying great ashen roses with countless petals. In Potterbur Field in Ramsbury Barlow borough the residents amassed with excitement. Mister Breggins and the men of his employ were also there together among the diverse array of peoples.

Cecil joined his friends and sat on the corner of a table alongside Burney Yarborough with a wary eye over the crowds. They were situated on an end of the carousing near wide trees and the great fire, even at a distance, shone brightly on them.

The tallow torches erected at each side of the marionette stage drew children like moths to its light. Red curtains, miniature versions that resembled those of the Duke of York's Theatre two hundred years before, parted to reveal a beautiful backdrop scroll painting that set the performance's opening location in the gardens of Coombe Abbey.

From tiny stage right, a lovely young princess marionette strolled in wearing her plush gown with ornamental beads that glistened in the light.

"Oh, hum," the puppeteer man spoke in a feminine voice as he was hidden above in the rafters of the wee theatre. "I wonder what I shall do? The birds are singing. The meadows are so very lovely and I am in fits for what I shall do to day. I cannot waste such a day where there would be so many grand experiences to discover!"

Another marionette girl entered from behind her. "Princess Elizabeth!" she cried in another feminine male voice. "I thought I would not find you in the splendor of these gardens!"

"Ha ha ha!" laughed Princess Elizabeth. "This is where I always am on such wonderful days as to day!" she giggled. "Isn't the sky a colorful blue of peacock plumes and frothing clouds of white egg whip topping?!" the marionette said joyfully as she raised her head with a taught string and gazed upwards to the master who controlled her.

"It is indeed, My Princess! Here, I bring bonfire toffee as a gift for you." The doll lifted her hand in a make believe passing of invisible candy and Princess Elizabeth brought it to her mouth and chewed.

A helper from the production dressed as a court jester went through the children that sat on the ground and dispensed toffee among them from a silver bowl.

"Why don't you visit your father, King James the First, to day?"

"That is a splendid idea, Temperance! I shall!"

The two dolls went away and a new scroll painting of a dingy hideout with little gray rats along the walls dropped to the floor. In came a fellow wearing a slashed doublet, a wide reticella lace collar and cuffs, and a broadbrimmed hat. His face had a long black curly mustache and his chin had a long pointy beard. Much care went into his costume and the little devil put on a show.

"I am Guy Fawkes!" he said boldly to a new cluster of onlooking fellows that stood on the opposite end. "I have put thirty-six barrels of gunpowder under the House of Lords and we shall blow them up during the State Opening of England's Parliament on November the Fifth, sixteen hundred and five! Afterwards, when King James the First and his Parliament are dead, we shall kidnap Princess Elizabeth and install her on the throne as Queen!"

The audience of tiny men cheered at his idea.

"Follow me!" Guy Fawkes shouted to his plotters and the stage was cleared for the next scene.

The king's throne room backdrop unrolled to the ground. A very royal rendition of King James entered from stage left wearing a tiny golden crown.

"Father! Father!" the princess called, "I have come to visit you!"

"My dear Elizabeth! My child, what has brought my lovely daughter to the royal throne to day?! How grand to see you!" the king said with a wiggling wooden jaw beneath his fuzzy beard. The marionettes leaned forward at their waists and gave a very precise and pretentious peck on the lips.

"Nothing more than my love for you, father," Princess Elizabeth answered sweetly.

"There is none in all my kingdom as beautiful and desirable as you, my darling!"

"Oh, father!" she giggled.

At that moment, from behind the king, two armed guards of his court abruptly entered wielding their tiny shields manipulated by a second puppeteer in the ceiling.

"Sir, come with us at once! There has been an evil plot for your life!" they exclaimed in urgency.

"What shall we do?!" cried the princess.

"Have no fear, my daughter! You shall be safe with me!" the king valiantly proclaimed and the royal party quickly jumbled their legs and scampered off the stage.

The backdrop of a grim courtyard fell to the floor of the dramatic presentation. Upon it was painted the gallows and a guillotine was in the distance. A new version of Guy Fawkes was pulled on stage by guards. He was now shirtless, dirty, and in chains. An executioner entered from the other side and pronounced judgment.

"Guy Fawkes, because you have plotted to kill the King," he said, "I sentence to you to death where you shall be hanged, drawn, and quartered!"

The executioner, wearing a black hood, held a shiny axe that he quickly raised into the air over Guy. Guy fell to the ground and screamed out as the axe chopped down on him and rent his torso in two. The marionette twitched and jerked as the executioner raised his blade and dropped it down again onto his legs. Guy wailed in agony and died as the puppet's limbs separated and came apart with a trigger switch activated by a thin thread.

The arms, legs, and torso with head were dragged away in sections as the children were captivated by the drama, zealously chewing their candies with sticky teeth.

As Burney Yarborough and others of Cecil's acquaintance carried on with smiles and laughter over the ridiculous 'Guy' effigy that was then paraded on a perishable straw chair around the blaze, Commissioner Howe, Detective Graneere, Detective Allcott, and four other constables from West London entered in on foot from the outer darkness. They were not in casual clothing, but were suited in their midnight blue police uniforms. The glow of their faces was intimidating in the fire's light. They were not arriving to enjoy the historical significance of the celebration, but to scrutinize.

"Oh, welcome gentlemen!" Commissioner Belamie cried with great cheer. He was very relaxed and disregarded any obligations to duty. "Commissioner Howe, Detectives," he said with a nod and a handshake to each man, "I am honored to be host to you this evening and happy you were able to make the journey!"

"It is our pleasure," Commissioner Howe stated directly without the appearance of amiability. After he shook hands, his eyes turned to scouring the crowds.

"Please," continued the Ramsbury commissioner, "how may I first assist you gentlemen?"

"I would simply like to speak to a few cornerstones of your community and ask some very general and brief questions if that would not infringe on the spirit of frivolity," Commissioner Howe said with a higher level of volume in his voice to cut through the cheers.

"Do as you wish, my friend. You have the respect of all in our borough," Belamie said with another handshake and a wink.

Commissioner Howe nodded with a short smile and Commissioner Belamie led the men in further among the people.

Morton scanned over every man's face that he could find and watched the reactions to his men's presence as they traversed with determination. He looked to the outer edges of the field to the people that naturally faced him because of his position with the fire. He carefully watched for anyone that attempted to depart from the party and retreat into the forest.

Commissioner Belamie approached Mister Holling, who sat smiling at a table with his friends.

"Mister Holling, this is Police Commissioner Howe from West London. Sir, would you mind answering a few of his questions?"

Mister Holling looked surprised as he turned in his chair and raised his eyebrows.

"No, sir. Not at all."

"Commissioner," Belamie said while turning back, "Mister Holling is the owner of the Watermill Inn. He would be one to speak to about your concerns. Please, excuse me, gentlemen."

"Obliged," Howe answered as Commissioner Belamie was dismissed and his men surveilled the entire area from where they stood. "Sir, would you happen to have come across any persons of suspicious nature, boarded them, spoke to them or of any such instances where you might have been in contact with an curious character of questionable or unknown history?"

Mister Holling's mouth slightly opened as a name gently touched on his thoughts, but before he spoke it, Morton continued.

"Someone that comes and goes at strange irregular hours or sleeps at odd times of the day?"

The innkeeper then shook his head as the newer

options faded the idea that had been in his mind. He pondered the latter question for a moment and shook his head again.

"No. There isn't anyone like that that presses me, Commissioner. Not as far as I can suggest. The current tenants of my establishment adhere to strict work schedules and have been for quite some time."

Commissioner Howe nodded. "Are there any of your current tenants that may not have attended to night?

"No, sir. My assistant was good enough to offer everyone a courteous transport here to which all accepted.

"Very good, sir," Morton responded. "You have been most helpful. I appreciate your assistance. Enjoy your evening."

"Commissioner," Mister Holling quickly injected as Morton took two steps away, "Um, there is a Mister Breggins who operates a large farmstead nearby who also does much of the hiring of hands in this area."

Commissioner Howe looked on with a changing expression of interest.

"He would be one to speak to as well, sir. As a matter of fact he is here and many of his men I can see sitting there along those trees," he said, pointing his finger.

Commissioner Howe quickly turned around along with all of his men and looked upon those who had congregated there. "Again, in your debt, Mister Holling," Morton said.

"Good luck, sir," the innkeeper added as he returned to the comical conversations of his table.

Detective Allcott and Commissioner Howe quickly went in the direction of the men that sat at tables arranged under the trees. He approached Burney

Yarborough first because he appeared to be a man of more experience by age.

"Please excuse my intrusion, gentlemen," Commissioner Howe said politely, "I wonder if I might have a word?"

Howe's men approached and studied their faces with discernment.

"Certainly, sir," Burney replied.

"I am Commissioner Morton Howe of West London. These are my officers. I have a few inquiries that I hope you may interpret, sirs," he said while looking upon all the men at the table. They nodded to him.

"I understand that you men are employed by Mister Breggins."

"That is correct, sir," Burney responded.

"Could you please tell my detective here which of these gentlemen here would be him?" Howe asked.

"Yes, sir," Burney answered. "He is there beyond those tables," he pointed, "seated with his wife. Wearing the top hat with the gray-white beard."

"Thank you, sir," Detective Allcott answered with a nod and went in his direction.

"Are there any of your fellows of Mister Breggins' employ that you have not observed here to night?" Howe asked. "I mean to say that would everyone be accounted for here to where my questioning would be exhaustive and all-encompassing as far as your associates are concerned?"

"Oh certainly, sir," Burney explained, "Every man of our affiliation is in attendance to night." He looked around side to side, but did not see Cecil nearby.

"There has been some suspicious behavior in London city and we are here on a succession of tours to the neighboring boroughs for inquisition and examination," Morton clarified.

Burney looked around and back to the others. "Guido, where's the good shepherd?" he said softly and then turned back to Morton. "I can only see one who isn't standing here now, but is hereabouts somewhere, Commissioner," said Burney. "Mister Griffiths."

Morton turned to his men. "See if you can locate a Mister Griffiths, Detective Graneere, gentlemen," he requested with a nod to his subsidiaries. They parted and stepped away, heading toward the massive bonfire and the people that rejoiced nearby it.

Cecil leaned against a wall in the middle of London city as revelers charged down the street past him in riotous mischief. Burning barrels of tar rolled by gravity down the cobblestone avenues as torch bearing vandals threw stones into shop glass windows for personal vendettas. The common people were terrorized in that section of London and retreated to their homes.

The mounted police were overcome and their horses reared and jumped as the crowd ignored them. Constables on foot pushed back taunters that hovered at the outer edges of the blaze while the buildings overhead echoed cracking booms of fireworks.

Drunken enthusiasts paraded a massive hay-stuffed Guy that was ten feet in height and set it over the blaze on opposite poles. It immediately caught fire and fireworks shot out from its head and whizzed and crackled over the buildings in the night sky.

Detective Shipley raised his pistol and fired into the air from his horse as the ungovernable river of shouting rabble-rousers flowed past him. Cecil stood unmoving against the building of the street and stared at Detective Shipley who was pulling on his horse's reigns in a struggle for control just a few feet away. He studied him, unnoticed, with a face of stone and the chief officer was forced to temporarily relinquish his effort.

At that moment, a brick struck Detective Shipley on the side of his face and threw him from his horse to the ground. He landed on his back and was still, trying to focus on the things happening over him. His horse reared and twitched, but remained near him. He was dazed and tried to remember what he was doing on the ground as the legs of runners jumped over his body. The perpetrator, a wild and dirty man with a wide round face, crazed with tangled black hair and unshaven with only a few teeth came and stood over him with a malicious smile. As Detective Shipley closed his eyes and began to black out, the lunatic raised a large flat stone over his head to crush him.

In an instant, Cecil rammed him from behind with lightning speed with the force of a steam engine. The man shot forward as from a gun through a large shop window on the curb and his head broke through the oak business counter that was situated in the back. He was killed instantly on impact and his body sat with the knees on the floor and his head peculiarly held secure in the hole.

In the chaos and explosions no one saw him and he took Detective Shipley by the arm and pulled him from the street into an alley. Cecil took him around the chest from behind and carried him up a wood stair to the rooftop above his horse and gently laid him down on his back.

Detective Shipley opened his eyes again and a beautiful display of exploding color lit the sky in front of him.

Morton prepared to address the men at Burney's table and the words were in his mouth. Detective Allcott was introducing himself to Mister Breggins at a distance as Detective Cornwall rode hard to the property behind them with pained urgency.

"Commissioner Howe! Commissioner Howe!" a voice cried desperately in the distance over the noise.

Commissioner Howe stopped and turned away to search for the caller.

"Commissioner Howe!" Cornwall cried again from atop his horse on the edge of the field.

Morton spotted him and raised his hand. He turned around quickly to Cecil's companions. "Please excuse me, gentlemen. Deepest apology for your disturbance."

Detective Cornwall waved his arm for them to hurry.

"Come!" Commissioner Howe ordered to his officers. "Something has happened!" The men departed in haste and Detective Allcott quickly broke away from his introduction and joined them.

The men gathered to Detective Cornwall who was frantic.

"Zone Three is under assault!" he stated. "North London has lost control and requests emergency aid! I left Detective Shipley at his request to bring you, Commissioner, and vandals have assumed authority of Blateney Street!"

The commissioner and his men mounted their horses alongside him with speed.

"I should have known better than to come," Howe said softly to them in regret and pulled his horse away and rode off with his officers into the night.

Davey and a bunch of school boys ran over the grasses on the edges of the field, chasing each other with playful shouts. They waved sticks in the air like swords and charged the imaginary enemies ahead that would threaten to storm their gates.

In the solitary darkness of the countryside, Cecil walked the lane that parted the forests and rose slightly to higher ground. He went quietly with his hands in the pockets of his coat. At the far incline ahead in the dark, a group of riders galloped at full speed toward him for the city. He stood still in the middle of the path for only a short moment in the shadows of the trees and the horses ahead immediately halted in alarm, sliding their hooves into the mud. The riders were nearly hurled from their saddles.

Commissioner Howe and his officers were confused and looked at one another in uneasy wonder, but they did not speak. They knew the horses had seen something ahead on the edge of the lane. The men drew their pistols and held them tightly.

Morton kicked his horse gently to make her continue on slowly. The others followed behind and he searched the shadows. The horses neighed and whinnied and the men had to wrestle them under submission as they peered into the black around them. Morton's horse came to a stop on the lane and was restless. She stamped and whinnied, startled by something in the dark. The others waited behind him and became lightly calmed and quieted down.

Morton became still.

Cecil hid in a thicket very close beside him and everything went dead silent. He watched him from within and Morton unknowingly fixed his stare directly at him in the leafless brush.

The horses in the rear snorted and nothing moved. Cecil squinted his eyes as he looked upon him with calculating concentration and readiness.

In the immensely heavy still, fireworks from the distant city lit the scraggly trees and sent crawling shadows over the jagged sticks of the dry undergrowth. Cecil's unmoving features seemed to dance in the faint highlights that tried to surrender his ability of unequaled stealth. Morton sat completely still on the path, listening, and looked for him intensely without relent with only his moving eyes. He raised his hand and pointed his pistol.

The wind changed on Cecil and the horses began to smell him. Morton's horse backed away to the opposite side of the lane and stamped with a nervous whine. Morton leaned to the side in the saddle and lowered his head and focused on the moving shapes brought on by the lights in front of him. He knew that what he hunted was near, but did not suspect that his greatest enemy was upon him in the dark. He remained silent and with much heed to the warnings within his soul, was too afraid to call out to it.

Cecil resembled an animal that was ready to pounce on its prey from the sprawling fingers that reached up from the twisted arms around him and the commissioner, buying himself more time, chose to ride on in his plight.

Chapter 15

$\mathfrak{M}$orton Howe kept in continual acknowledgement being in the position that he was in. He and his wife Julia spent much of their free time at dinners or other honorary functions that would associate them. She was a virtuous woman and fair, a proper wife to possess for a man who was the face of the police organization. He loved her and held her in high regard and she was good for him. They never had any children of their own which at first was a great disappointment for the times at their age. They both agreed it was probably for the best in the end as Morton climbed the ladders of notable police work in his youth through his thirties, which had significant domination over his personal life. To this, Julia did not mind and chose to support his accomplishments and betterment that gained him much respect from lawmakers and leaders; ultimately putting her into a beautiful home that she adored.

He had found himself at ease at the lavish celebration of the Lord Mayor of London Sir Lambert

Jules Rowland and his lovely wife, Lord Mayoress Ambrosia's thirtieth wedding anniversary. Morton's wife accompanied him to a dinner ball for the aristocracy of West London, held at the Lord Mayor's glamorous mansion by special invitation. It was these highly anticipated rewards that the women attached to such gentlemen were so able to relish. Brannigan Allcott, his wife Marilynn, Robert Shipley, and his wife Toulouse were those to be honored to accompany Commissioner Howe to the event and Julia could not have been happier. The affiliates not only got on so very well, the Howes had also been elected godparents to their children.

It was very different, but not unusual to see the men together in sharp black suits in addition to the silk top hats that made each man occupy the character of a distinguished partygoer. The guests were escorted to the cloak room where their wraps, shawls, and overcoats were courteously handled to which the men and women parted. The men found their way among some one hundred or more guests to the Refreshments Room where they were immediately served a fine Portuguese port to their well-being and the women to the chaises of the Ladies' Lounge for primping.

The ballroom's location was clearly identifiable by the outflow of music along the golden ceilings overhead. A sizeable orchestra was at pleasing fulfillment, expelling the works of Mozart to the enjoyment of anyone with a trained ear. Along greatly embellished tables of before dinner snacks for the dancers, many dozens of silver bowls and trays held fantastic assortments of tea sandwiches, biscuits, cold tongue, bonbons, coffee, and cake with punch fountains. At the gathering of nibbling men at the presentation, Morton came across an acquaintance from another side of London that he was pleased to see.

"Detective Samuels," Morton said with a handshake.

"Commissioner Howe," he said cheerfully, "good to see you, sir. How are things coming?"

In polite and light conversation, Morton admitted nothing. "As well as can be expected," he answered.

"Criminals still multiplying like rats," he stated with Morton's agreement.

Morton raised his eyebrows with the attitude that could be expected from a man who continuously saw it all on a daily basis. "Sadly, it is true," he answered.

"Commissioner, I would like to introduce you to my friend here - an American."

The gentleman Detective Samuels referred to was memorable by appearance. His eyes seemed a bit sad and it was not only because of their natural shape. It was an impression that Morton perceived at first glance. He had curly black hair that started at a high hairline and wore a neatly trimmed mustache that was a remarkable accentuation to his face. The circles under his eyes were analogous with them where he naturally appeared to be troubled and tired although Morton could recognize a man who chose a glass of laudanum over all else for whatever reason when he saw one.

"...from the United States, Philadelphia, Pennsylvania," Detective Samuels said. "...Works for the popular *Graham's Magazine* and intends to start a literary journal.

Uh, Mister Poe...Edgar Poe," the man answered, changing hands with his glass and extending a quiet handshake to Morton.

"Morton Howe. Pleasure, sir."

"Likewise."

"Mister Poe here is a celebrated author and poet," Detective Samuels continued in his introduction. "Perhaps you might have heard about his success of '39,

The Fall of the House of Usher?"

"Oh? Very good," said Morton. "My compliments. How very interesting. What brings you to Great Britain, Mister Poe?"

"I am incognito; running away from scenes of the tested truths that I have so meticulously exacted before I am found guilty of the very things that I have written," he said with a mixture of both sarcasm and shocking genuineness.

Morton and his fellow detectives laughed at the gentleman's odd response even if it were to be true.

"Let me remind you, Mister Poe, you are in the presence of many very cunning police detectives," he said and all men of the conversation chuckled.

As Mister Poe took a sip of his own mixture, he responded. "I would hope that the commissioner would grant me this one final evening of impunity before placing me under the careful scrutiny of his office."

The men laughed again.

"With that, I must now pardon myself, gentlemen," Detective Samuels said with an entertained smile. "It is now left to your discretion, Commissioner," he laughed. "I bid you all a good evening."

As he walked away into the crowds to kiss the hands of multiple ladies, the other men of the company excused themselves away to the summoning of wives and other business professionals. Mister Poe was left alone with Commissioner Howe at the tall heated silver server of tea.

"I am sorry to hear of your late President Harrison," Morton stated as a transcontinental peace offering.

"Yes, a tragedy, but I am happy to say the now President, John Tyler's son, Robert, is an acquaintance whom is to appoint me to the Philadelphia Custom House."

"Indeed? I pray good fortune in the matter," Morton

replied with a sip of red port. "And of your writing...is there anything now currently in the works?"

"Certainly, Commissioner. A true storyteller never retires. There is always something currently in the works," Edgar stated quietly. "A tale entitled, *The Murders in the Rue Morgue*."

Morton raised his brow at the name. "I can see that you deal with the world of the macabre, Mister Poe."

"Not unlike you, Mister Howe," he answered with a penetrating gaze that seemed to read Morton's very thoughts and expose all of his intentions, past and present. His mood had slightly changed. The commissioner did not answer him, but remained fixed in a mutual stare into the eyes of the mysterious.

"Men who have experienced bitter processes of death," Poe continued, "have a finalizing yet eternal secret bond with coequals. Men who *are* death even without the luxury of experience also carry a bond, but it is something of another sort; bestowed with the diabolical gift none so many would be enriched with to see into the hidden plane of Hell through curtains which are continually opened for all, but it is only they who acknowledge them."

"Do you imply anything, Mister Poe?"

"Not I, Mister Howe. I would not be so bold. It is the consciousness of men that press them to see the twisted faces in the mirrors within."

Edgar Poe gave Morton his undivided attention and it seemed to them both that there was no other sound but the words that came from their mouths.

"Like I, you also understand the meaning of these things," Edgar said slowly. He paused. "What was it really, Commissioner, that made you do what it was you have done? Or what was it that made you do what it is that you do?"

Morton looked at him with cloaked surprise, not

having such a question cast at him in many years or ever as far as he could remember. He looked at the man and he was right; he did feel some peculiar connection to him and for what reason in the natural realm he did not know, but felt it was from some unseen parallel universe that crossed all mainland and landmasses, globes and cosmos. The man had him pinned down without mistake and he wondered if he could put it into mere simple human words. He thought about Mister Poe's origins and his distant home, how it was another world away and chose to be candid without fear. Instead of other possibilities for the discussion or to deny the charges that left him naked, he gave him his answer.

"We do not choose what we will do, Mister Poe. It chooses us."

Edgar looked into his drink with thought; a concoction that the world had put into his hand and returned his eyes to Morton.

"You have spoken well, my friend."

Morton looked upon him intently and studied the man's face with a burdensome curiosity.

"What was it really, Mister Poe? Why did you make the journey to Britain - so far from your home?"

Edgar looked upon Morton with decisive valuation without moving for a strangely amount of time and then answered in a soft but deliberate voice. His face was as straight as stone.

"It was to stand here and speak to you, Mister Howe."

Morton snorted a quiet, but nervous laugh as his company surely jested with him again, but Edgar did neither smile nor laugh at fate. He looked into his face and quickly became somber within his own afterthoughts and recollections which haunted him like devils from long past.

At that moment, their generous host called his guests for announcement.

"My dearest colleagues, friends, and closest family," he stated from a podium temporarily placed at center stage of the ballroom above the orchestra. "It is tonight that my captivating wife, Ambrosia, and I celebrate our thirtieth wedding anniversary!"

"Huzzah! Cheers! May you have many more!" the party shouted.

He and his wife smiled with great pride and honor at the enthusiastic plaudits.

"It is as some of you may already know an extra special occasion, for tonight is also our youngest and most beautiful daughter Rayna's sixteenth birthday!"

His guests cheerfully applauded with a roar and their claps were the muted beats of hands in white gloves.

"Sixteen wonderful years ago," the Lord Mayor announced, "a precious gift was brought into our lives and it has been nothing less than marvelous." He held his glass to her and his guests did likewise. "Your mother and I love you, my dear. Happy birthday," he said nearly shedding a tear.

The ladies and gentlemen clapped and the musicians tapped their bows upon the strings.

"Now for a memorable gift," he said to his daughter. He turned to the extravagant staircase that curved beautifully to the second floor in the great foyer and upon it was the famous and very handsome young opera singer, Angeloni Bellanicio.

The man was dressed for the stage. He wore an iridescent blue velvet outfit embroidered with green silk thread with matching buttons and cape which he slung over one shoulder. His hair was gloss black and he had the dark eyes and face that all young ladies and their mothers would hope for. The guests immediately cheered for him as he stepped to the stage with a great smile, waving a silk kerchief and began the girl's favorite British broadside ballad.

Immediately, the men took the hands of the ladies who were dressed in the very finest off the shoulder gowns of all colors and styles of bell-shaped skirts. Some of their hair, including that of Julia Howe, was styled with a part down the center with ringlets that dangled from the sides. Some were fashioned in loops around their ears and pulled into buns at the back of their heads. The couples, which were everyone in attendance, began with a brisk and lively Waltz to suit the music.

Upon turning his wife by the hand, Morton's thoughts were far elsewhere. He was severely pained and tortured by it all. Mister Poe's words rang in cold remembrance as the night wore on. He unintentionally searched the rooms for him, but could not find him.

Chapter 16

There was nothing on Cecil's mind except his cycle. The hour was at hand and it meant more to him than what would take place in the physical realm. It was the cycle of balance - an eye for an eye and tooth for a tooth. He stood from his bed and in the light of his lamp he stared into his own eyes at the mirror. His chest swelled and contracted as his breathing became heavy and he started to sweat. He snapped up his coat and blew out his light. The room went black, but the moonlight shone strong from the slats of the shutters in the darkness.

Cecil went hard and fast through the street alone. He quickly escaped the small town and, in the faint white light overhead, darted like a hind into the forest. As he entered the trees upon a hill that overlooked London at a great distance, he pulled off his raiment in the cold night. He growled and grunted with steaming breath while he stripped naked and threw his clothes to the ground. He trembled with madness as he scoured the surrounding woodland with wild eyes to the sky. His nostrils flared and his demeanor heightened into rage. He ran swiftly over the forest floor going deeper within. In a small opening in the massive trees above, Cecil stopped at the sight of the Full Moon. He breathed like a wild beast through his clenched teeth and stared down at his arm. Thick black hair began to slowly sprout from what seemed like every pore and he grunted and hissed. He tightened the muscles on his entire body as they slowly bulged and enlarged. The tissue and tendons around his neck and throat strained and flexed as his grunts and howls altered into much deeper and lower tones. After a moment, the color of his flesh had become obscured by the heavy covering of hair. Cecil moved side to side and stepped forward as he gradually grew in height and mass. His face mutated and was deformed, elongating slowly as he stomped his foot with a great thud upon the earth. He turned his head and looked into the darkness around him as he transformed into the eight-foot wolf beast with gargling growls. He fell forward onto his long and powerful arms and beat the ground with a menacing fist. He snarled with a wide open mouth and saliva dropped from the row of teeth that had protruded from the long jaw of his head.

The wolf shook as he stood fully up and raised his terrifying face to the night sky. He inhaled a massive draught of air under the moon and let out a howl that trembled the forest. His eyes widened with the thoughts of what was to happen and he turned in the direction of the city. With a shattering roar he jumped forward and flew through the trees at super speed, breaking limbs and snapping the fallen brush of the undergrowth. Like a shadow on the wind, too fast to see, the wolf shot through the tree line into the open and leapt over the hillsides on the infallible path to London.

The fire in the brick hearth warmed Morton Howe's study in his home. He sat alone in a comfortable leather chair, facing it, as the distant streets were quiet in the night outside his windows. He rubbed his forehead with both hands and quietly wept. In his lap lay his flintlock pistol and he reached again for the Scotch whiskey that sat on the arm table.

The clock on the mantelpiece struck nine o'clock with a musical chime and he quickly wiped the tears from his face. His wife entered the door behind him.

"Morton…dear…are you well?" she asked softly.

"I am," he said plainly while raising his hand.

She turned and left him, not knowing what to say.

He rose, put on his coat that hung from a rack beside the door, and found his wife in the parlor. She looked lovely to him, quiet and still in her lime colored chemise with her shoulders wrapped in a cotton shawl with lace. She was reading a book by a lamp on the end table and was warmed by an inspiring fireplace. She noticed him watching her and they both smiled. He became sincere.

"Remember when we went to your father's summer cottage in South Wales? You were so young then," he said with sentimental melancholy.

"We both were," she answered with a smile.

"We walked barefoot on the Pendine Sands of Carmarthen Bay and took a boat to Caldey Island."

"The Old Priory Tower and Saint Illtyd's Church was so beautiful and ancient. I can still remember the Benedictine monks that lived there," she answered.

"I wonder if the lighthouse is still standing? I wonder if things have changed?" he said.

"In that old place? Certainly not. Some things will never change."

"And some things do," he said. "It was so much simpler then."

"It was another time," she said with a smile.

She was a woman in her early forties, but her eyes were still bright as when he first met her.

He paused for a moment in thought and then spoke again as the logs crackled in the hearth. "Those men…the monks…do you think they will ever win their salvation?"

She set down her book and stood from the cornflower blue sofa settee to meet him. "I think every man must continue to strive for honor. No one can change the past. …And in the end he has to work it out in his own way. No man can earn forgiveness no matter how hard he may try," she said softly. "It is a gift, given by the one to whom is owed."

She came near and he took her hand. He pulled her to him, embraced her gently, and kissed her cheek. After a moment of quiet together in his reflection and hope, he finally spoke.

"I am sorry, Julia."

She pulled away. "Sorry for what?"

"For the times I let you down."

"You've never let me down, Morton," she said, reading his troubled face.

He looked down and would not look into her eyes.

"Look at me," she said tenderly. "I have always loved you. Everything about you. I've not been disappointed in you a single moment that we've been together. You are my love and I will never have any regrets."

He looked at her, moved with compassion towards her and was deeply remorseful; more than he could ever remember and it travelled far into the uttermost depths of his soul. "You are the *one* light…in my life."

She leaned against him and put her head down on his shoulder. "Will you come and sit with me?"

"There is nothing more that I would rather do in all the world, but I am sorry…I must go to the offices for a bit, my dear. I have most important work that needs immediate attention," he said with heartfelt grief.

Her face easily revealed that his news was greatly upsetting. "Now? It can't wait until tomorrow morning?" she asked.

"I am sorry, Julia, I truly am…but it cannot."

"You've left like this every night for three days," she noted to him in her soft voice. "And it is Sunday evening. Would you not even rest on this night?" She stepped back as he held her arms and looked into his face. "Is everything alright, Morton?"

"Of course, darling," he replied with a small smile. "It is a matter of police business." He held her tightly again. "I love you," he said slowly and intently while looking into her eyes. "Lock up behind me."

She was disappointed as he turned and went out the front door and left her alone. She had only a few more words that she longed to say, but he was gone and the time she had to speak them had slipped away.

Morton crossed over his front porch and went through the front walkway gate to an unmarked carriage that was waiting for him a short distance from his house. Four officers met him on the walk, armed with guns.

"Keep sight of the house and let no one enter," he commanded them.

"Aye, sir," they responded firmly and went away into the shadows.

Commissioner Howe climbed into his carriage and the driver quickly whisked him away.

He entered his office and turned up the gas lights along the walls. He stood for a moment in silence and listened. He looked over the room carefully from the door to discover a clandestine intruder, but all was still. At his desk, he pulled a stack of papers from a locked drawer and spread them across the entire surface of it. He took a glass from a mahogany drink cabinet and poured another Scotch whiskey into it. He lit the oil lamp on his table and turned up its flame to see.

He paused for a moment in complete silence. The Royal pendulum in the longcase clock at the far wall clicked with irrepressible rhythm. He exhaled heavily in a nervous sigh and the sound came from his nostrils. A tiny key in his shaking hand unlocked a tiny compartment within the drawer and he removed the single piece of parchment hidden inside. It was folded and worn and was very old. He opened it and looked upon the words written therein with great hesitation and fear. It was a simple list of names…

garrick winchester

jack todd

hugo faulkner

eaton barrett

albern partridge

He held it in one hand and laid his head in the other as a tear streamed down his cheek. He placed it on the table next to his pistol and took another paper from his private drawer. He was remorseful and sadly stared down onto the handwritten note. He folded it and sealed it inside an envelope. He took up his pen from the ink well, wrote something on the front, and put it in the pocket of an old ragged coat that hung on a rack beside his chair. From his private drawer again, he pulled another already sealed envelope and wrote upon it:

to my loving wife.

He placed it on top of the other things in his drawer and took a drink of the liquor that was at hand.

Davey sat at a tiny desk beside his upstairs bedroom window. He looked out past the old oak tree on the corner of the house and then to his paper, drawing what he saw. The image of the Full Moon was reproduced in his ink. He paused and stared upon the harmonica that lay just a few inches from his hand. The pen fell slowly over as he became still and went deep into his thoughts. His face reflected a great measure of sorrow and he stared long upon it. He looked down onto the wood grain of his table and ignored the admirable sketching.

The squeak of a wind vane on top of a pole in the middle of the farmyard collected his attention and he looked out to it. Fashioned in the black iron was the image of a beautiful Ballet dancer with a long dress blowing in the wind. She turned on her pointed slipper and faced another direction as the wind changed.

Commissioner Howe read over the official death reports of Jack Todd, Albern Partridge, and Hugo Faulkner; starting with Hugo. He frantically searched for any clues that he could find upon the pages. At the top corner of each report the suspected or known date of death had been written by the police coroner. It flagged his concern and out of curiosity took out a calendar to examine it. The date on Hugo's report was August the Second and Jack Todd's was September the First. He flipped through the papers and read that Albern was October the Thirtieth. He became distraught and examined the calendar key chart. The moon phases appeared to show Full on each of the recorded dates. Quickly, he thrust his hand into the drawer and pulled out a small scrap of parchment with *Eaton Barrett ~ September the Thirtieth* scratched upon it. The calendar shook in his hand as he hurriedly flipped its pages to September. It was the night of the Full Moon.

Morton was stunned and he froze in horror. He smacked the calendar to the table and threw the pages back until November looked him in the face. The days had been crossed off with an X all the way down to the night he sat there - the twenty-eighth – the next Full Moon.

Morton's heart pounded in his chest and he jumped back out of his chair, knocking it to the floor. There, outside the window across his room, the enormous black wolf stood in the darkness, breathing on the glass. Morton's face went white. He trembled in great fear and instantly took up his pistol and raised his arm. The wolf swiftly turned away and disappeared as Morton missed his opportunity to fire.

In the steam that remained from the wolf's breath, MORRIS HARROW was written with a finger, revealed in the light of the moon.

Commissioner Howe took up the old coat, ran from

the room, and flew down the hall of the empty police building. He busted into the lounge where his originally selected team of five detectives sat armed with guns and crossbows on standby; waiting for what, they did not know. Detective Shipley was recovered and had only traces of his misfortune in the bruising of his cheekbone and blackened left eye. Detective Olterman was dressed in a matching commissioner's uniform and wearing the proper hat.

"Now! Ride! Go!" he shouted to them in a panic.

The men jumped from their chairs and sprinted across the lot to the police stables that stood in the protected rear of the offices building. Morton extinguished the lights and began to quickly change into derelict clothing as he watched them from a dark window inside.

After a strained moment of waiting, the men rode out on horses from the dark and charged down the drive past the windows.

Upon the rooftop, high above the street, the wolf stood with his hand on a chimney, watching them. The riders turned to the right and the loud clops of the horses' hooves against the cobblestone streets echoed over the quiet city. The wolf crouched and leaned towards the ledge, quickly scanning the men with his eyes as they retreated into the fog, growling and showing his teeth. As they turned a corner of a street two blocks away, one of them called out to the man at the rear.

"Commissioner Howe! This way!"

The wolf got his long fingers onto the ledge and leapt forward from the roof to the top of the next building, after them.

Commissioner Howe ran from the police building under the cover of darkness into the stables and mounted his horse that was made ready. At high speed, he burst through the opening and turned left onto the street. He rode hard and swiftly away, passing the perpendicular lanes of London with his thoughts propelling through his head as if they were in a hurricane. He turned and looked back over his shoulder in fear.

The ferocious wolf grappled with the arduous slopes of steeply pitched roofs and jumped from cross-gabled rooftop to rooftop above the fleeing horsemen. He turned this way and that, tearing off portions of split thatch and clay tile, but the men never heard or saw him coming against the smoke in the dark sky overhead and the thunderous clap of hooves upon the streets. He nearly lost them in the heavy fog that had pitted itself against the city and sought to isolate him from the chase if it were not for the sounds they made.

Detective Allcott called to the other men. "Come! This way!" He steered his horse away from the main roads and pressed toward a portion of the city that was less inhabited.

"Are you certain?!!" Detective Shipley cried, confused.

"Our own shortcut!" he shouted as he kicked his horse and leaned forward upon its mane.

The men turned after him and whipped their horses, gaining speed after the beasts' hooves touched soft earth.

The wolf leapt from the final rooftop on the edge of a cluster of houses and hit the ground running, away from the hazy light of the whale oil lampposts into the dark.

The riders drove alongside a small pond in the cold air and followed the carriage tracks in the dirt in front of them to Highgate Cemetery. Once the men entered through its tall open wrought iron gates, they split apart, three and two. One group followed the center lane down over a hill, out of sight, and the other went over the right lane along the twelve-foot stone wall into the silent swirling mists of the inhabitants' gravestones.

Each group immediately dismounted and pulled their panting horses to hide in the fern and ivy leaf covered labyrinths of catacombs and mausoleums. Straightaway, the men drew their weapons and took positions behind the tall sculpted memorials, facing the direction of the front entrance. No one made a sound as they crouched and watched the statue silhouettes in the illuminated fog.

Within seconds, the unnerving sound of galloping thuds against the ground followed after them. The men became alarmed and prepared themselves to shoot. As the sound came closer to the entrance in the wall, it immediately fell silent. Their eyes adjusted in the moonlight after a moment and they stared long about the giant winged angel on top of a monumental headstone. There was complete silence among the living and the dead and only a single distant foghorn of the Thames cut through it.

Slowly, the silhouette of the angel began to move in the mists and its wings changed into what appeared to be long arms. The thing hunched forward as it stood beneath an arch on a platform of stone.

The detectives, for the first time, became sore afraid and did not know what they were looking at. Detective Allcott, who at first kept a small smile on his face for the thrill, went pale and was overcome with terror.

"We should not have come here," Detective Graneere whispered to him in a wavering voice.

The wolf stepped down to the ground and sniffed the air for them and kept himself pressed into the mass of looming architecture as he went forward.

Detective Allcott and his men could see no more but

shadow and he turned to the only man beside him. "We *must* fly," he whispered nervously, looking into Graneere's eyes. The two men crouched and made their way quickly to retrieve their horses through the crunching leaves.

At the sound of it, the wolf turned and quickly followed. He crept quietly and stepped rapidly through the fog-emphasized moon beams that penetrated the long cold fingers of the treetops. The steam of his breath split across his snout from his nostrils as he climbed to the top of an entrance to the catacombs and stood partially upright to see. The sound of disturbed horses echoed through the stone and his ears perked up to locate them. He unwittingly moved upon the three remaining detectives who were huddled low beneath him in the crevices of design of a mausoleum.

Detective Shipley fired a crossbow from his hip and the dart struck the wolf deep in the shoulder as he dodged to one side. The men did not remain to see the result of the shot and fled in fear for their horses. The wolf fell backwards from the wall to the ground and hit it with a great agonizing roar.

Detective Allcott and his partner whipped their horses and went wildly over the cemetery lane that took them out a small side exit in the wall. They looked back as they went, frightened at the sound of the wolf's pain. Detective Shipley and his men followed and quickly drove their horses through the mists to the way out.

The wolf stood and immediately ripped the arrow from his flesh. In his rage, he squeezed and broke it into splinters with one hand. He threw it down to the ground and something moved beside him.

There, upon a stone slab with a smiling cherub at the base of a giant ancient tree was a dirty and disgusting little child. He spun in a dance upon the grave marker and tapped his feet. He stopped and clapped his hands together then kicked out one shoe, holding out his arms with a slight bow. As he raised his head, he appeared to be starved and both an old decrepit man and a young boy at the same time. The wolf breathed in with a short gasp and was afraid.

"Hello young, sir!" the little boy said in a heavy English accent with a tap of his shoe. "You wouldn't happen to have a Penny to spare this time of night?!" he said with a fiendish smile. "I collect 'em, I do! My treasures has a Queen Mary the Second!"

The wolf growled and showed his teeth as he backed away slowly from it. What frightened him was that the little devil had no scent at all.

"Not seen a guttersnipe before?!" the ragged child laughed loudly. "Ol' Blackheel, what say ye to 'at?!" he said laughing as he turned to his side and looked towards the ground at the gnarled roots of the tree. In the black mud beneath a heap of leaves, a miniature deformed face of some person moved around. It had no teeth and mumbled something unintelligible without being able to fully open its mouth.

The wolf backed away further in fear.

"Ha!" said the lad. "He agrees! A street urchin would make any kind 'o trick for a silver coin!" He removed the stained rag over his head and held it out for money with a bow. The dim light revealed in his deteriorating hair a puncture hole in his head.

The wolf roared in fear and hatred for the little filth and ran away from him, but he was already gone long before.

The detectives traveled fast in fright and determination for the Thames. They had not time to speak. The wolf could hear their horses and tracked them in the darkness. Detective Allcott turned on his horse and thought he could see a black shadow coming through the fog far behind them.

"Hurry!" he shouted.

The men turned to the river and sped down Old Wharf Street in the fading light of the lampposts.

"Commissioner, up ahead!" Detective Shipley called.

Each man clung to their horses' neck as the sweat-soaked beasts carried them through the paths of the cluttered docks and warehouses. There was a narrow wood bridge that rose over a portion of the water going from their left and connected to a small pier that attached to the opposite shore. They slowed the horses and turned onto it. The galloping hooves reverberated upon the veiled face of the waters and the wolf was signaled.

The fierce creature flew with great speed in the darkness along the Thames and leapt from the brickwork of the quay onto a moored ship. From there, many other ships and barges lined the Berkdinshire Staithe and the wolf, as a shortcut, exploited them. With marvelous agility, he maneuvered the weather decks of cargo holds and webs of ratlines and backstays, leaping from bulwarks to gunwales. He gained on them with perpetual strength.

Detective Allcott and his men crossed over to the waterfront of the fuse mill and turned down its alley. The men were shaken and fumbled with the simple bar that held the massive wooden doors closed at the street side of the building. They were too afraid to further fulfill all of their orders and made every effort to get inside. They swung open the bay doors and drove their horses into the dark opening as the wolf came over the rooftop above them to watch.

In the light of the moon, the wolf paced along the levels of the roof's construction. He looked down and back, listening to the horses through the walls beneath him. He turned away from the high ledges above the open doors and went towards the river side. There, a long row of factory windows stood upright from an extended portion on the top of the roof and he stopped. The wolf smashed the glass with the back of his fist and heard the shards drop to a floor only a few feet within. He knew it was not a long fall and jumped in.

As the enormous creature broke through several windows with his body, he and the glass hit the floor inside together. He looked around in the extremely vague light as he stood completely still in a short storage room. The wolf had to crouch to walk forward from the windows that were higher than his head on his hands as his back rubbed along the wood beams of the ceiling. He came to a tiny stair corridor and squeezed himself through, going down into a larger space.

From there, he began to hear the echoing shouts of the men somewhere far away. He turned through halls and travelled down stairs quickly by the faint light that came through small windows on the ceilings. He could smell something in the building that was familiar and he made his way to it.

The wolf came to the ground floor into a large open warehousing area. Along one wall was an additional small storage building made of wood that went to the roof in height with a door on one side. He went to it, sniffing the top corners of the door. He turned the knob and it was locked. The wolf knelt slowly to the floor and placed his eye to the keyhole. He pulled away, put his nose to it, and sniffed. He raised his fist to the latch system and softly and effortlessly punched it from only two inches away. The door broke inwards with hardly a sound, splitting the frame apart just at the dead latch - his favorite trick. He stood, leaned over, and stepped into the room. It, like all the others, was lit within by nearly horizontal glass windows on the ceiling.

Just as the wolf expected, there were large casks labeled GUN POWDER laid on their sides and stacked to the ceiling. His eyes scanned them quickly, looking up and down. Upon the wall beside the door was a large axe that hung on nails. The wolf turned and went out into the warehouse room.

Small wood boxes marked SAFETY FUSE were stacked in crates along the walls ready to be shipped. The wolf took one up in his hand and smashed it open. Unreeling the cord from a spindle inside, he stretched it out to a determined length using arm breadths. He pulled it into a coiling heap and bit it in half. He ran to the separate storage unit and took up the axe as banging sounds and shouts came through the long walls from the men. He swung it into the tops of the casks and broke most of them open in his reach. The tiny black grains poured out onto the floor in great heaps. He took one end of the fuse and ran it into a small puncture hole he made with the axe head in a cask in the center of the room. The wolf backed away, running the fuse in one hand out the door into the fuse warehouse. He watched its length as he went far out with it, going backwards fifty feet to its end. He laid it down and looked up and around to the walls. He quickly reentered the room and put his hand to the barriers and looked upwards. He searched the floor and the corners. He turned out and searched the floor and walls of the entire place. There was no lighting system anywhere in the building.

The wolf swung the axe against the floor and it made no spark. He smacked the wall and it was the same. He went to the doorknob and struck down on it and broke it off with no reaction in the dark. Entering the powder room again, he found a heap of cask rings against the wall and brought them out. He threw them to the floor and struck them with the axe again and again making a lot of noise, but there was no spark. He growled and huffed in anger and his lip rippled over the pointed teeth in his scowl.

The shelves behind him, hidden in the shadows, caught his attention. He could make out the dark markings painted against the light colored pine boxes they clung to: AMMONIUM NITRATE – and beside those: ZINC POWDER.

The wolf punched one hand into each box and pulled out a fistful of powder in both. He knelt to the floor where his fuse line began and mixed them together. The wolf stood and dragged the axe blade along the floor in front of him. He leaned forward and put the handle into his mouth. He quickly bent his stifle and hock joints and jabbed it down his throat. Immediately, he pulled it out and vomited with an awful sound, hunching over. His eyes watered as he slung stomach fluid acids across the powder at his feet.

A light flared up and the humble flame softly illuminated him. He dropped the axe to the floor and quickly pulled the fuse into his chemical fire. It sparked and began to burn slowly as Detective Cornwall entered the far end of the warehouse on his horse, holding a burning torch above his head. The horse whinnied in fear and backed away as he fired a shot.

The wolf turned to him, hit by the ball in the chest, and roared with a great echo in pain and anger. The Thoroughbred panicked and reared up on the man, throwing him off. It turned and left him, retreating the way it came, slipping in its hurried rotation. The wolf sprinted across the open aisle in the lingering moonlight and the detective ran for his life through the connecting doorway with a scream.

Charles Cornwall dashed through a long dark square-shaped tunnel behind his horse towards a light as fast as he could go. As he passed a certain point, he stepped over a fuse line that lay across the floor of his path.

The wolf was only a moment behind him and noticed that the furthest end of the fuse mill, beyond the passageway, was illuminated in torchlight. He roared as he swiftly flew over it on all fours with frightening speed. Detective Cornwall broke through the open end and the fuse line pulled taught and raised across the passage behind him.

The wolf broke through it as he came and the tiny metal switch released the unraveling movement of several heavy chains. Immediately, an iron door dropped down from the top of the opening, ahead of the wolf, and locked into place. As he smashed into it like an attacking locomotive that had lost control, another door dropped down behind him. The boom of his impact was deafening and seemed to shake the distant walls. The entire container rose rapidly from the ground into the air on massive counterweights of iron as the second door locked into place.

The massive solid iron steamship boiler was lifted straight into the air fifty feet to the ceiling as the beast roared in intense rage and beat against the panels.

The detectives spun around and circled on their panicked horses underneath it, watching the massive swinging pendulum in terror.

Detective Olterman rode out through the open warehouse doors behind them to the waterfront. He jumped his horse from the dock to the deck of a paddle steamer harbored there. He leapt from the saddle and ran to the pilot house where the men had started a small coal fire in the boiler. He took hold of the steam whistle cable and blasted three hard blows.

Commissioner Howe raised himself up in his saddle a half mile away across the Thames when the sound of the whistle blasts startled him. He shook in the nervous cold and anxiously looked to the position of the fuse mill in the heavy fog.

"Hyah!" he cried out to his horse and kicked in his heels. She cut across the water's edge quickly in the night and took the commissioner in the direction of his men.

Detective Olterman remounted his horse and joined the others inside the fuse mill warehouse, shaking in complete amazement.

"What the devil is it?!!" Detective Allcott shouted as the men struggled to control the frightened horses that reared themselves and whinnied in the presence of the monster.

"What made it draw near?!...How did he know it would follow us?!" Detective Shipley cried as the beast inside the boiler roared and vehemently pounded upon the rivets of the lower seams in a fit of unrestrained wrath.

There was a thin horizontal slot cut into the front side of the thick iron panel for looking in and the wolf could see them circling below while he swung in the air. He heaved a great roar of anger as a warning to them and it reverberated over the rafters of the massive expanse and rattled the windows of the ceilings.

The spark had traveled along the gunpowder fuse and entered the powder room. The crackling light it made revealed the surrounding barrels in tiny flashes. It advanced one foot every thirty seconds and finally crawled up over the rim of the cask and went down into the hole; a quality and reliable English fuse.

The wolf ceased pulverizing the floor, weakening the seam, and stood with his arms braced against each side. When he leaned forward and peered through the hole at the men, the entire building exploded.

The detectives were consumed in a blast of fire that immediately melted off their flesh. It disintegrated them and their horses instantly as it blew their bones apart.

The wolf jumped back from a short burst of fire that came through the slot at his face. The massive iron boiler was propelled slowly upwards into the sky through the windows and rafters of the roof while multiple explosions shattered the remainder of the mill.

Commissioner Howe's mouth dropped open in complete awe and disbelief as he rode hard along the Thames and drew near. Flames spiraled up into the night sky in every direction over the water as the blast broke every window for ten blocks and shook the entire city.

His horse skidded to a halt in fright and he yanked back on the reigns in gut-wrenched horror. Burning fragments of the building shot out into the Thames like ten thousand falling stars and a huge fireball rolled vertically into the sky. Commissioner Howe gasped and moaned after the combustive flames receded and kicked his horse again towards it. His long dirty coat took to the air behind him.

The heavy cylindrical iron boiler plummeted from the air at an angle to the ground. The wolf held on to the hole and watched through it. As it headed for an impact upon the brickwork pavements, the wolf dove against the weakened rivets and tipped that end downward with his momentum and weight.

The boiler hit the ground on its initial impact with so much force that it split open the seam of rivets in the iron. It smashed the bricks with a boom, sending them in all directions as the speeding projectile skipped and rolled over the crates and barrels of a ship yard. The wolf roared inside as he was held against the wall when it spun and ripped through everything in its path. The boiler hit the ground as it skipped one final time and the top end spun around horizontally to the other side. It smashed through the wall of another warehouse building that sat two buildings down from the fuse mill and came to rest inside. The wolf huffed and growled inside, recovering from the ride, and his fingers came out of the dark hole on both sides of the split. He roared with great physical strain and bent it apart.

He crawled out and hurried to the gigantic hole in the wall at the sound of galloping horse hooves. As he looked out, Morris Harrow swiftly rode past on the cobblestone bank along the river towards the fire. The wolf snarled, lowered his head, and put his hand on the threshold of the demolished wall with a deep rumbling growl.

Morton Howe rode helplessly upon the destruction. His men were nowhere to be found and he feared the worst. There was no sign of life in or around the blaze. The boiler was missing and he searched desperately for it; certain that it held his answers within. His horse became spooked by something in the surrounding darkness and Morton recognized it. He looked over the water and along the walkways quickly, but found no one. The horse neighed and turned away and Morton knew it was a good idea. He kicked the horse, allowing her to flee from whatever was scaring her.

Morton took off and looked high and low for the creature as he rode hard away. Somewhere in the darkness, the low barks of the wolf came after him. He whipped the horse and tried to go faster in the failing visibility of London's night.

In the cluttered shipyards and dense smoke and fog, the horse became disoriented and lost. As Morton would attempt to turn into certain known exits, an eerie bark would come from the dark avenues and thwart his horse. He attempted to retreat from the burning waterfront and hide in the city streets, but was routed quickly into a long brick passage under a dry bay roof shelter that brought him back. The horse went through the darkness quickly to the opening on the other side as if it were a long covered bridge. She came to the end of the road, a drop at the side of the Thames, and stopped. Morton panicked and drove her along its edge at the end of the alley and searched for another escape. The horse breathed hard with great draughts in the silence and Morton pulled the pistol from the case on his saddle.

Both he and the mare shook for fear in the quiet dark. Distant voices of shouting traveled from all parts of the water as people hurried to the scene. The horse turned and faced the long black tunnel, the only way back, but could not take it. A growl echoed against the brick from within the darkness and Morton raised his trembling pistol hand with the look of an absolute fear of death. He shouted at the dark.

"What do you want with me?!!"

The wolf looked straight upon him from within and hissed. Saliva dripped from his teeth to the ground.

The mare immediately went wild and neighed and whinnied, backing up. She reared straight up on her hind legs at the water's edge and Morton Howe fired a shot into the wolf point blank as the beast jumped onto him from the darkness.

Both he and the horse were thrust far from the ledge and splashed deep into the river amongst the surges that obscured their enemy. The mare landed on her side in the water and plunged upside down, then rolled and swam for the dark surface. Further away in the depths, Morton screamed beneath the freezing wake. He twisted and spiraled in the light of the raging fires above and attempted to reach the air.

His hands almost breached the surface. He was within inches. Great crowds of people scrambled along the waterfront from the city and cried out as they worked to douse the fires. He could hear them and was scraping frantically at the brittle partition between life and death with his fingernails.

It was too late. The wolf grabbed hold of his ankle from below and yanked him down into the deep. A small envelope dislodged from his coat pocket and was lost in the turbulent water. He pulled on the commissioner's clothing, one hand over the other like climbing a ladder. Morton screamed half of his last breath in his nightmare and the bubbles rose away to the bright swirling yellow light above.

He faced away from the beast in his dread and kicked to get loose, but was powerless against him. The enraged wolf finally got his arms wrapped around Morton's chest from behind and slowly squeezed the air out of him. The man groaned in pain as the remainder of his last breath was expelled through his clenching teeth.

Morton's eyes reflected the true meaning of horror when the wolf turned him around to look him in the face. The wolf held him under with one hand by the throat and felt Morton suck in a great draught of water. Morton Howe rolled his eyes up into his head as he shook violently to death and the wolf watched him.

The mare swam hard and kept her head just above the water. She raised her muzzle and gave a short struggling whine.

"A horse has fallen into the river!!" a man shouted, pointing from the quay. People of the area lined the bank beside the fire and looked on as two men got hold of the mare's reigns and pulled her towards the ways.

In the reflection of fire in the middle of the harbor, the wolf's head rose from beneath the black surface. He did not move and watched their chaos.

"Here!" shouted a man. "Something in the water!"

Several men hurried to assist him as he pulled the body of a pauper from the icy water and rolled him over.

"God's Mercy!! It can't be!" one of the men exclaimed in disbelief. "It's the commissioner!"

The wolf turned towards the other side, sank beneath the floating debris on the Thames, and swam away at the sirens of the oncoming fire brigade.

An envelope addressed to Garrick Winchester floated on the surface of the darkness into nowhere.

Chapter 17

The workmen of the Breggins Farm were fitted for the cold early morning and prepared wagon loads of hay for the animals. Cecil rode out into the fields on top of them with the others and distributed it with pitchforks. Mister Breggins had so much livestock that it would take them half of the day. Cecil didn't mind the cold air. It was something he had always been accustomed to, being affiliated with farms or some type of merchant loading service all of his life. As the men distributed hay to the sheep that gathered around them, Guido, a middle-aged Englishman named after his Italian father, and long time member of the Breggins enterprise, was first to mention the inevitable topic that was on everyone's minds.

"Did you gentlemen hear the blast last night?" he said.

"Aye!" nearly every man answered.

"Who didn't?!" another said.

"I thought the French had finally invaded London

by sea for an bygone squabble and sacked the Royal Artillery Barracks!" Guido laughed. "It is amazing that it could be heard from here."

Cecil looked at him while he worked from the corner of his eye.

"I hope no one was injured," Guido remarked in a change of unadulterated earnestness.

"There *was* some ill news to emerge from the event as a result," said Theodore Tillmire. "I heard from the men of Saint Katherine's Docks that the West London Police Commissioner and several of his men were killed."

The men stopped their work for a moment and stood silent. They were all dumbfounded. Cecil continued shoveling the hay from the wagon and could not be concerned. He was stripped down of nearly all human empathy and saw the pitchfork in the hay of no more or less value or importance than the workings of mankind and their cycles of life and death.

"Morton Howe?" Burney said, amazed.

Cecil looked to him and wondered how he came about that name and then remembered the Fifth of November.

"That is ill news indeed," said Everard Abraham with a solemn face.

"I thought him to be a good and honest man by first impression," Burney said in frustration.

Cecil stopped what he was doing and looked on Burney and the others with a new and wary position of distrust. He would be more mindful of how he further handled things.

"I wonder what would have caused such an unbelievable disaster?" Guido asked.

"It was a fuse mill," Theodore answered, "and we can only speculate that the gunpowder store was improperly warehoused."

"I expect the commissioner and his men were slain in their attempts to control the situation at hand," said Everard with compassion and exalting respect.

The men returned to their work in contemplation and Cecil's face was without any nuance of emotion.

"God be with the souls of those men," said Robert Henry Young, who seemed to be most sensitive to the report.

Cecil stopped and quickly looked upon Robert from a distance as the men worked and quietly huffed in discord.

The majestically beautiful Guildhall building of the City of London was buzzing desperately with large crowds of citizens and representatives of surrounding boroughs, local manufacturing, and harbor trade. The exterior of the structure was quite a spectacle. It was very old, built in 1440 with many tower pinnacles. Its face was lined with four stories of glass windows and the entrance to it went between two equally high and imagined buildings of architectural splendor that mimicked one another. On the interior were magnificent arches of stone to the great ceilings of ornate woodwork in the room of meeting. High upon cavities in the walls were sculptures of kings and queens writing upon tablets of stone and tall ships at sea. Lofty windows of elaborate stained glass let in the light of the afternoon as members of local parliament stood to address them. Chamberlain Cornish James began the meeting.

"The Right Honorable the Lord Mayor of London, Sir Lambert Jules Rowland will now communicate a statement," he said.

Many officers of the City of London Police as well as other constabularies of Greater London were in attendance and stood along the walls of the platform.

The Lord Mayor of London was a mostly serious man when not giving parties. In his late sixties, he still had a younger appearance and his hair was light brown. He grew a heavy mustache on his face and it traveled down on each side of his chin. He wore a long maroon and cream greatcoat that came near to the ground with white gloves and he set his brown top hat upon the podium when he spoke.

"Good afternoon to all," he started. "As many of you know last night there was an explosion at the Frederricks-Britannia Fuse Mill upon the Thames. Fires broke out among several local buildings in which the West London General Fire Brigade quickly abated with much expertise and precision. We do not know the cause of this disaster although it is known that there was a substantial amount of gunpowder and other potentially dangerous materials stored for the manufacturing process. I would like to recognize that it is a grievous loss to the Berkdinshire Staithe area. The management of the mill has been an integral part of the economical advancement of our beloved city. We all certainly hope to support their rebuilding efforts. Furthermore and foremost, I am deeply sorry to inform all of you that Commissioner Morton Howe and his top notch team of detectives were killed either in or as a result of the blast."

A wave of dismay swept over the room and the people groaned in regret.

"Six men in total – Chief Inspector Brannigan Allcott, Detective Robert Shipley, Detective William Graneere, Detective Edgar Olterman, Detective Charles Cornwall, and Commissioner Morton Howe…may these men rest in eternal peace."

The people began to speak softly to one another as many of the names were familiar to them.

"Commissioner Howe and his men must have been hunting some criminal of sorts. Who, we do not know or why they were there we do not know. The owners of the Frederricks-Britannia Fuse Mill have reported to us that Commissioner Howe and a small group of detectives had been granted an area to which what they had organized inside was restricted for an allotted time by arrangement for police matters. During this time, Commissioner Howe's team had kept their intentions confidential from all others within the precinct for what we believe to be security purposes. I know these men had been working on numerous homicide cases as of late and we can only speculate that this may have somehow been related...but turned out awry. We have absolutely no idea why, but a steamship boiler had also been inside the building – for repairs or salvage or what other reasons we do not know.

This is a terrible tragedy and our condolences go to the affected families. A ceremony of commemoration will be held publicly to honor these great men whose service to our city is renowned."

The Lord Mayor of London, Sir Lambert Jules Rowland, closed his address.

𝕴t started to lightly snow in England and the landscape became much different. After the countryside took on its new appearance for early December, the people somewhat welcomed it for the anticipations of the oncoming new holiday seasons. There were large numbers of children on the steep inclines of Millwrights

Row attempting to sled in the snow, but they were much too ambitious for the time of year as there was not enough to work with.

Cecil and his fellow workmen continued their labors at the Breggins Farm and the old man prospered. His livestock numbers always flourished and the men were satisfied to be employed there. It had been a good year for him and his merriment would occasionally show through his strict business mannerisms. The man was well-known and well-liked.

In the streets of the city it was business as usual for the establishments of wine and spirits. There was never a shortage of intoxicating drink nor the people who lived by it. Prostitutes and drunken gentlemen callers kept the nights awake with their cold-aired clamor and careless laughter, but this time with one less troubled soul.

Several less than savory characters of Cecil's work companions had coerced him with much effort to darken the doorways of the Chatter Box – a pub where Britain's wanting could have a hot meal with their amber ales. They had gathered together for the celebration of one of their own's birthday and the men made a cheerful ruckus from the two round tables they had consolidated in the back room. They drank heavily, including Cecil, and the levels of their mirth crowded the opposing bar through the open doorway of the partition wall.

They worked themselves through several pitchers of golden sack mead and as the last one went dry, Pennant Athelwold, the party's host, bellowed a suggestion for the imminent twelve o' clock hour.

"Now, my reputably magnificent and fair fellow partners," he slurred loudly, holding up an empty lead stein, "for the thorough merriment of the approaching midnight hour we shall attend the magical courts of the sorcerer, Bingwen Peng, for a reading of the future!" He belched from a foam-filled throat and laughed.

His friends laughed at what he said and what he did and rose from the table as Cecil's demeanor shifted to unrest. He reluctantly followed the staggering group down the street in the diminished lamplight and passed off his trepidations with the onset of amusement.

Children of destitution ran the streets, even in the chill of night as lone carriages rolled along them. One approached them in the dense smoke and fog of London's coal fires and factory smoke stacks carrying a lighted torch. Its mysterious fire glowed only a few feet from the ground as the group discovered it was a young lad. Up close, his emaciated features could be seen while he enlisted them with dry and hollow enthusiasm. His front four teeth had been knocked out and his shoes were splitting apart at the seams. Cecil shuddered with the familiar image of him and kept needless distance.

"A wonderful night to be out, gentlemen," he said, walking along beside them raising his torch. "Permit me, sirs, to chaperone thee to thy privilege. 'Tis a bit dank this night and one could use the helpful assistance of one with clear eyes and a navigable knack for the street."

The men ignored him and continued to laugh at one another. The boy remained in their company with further solicitations.

"I'm glad to be of aid to you, sirs. I am at your disposal for the evening and am quite skilled in many forms of helpful service. If you be in want for anything I am the one who will do it for you. If you need a drink to your satisfaction delivered at your requests I am at attentive charge. There is nothing I can't handle for you fine gentlemen with utmost regard and will assure you your matters are in confidence."

The men approached their destination and they began to call out to the one they desired to meet inside with comical expression.

"We are here, Mister Peng!!" they shouted at the sky. "We are to your door! At long last! But of course you knew we were coming!" They let out a great howl and one man slipped and fell in the snow. The boy pulled on his arm and somewhat helped him up.

"Ah! Good. We near your destination. I am sure it to be warm inside with the benefit of much food," the lad said with uplifted spirits. With his light, he showed them to the door of a building with many dozens of odd candles burning inside through exposed windows and attempted to go in with them. He set his torch to the ground and an Asian woman stopped him in front of the men in the foyer.

"No boy," she said to them.

"I am party to these fine gentlemen to assist them to night," he answered. "They have asked for my participation."

The men looked at the lad who came in with them and Pennant became angry.

"Be gone with you!"

"A Halfpenny, my dear sirs," he said with his hand open. "I…I have brought you here with my light and my young sister has no food or warmth. She starves, sirs. If I were to have two Farthings for a bite." He pleaded with the men and looked to all of them as he held out his hands.

Pennant grabbed him by the hair and pushed him through the door behind them.

"Get away, rat, 'fore I put stripes to you myself!"

Pennant shut the door and turned away. Cecil watched the lad go with small pity, knowing that he had his own difficulties as well as everyone else.

The soothsayer and palmist, Bingwen Peng, was popular among those in London with an alternative means. He offered his services inside a strangely lit parlor of oriental magic. In the back, the main room of meeting was situated wherein he sat upon a raised golden throne on a platform of extravagantly carved teak sculpture. There was wild excitement among Cecil's cohorts and its intensity was heightened by the fuels of association.

Each man paid his fourpence to the middle-aged Chinese woman and was led to the back through chiming and sparkling gold curtains of the orient. The men were seated at tables in the room illuminated by a thousand candles and in the orange light the red sculptures of great dragons stood menacing against the walls. The sorcerer was not yet present and Cecil gazed upon the exotic creatures that were displayed in hard wood all over the room.

The men became quiet in wonderment when their mystical artist entered slowly from a dark curtain and seated himself on the intricate gold. He was Chinese and wore heavy robes of red and gold silk with a belt of silver with settings of jade. On his fingers were large rings of gold and precious stone and hoops of gold rings were in his ears. His eyebrows were pierced with gold rings and his beard grew in a long black point from his chin. His head was adorned with a beautiful blue Phoenix Coronet with silver and gold conches of pearl and jade, draping strings of pearls

The woman who had seated the men began to play upon an ancient wood Guqin, a long stringed instrument, from the shadows of a corner and surprised them. The men were still and silent as she plucked the seven silk strings and began to sing softly upon its hypnotic and soothing tones. The sorcerer did not move and was like one of his statues; his eyes fixed upon them, appearing kingly in his aura. For a moment, the party was transfixed by the delicately lingering harmonics of her music and no one moved or made a sound. Her words were in her native tongue and she sang of a beautiful heron that fell in love with a human girl and was granted humanity by a wizard to fight and die for her in the Great War.

As she played, Cecil became quietly fixated on a biting wolf carved into the framework of a large mirror. He sat still and saw himself in it from the distance.

After six minutes of uninterrupted repose, she laid the instrument aside and disappeared through folds of embroidered silk.

"I am Bingwen Peng - the soothsayer, the sorcerer of the order of the Chinese Ming Dynasty," he stated with a Nanjing Mandarin accent, but with impeccable English. "You have come to learn of your future. I will show you."

The men looked at one another with a laugh and each had an amused smile on his face except for Cecil.

Bingwen Peng rose from his seat and stepped down to the men who were anxious for their turns. "Who would like to be first?" he said.

The men began to laugh and slapped the shoulders and back of Joseph Hemus Wells, the one who was celebrating his birthday.

"Stand," said the fortune-teller.

The man rose and Mister Peng looked into his face and then took hold of his right hand. He turned it over and read the lines of his palm.

"To day is your birthday," he said with no expression.

The men burst into laughter and cheered. Joseph smiled and raised his eyebrows, looking back at them.

"To day, you are thirty-nine," the Chinaman said with accuracy.

Again, the men laughed in disbelief. Joseph blinked hard and laughed with them.

"You old codger! We shall fetch you a nurse!"

shouted Pennant, who was much older by more than a decade, from the tables as they cheered.

"Your name is Joseph," Bingwen said after he looked deeply into the man's face.

Everyone beat upon the tables and whistled as Joseph shook his head and turned to them again.

"All right! You got me! You had me goin' all night, you conniving bastards!" he said, laughing.

Pennant and his friends wiped tears from their faces and cried out, "No! No! No! We swear it! We swear it! We've not told him anything at all! We swear it!"

Bingwen remained austere and continued with his craft. "You tend goats and are a man of farming."

"Goat man!" they shouted with applause and their rendition of the animal's known voicing.

"You will not tend goats for long. Something will come and make you rich," Bingwen stated with solid position.

The men quickly quieted and stared upon Joseph in amazement.

"Your daughter is in North France."

The men were silent in disbelief. Joseph breathed heavily and his lip quivered as a tear streamed down his cheek.

"She will write to you and want to come home."

Joseph began to weep and they cheered for him again.

"I hope your birthday will be a happy one," Mister Peng said with a short nod and tiny smile.

As they applauded, Joseph turned away, wiping his eyes and the faded hope had been breathed new life.

"Go! Go!" the men shouted to Pennant, pushing him and clapping their hands. He rose and went, somewhat nervously, to the soothsayer with a smile.

Bingwen looked into his face and into his hand. "Your name is Pennant Athelwold."

The men began to laugh and clap as Pennant's face went long in astonishment.

"Your brother is in Manchester and you do not speak to him."

Pennant became serious and reluctantly responded. "It is true."

The men laughed and shouted. "Why don't you speak to your brother, Pennant?! Did he steal your goodies when you were a wee one?!" they teased.

"It is over his wife. She used to be yours," the magician said and Pennant became grieved.

The men's eyes got wide and their mouths hung open as they went silent. Cecil watched from the back corner with rigid study.

"I tell you this," said the sorcerer. "Go to him. He has something for you and it will alter your destiny."

The company cheered for him with loud whistling in a joyous riot. The sorcerer looked into his eyes and spoke softly beneath the noise and no one but Pennant and Cecil heard him.

"You should have given the rat two Farthings," he said.

Pennant became changed.

"…it would have saved his life."

Pennant walked away from the sorcerer and his face transformed to regret. He did not laugh with them as they patted his back and shook him as he sat.

They turned to Cecil, behind them, and beat upon the tables. "Cecil! Cecil! We want Cecil!!"

Cecil became uncertain and tried to prevent them.

"No. No. I am here only to observe the ludicrous actions of fools when their fortunes are told them," he stated with responsive banter and shrouded apprehension.

"We won't go until you face the Emperor!" they laughed with elevated protesting.

Cecil stood to his feet, smiling, and walked to the palmist, turning a dark countenance. Cecil stared into the sorcerer's eyes with defiance to challenge his looking within.

Bingwen Peng became unsettled and breathed in heavily. His eyes widened in alarm of deception. He spoke very softly and the other men could not hear him. "Your name is not Griffiths."

Cecil did not move and looked upon him with imposing weight.

The soothsayer began to quake with fear and quickly took hold of Cecil's hand out of curious compulsion, repressing sound judgment, and looked into his palm.

Immediately, the man hastily pulled away from him like a hand from fire and fell over the golden throne. The Coronet fell from his head to the floor.

"Nǐ qīzhà zhě! Nǐ hēi'àn de xié'è hé nánrén de shāshǒu!" he shouted in his language in terror, pointing at Cecil.

The men's mouths dropped open and they looked at Cecil in complete surprise, on the verge of laughter, ready to ridicule him.

"Gǔn kāi!" the sorcerer shrieked.

Cecil shouted to him in anger. "What did you expect to find in the future of another man?! We're all sinners in the eyes of God! You warlock! You abomination!"

All the men except for Pennant and Joseph, burst with howling laughter and pointed as the sorcerer continued to scream at him and retreat toward his dark curtains.

"What have you come forth to see?!" cried Cecil. "You foreseer of evil in an evil world! If you seek it you shall surely find it!"

Their tumult was of deafening magnitude and nearly

drowned the charges of the magician.

"Gǔn kāi! Líkāi zhèlǐ! Líkāi zhège dìfāng! Líkāi zhège dìfāng!" he screamed frantically. The Chinese woman rushed in and saw his dread and shouted to them.

"Get away! Get away from here! Leave this place!"

She pushed the laughing men from the parlor and through the front door into the street as the sorcerer continued to yell at Cecil from beyond the curtains.

The party fell in a heap on the street in the snow and moaned with pain and hysterical cheers. Cecil stood over them with a grim face, glancing to the door that had been shut and locked behind them.

"He wouldn't even give Cecil's reading!" they laughed. "I've been sayin' for months he's got secrets!" one said. "It's because he's killed Chinamen in another life! He slew them in great heaps in battle with one sword!" they jeered. "Never have I gotten so much for fuppence!" another said and they all began to choke on the cold air in their laughter.

Cecil put on a smile and helped them up, but quickly became withdrawn into his own thoughts. The sorcerer's fear had reminded him of who he really was inside and it made him sad - only because he felt no sensitivity to it. The road was long and it had been hard; much too hard and it had left him lingering outside on the edges of life and looking in at others from a cold window from the outer darkness like he was now, shut outside that door. He turned and looked to the night sky. The Waning Crescent Moon cut through the winter clouds above and he could not think of a reason for it for him.

Pennant stood to his feet in laughter, but immediately became troubled with what he wanted to take back. He looked for the boy and did not see him.

320

Chapter 18

The holidays of December were evident in the season that was cultivated and increased by the peoples of London under their leadership. The street corners of the shopping districts brought many casual singers to the groups of carolers that elevated Christmas cheer. Traditional melodies were the favorites and wreathes hung on business doors with welcomed introduction. Carolers in groups of two and three were a common sight strolling along the residential streets in the evenings with lifted voices remembering the Christ child.

The pleasing aroma emerging from the bakers lingered at face level through all of the streets and caused the purchasers to be urged to indulge in sweet gratifications of caramel whips and pecan tarts, apple nougatine and pumpkin croissants, brioche buns and cranberry walnut bread, bite-size almond cakes and Yule pastries, rout drops and orange muffins, ginger snaps and lemon madeleines. Very few folk at all were so impervious that the lure was an ineffective ploy. The butchers had their game as well to all that passed their doors with sugar glazed hams and steaks stuffed with mushrooms, peeled apple lamb and special bacon dumplings, spiced kid and ox tongue with pigeon for pie. The jewelers were fully prepared for the slew of ladies that flocked within their exquisite walls to dote and sometimes gain bracelets of gold with cameos in black and white sardonyx stone, fringe necklaces in silver-topped gold with graduated rows of diamond set ornaments of leaf motifs, and multi-karat pale yellow sapphire rings encircled in rose-white pearls. Hatters were armed with custom delights hailing from France and Germany of fragile feather tufts and tussocks of lace ribbon. People put their worries away and delighted in the fleeting moment of warmth of that joyous season.

A jolly fellow fiddled at the window of a popular toy store and danced in the small bits of snow that dusted the sidewalk there. Cecil approached and gazed into the glass alongside a small lad who dreamed about Father Christmas and what he would bring to him. Cecil looked on at the boxes of colorful candy and complex toy trains and could remember being the same way when he was young. He remembered the feelings that even the smallest gift would instill in him when he was a boy. He turned again and looked upon the small lad who had not even noticed him standing there in his smiling happy vision of Christmas. Cecil was reminded of Davey and missed him. His own Christmas wish that was fading was in the frail and distant hope that everything would be alright.

He stared intently at the tiny tree in the window that was covered in miniature flickering candles as the fiddler's rendition of the Austrian's *Silent Night* caused him to be both nostalgic and remorseful for the past and for the future.

The Covent Garden Theatre in Westminster was astonishing in its prestige and elegance. Since its second rebuilding in 1809 many masterful presentations of opera and ballet were performed there. The auditorium housed four tiered balconies of grandiose splendor in which the admiring public would applaud the virtuosos of artistic aptitude.

On this night, the Paris Opera Ballet company performed Austrian composer Valentin Windischgraetz's recent work, *Le Loup Effrayant,* as a gift from Louis Philippe I, King of the French, to Queen Victoria and Prince Albert for the November birth of their first son, Prince Albert Edward. The ballet was inspired by the recent infamous events of England's mysterious wolf attacks. In a letter to Her Majesty The Queen, the composer regarded the occurrences as igniting the fascinating works of the imagination and assured the impression would ring with noble honor.

The members of the audience were notable in not only their attire but for their social standing. The ladies and gentlemen were dressed in the most expensive formal evening wear known to London and much of the fashion had been tailor made specifically for the performance. Over two thousand people looked on from the pigeonholes, boxes, and rows to the glimmering danseurs and danseuses.

Cecil carefully placed an open box on the floor beside the nightstand of his bed. Inside was an expensive French microscope that was beyond description for its cunning beauty. It was nearly solid golden brass and the shaft of the magnificent eyepiece was emphasized with black marble. Its stage was complete with various rollers of acute focus raised on golden legs styled into curls of spouting water in romantic design. There was a pivoting mirror glass beneath where the looker could direct light into its lenses. Beside it was a folded note that sat upon a smooth cedar treasure box. Within its tiny hinges was the most valuable thing of all. It was Cecil's entire life savings - what he had very faithfully and persistently put away with strict regulation year after year; denying himself continuously of material possessions and sometimes basic needs to keep it from withering or being lost. It was his suffering and his lasting legacy; the reason for a long hard life of wandering over golden hills and green valleys, along musty rivers in the mornings and bright ocean shores in the nights, within sweltering factories and dark mills, frozen dockyards, and majestic farmlands to procure it.

It was more than enough for someone to start a completely new life, free of want and care; more than enough to enroll in any college and become whatever they chose in this world. Cecil placed the paper brown lid upon it and attached a white paper label. It read simply: Davey ~ Harper's Lane.

Among the gaslight chandeliers that extended on arms of polished brass, the Royal family watched in pleasant anxiety the peril of the principal dancer - Prima Ballerina, Gabrielle Perusse.

A large articulating puppet of a gray wolf, played by six men of the Coryphée, crept in from stage left. The men and women of London, portrayed by beautifully costumed dancers, became frightful and pulled each other dramatically away. The spectators were alarmed as the innocent female lead alternately performed *pirouettes* with *deboulè en manège*, going in a circle around the beast - completely oblivious to him.

The Corps de ballet surged and bowed as the conductor's formula of sound swelled to the vaulted ceilings of neoclassical Georgian design. Bizarre and repetitive music of string dives and non-rhythmic percussive striking dropped over a slow crescendo of trèmolo of the strings.

From the faux carriages under the proscenium arch, the male Premiere, Rogier - the Famous Spear, leapt upon the wolf with a shining sword and battled him.

Cecil paced his room like a caged animal. Within, the fearless man and the unstoppable beast were at war. The Waxing Quarter Moon burned through his window and he counted the days. His skin crawled upon his bones. His nights were plagued with anarchy of time and he wrestled against it. Fire rose upon the timber of the hearth and his mind was bent upon the list.

He went to the drawer at his bedside and took hold of the black book. He threw himself to his knees at the stone and tore his damning testimony from the pages of its testament. He held the only evidence of his identity in his hand and in one motion of forfeit and justice cast it into the fire. In an instant, the thing was gone. He breathed in deep draughts and flinched as a heavy pool of water formed upon the ledge of his lower eyelid. His face was of regret for the past and there in the silent room he finalized all of his decisions.

Not finished, he looked down upon the words, *The Holy Bible*, etched on the book in his hands. He laid it onto the fire and it engulfed the pages of the Holy Scriptures. With a glassy stare, he watched it whither in the heat and his heart turned black along with it in the ashes.

A large woman in the audience gasped and covered her mouth as the wolf killed Rogier, the man who beset him.

In the midst of the dramatic heights of the Prima Ballerina's peril, Simon Harrow ran back into the treacherous trees in the booming blasts of the thunderstorm, alone. He ran with desperation and great fear and wept in the deep and dark forest as he was drenched in the unforgiving vigorous strength of the deluge. He flew over paths as quickly as his young nine year old legs could carry him. In the imposing threat of the towering darkness, he cried with bitter anguish and his tears washed into the rain that flowed down his cheeks. Over hill and valley, he searched for the hidden well in the momentary light of the flashing sky.

As he held his last breath, the boy saw lightning flashing through a crack and put his lips to it. He blew out the water that permeated and breathed in. He quickly attempted to place his feet on each side at the top of the well and press up with his back and shoulder. There was a footing and he tried, but slipped off and spiraled down. He swam up, blew air through the hole again, and took a couple of quick breaths. Placing his feet once more, he forced his neck and shoulders against the lid.

It raised an inch and moved over just enough for him to get his fingers in. The water flowed over the rim through them as he repeatedly thrust to get out. He had strength and leverage enough to force an opening where he could stick out his face and gasp for air. With that, he pressed further, enough to squeeze his shoulders through and wormed out.

He fell down into the flowing puddles of the ground and cried aloud with deep groaning for what had happened. He put his hands over his face and wept for his parents. He wept for his life. All was lost.

He stood in the storm and pushed the lid back into its place over the water that issued from the top and flowed down the rock. He looked up into the forest in the direction that his brothers had come and turned away and ran naked into that awful darkness that gladly received him.

In blasting thunder, Simon found his way to the old path and moved over it with speed. When he spotted the old stone well hidden beneath the ivy leaves in the dark, he screamed as he wept.

"Cecil!!!"

He took hold of the stone lid and tried desperately to move it. Water poured from its uneven edges and he got his fingers into one of them. He lifted and gritted his teeth. The lid managed to raise an inch, over the lip, and with unstoppable determination he slid it off to the ground.

He stood, horrified, looking down into the watery pit; into the black.

"Cecil!!!" he screamed frantically and splashed his arms into the water, slinging it from the edges, trying to feel for him. In desperation, he climbed onto the rim and took a deep breath. He was afraid of the darkness and dove into the water, head first. He could not swim, but tried to push his way into the deep tunnel upside down, reaching out for Cecil's cold hand. In terror of the hole in complete darkness and lack of oxygen, he turned away, helpless, and swam to the surface.

Simon's head breached at the rim and he cried with deep agony from the water as he surrendered his older brother to a cold and lonely death. He climbed out and slumped down onto his knees at the base of the well with his head down against it and could not forgive himself for letting him go.

"I'm sorry, Cecil…I'm sorry.."

Thunder oppressed the sobbing words of apology and regret to Cecil that came from his mouth as he clung to the rim above him.

The ballerina curled to the floor and bowed her head in sorrow as her friends, the young ladies of London, the mourning dancers of the Corps de ballet, comforted her.

On this warm night, the abnormal temperatures of the last two days had melted the snow, but there was something sinister in it. Winds suddenly elevated in power and a storm of historic proportions was unleashed upon England's countryside.

A family man and his wife immediately sensed an oncoming assault and the farmhouse began to creak and groan under gales that threatened to destroy it. Large pieces of the roof ripped away above his head and in dread he turned to his wife who was silent and paralyzed in fear.

"We must get to the cellar!!"

In terror, he took hold of a glowing lantern and grabbed her hand. They fled through the back door to the yard as one hundred kilometer per hour winds pummeled them. Forty feet from the house, he fell to the ground and fought open the double doors. Timbers on the upper portions of the house cracked and split as he took hold of her hand and pulled her in front of him. The barn, which was upwind, boomed and splintered fragments flew overhead in the sky like a thousand wood spears. She ran down the steps into the dark, turned, and took the lantern that lit her pale face. He stood above her at the hole, hunched over, with one hand tightly clutching the door that opened from the ground and his other raised to his head for defense against the blasting tornado winds.

"Where's the lad?!!" he shouted to her with great distress.

She did not answer and stared at him in a daze.

"The lad?!!? he screamed within the deep battering howls.

"He stays with Mary!! He is safe with her!!" she cried, disoriented with shock - her gaze frozen upon him.

The man quickly stepped into the hole and prepared to come down to her. The entire house groaned behind him and gently lifted one inch from the ground on one corner and then sat back down.

She became crazed as the cloud of bewilderment seemed to instantly disintegrate from her manner.

"Mother's jewels!!" she screamed. "God, no! I won't lose them!! Please! No!! We'll lose them!!"

He stared at her, unmoving, face to face - horrified at her words and her appearance. He turned and went back and slid the board into the slots to shut her in. Dried leaves of maize whipped past in tens of thousands from the surrounding fields and nearly blinded him while the distant barn was rent in pieces.

Then, in the bright spot of the burning limelight of Covent Garden, Gabrielle's character, La Beauté Félice Qui Pleure, rose and danced alone in the grief of her fallen lover. She turned on her slipper and her dress floated beautifully on the air.

The dancing woman of the wind vane spun wildly in the violent gales of a hurricane as the man passed swiftly beneath her to the farmhouse.

Winds immediately intensified with monstrous capacity to one hundred twenty kilometers per hour and the man threw himself inside the house and ran for the kerosene lamplight of the kitchen.

The upstairs bedroom windows shattered as he grabbed hold of the hand carved oak dish cupboard with both hands. It was filled and extremely heavy and he twisted one corner away from the wall as far as he could. From the side, he stuck his head into the narrow gap behind it and slid his arm along the wall as the house was coming apart. He reached for a secret flip down drawer with a trembling hand. The roof broke away from the house and separated from the framework upstairs with a catastrophic boom. He fumbled to open it and the dishware inside rattled violently beside his face. The walls shook as the sound of a distant steam engine began to rumble in his ears. He got his hand inside the tiny hole and felt them.

The black wolf busted through the kitchen windows behind him in the sprays of lightning. Glass shattered against the cupboard in the winds as he stood fully up to his eight-foot height with an ear shattering roar of vengeance. The man fell backwards along the wall to the floor in stunned fright and then quickly stood to run.

The light danced over the wolf as the six arm cast iron kerosene chandelier swayed rapidly at his face from the ceiling. The man turned to his right and the wolf smashed the countertop and porcelain sink into rubble with his fist and blocked him. He retreated behind the dining table to put it between them. The walls of the upstairs bedrooms disintegrated with a thousand crushing explosions and the wolf shattered the table into matchsticks with his fists.

The wolf stared down onto the man with complete rage and roared, his long black hair whipping wildly in all directions. The saliva was pulled from his teeth and slung around the room in the winds that tore the farm.

The man turned in to the pantry closet and slammed the door behind him. The upper floor ripped from the house and half the ceiling over the kitchen flew away. The front parlor was completely exposed from above and the Christmas tree disappeared into it.

The wolf jumped to the pantry behind him and repeatedly beat upon it with brutal force, demolishing the framing inside. He punched through the wall with overwhelming violence and a board of framework struck the man on the head and he slumped lifeless to the floor. The whistling roar of the steam engine shook the foundation of the house until it cracked. The wolf splintered the pantry door into ruins and took hold of the man's ankle that lay among the shambles.

There was a shot.

The wolf quickly hunched forward with terrible trembling. His hands drew up and writhed in front of his face in convulsions. Immediately, in one motion, he looked upwards to the shredded ceiling, gargled out a blood-soaked roar, and fell to his back on the floor.

A hand laid a beautiful silver harmonica to the blacksmith's dirty table. Even in the dull lighting, it glimmered in extraordinary artistry. The blacksmith, inspired by its loveliness, was heartbroken and reluctant to steal its prize of lustrous power, like marring the face of some delicate masterpiece. In a moment of regret that could never flee, he extended his worn and dirty hand, lined with the char of the heated irons, and put it to his fires.

What emerged, falling to the workman's table from a black slag-coated mold, was a simple and ordinary round ball - unpolished and of no beauty, lacking elegance and made plain; the etchings gone and its history erased except for what *one* would remember. Its resolution seemed to have a lost meaning and no more purpose.

Davey stood trembling in a dissipating cloud of gunpowder smoke, pointing a flintlock pistol in his hand. His eyes were wide, but his face showed a torment of awestruck grief as pieces of the kitchen ceiling were sucked away into the sky above.

The wolf was shot through the heart and lay writhing in a pool of blood as the climax of the storm escaped overhead. The beast shrank back and, slowly, in the conclusions of death, the man emerged.

The house reverberated and settled in the lesser forces of the onslaught with great groanings and cracking splits while Davey ran and took up Cecil's head and held him in his arms.

Cecil choked and gasped with strained breaths as he looked up into Davey's eyes with shame.

"I'm glad it was you," he said, dying, as a single drop of blood traveled over his cheek from his mouth. "I have sinned. I've harbored evil against my brethren. The Lord has repaid me evil for evil." He spoke with labor and his words were soft. "I have held them in a prison, shackled in the destructive chains of unforgiveness within my heart...a cruel and tormenting place where..." He gasped for air. "...all light had faded. In my vengeful lust I was blinded. And now many have suffered in my cruel wake...Forgive me."

He looked upon Davey with a broken heart. "I was happy there, under the yew tree...with you." He paused in deep remorse for his own life and for Davey's. "I'm sorry. Things should have been different."

Davey's eyes filled with tears.

"Please...don't tell them it was me."

Cecil looked upon him one final time to remember him.

"You're a good boy," he said and a tear fell from his eye. He raised his hand to Davey's face and touched his cheek. "You have your father's eyes."

Cecil's head slowly slipped back as the effects of the silver ran its course and he died upon Davey's arm. The boy looked into his face with great sorrow for his friend whom he loved and his lips trembled with it.

Simon coughed a puff of dust from beneath the remains and the old oak tree in the yard returned upright in the receding winds.

The End

From the author:

Thank you for buying this copy of *Revenge of the Wolf*. If you have enjoyed this book, please tell someone about it by leaving a book review online where you purchased it as well as your favorite book shout-out sites. It will help other readers discover an exciting new read as well as me. I truly thank you for it.

This book took me a total of twelve months to write because of its complexities. What brought about this tale was my love for wolfman stories since I was a kid...and how they were never done well at all. I have always hated every werewolf film and book ever made because, if you really think about it, they're stupid. This is frustrating because it is such a thrilling idea. So, out of wanting to see an awesome werewolf film that has everything an audience wants to see play out in my mind, I wrote this story...but it is only the backdrop of the real story. This book most reflects me in its ideas and feelings, the ambiguous nature of all men, and our eternal struggle to consistently do what is right even when it is against our very nature. I hope you've enjoyed this mad world set in a time long past as much as I have and grasp those most important underlying themes.

Remember the words of the dustman and that there is an Angel who looks on for *you* in hope.

To contact me about this book or if you have any other questions, send an email to: wyattdmichael@yahoo.com

Peace and Love and may God Bless you
~ Wyatt Michael

About the Author:

Wyatt Michael is a musician, singer, songwriter, suspense/thriller novelist, artist, actor, and screenwriter. He owns Michael & Company Pictures, a film production company that he writes for.

Throughout his teens and early twenties, his Alternative Rock music was showcased on many radio stations from Ohio to California (before internet radio was an idea). Later, he and his co-writer built a recording studio and taught themselves how to use it. Over the next six years, his band, Only Makebelieve, recorded and finally released *Message from a Mockingbird*, an Alternative Pop masterpiece album that received rave reviews from critics all over the world. The group set out on a tour and promoted the album, which also ran on national college radio. Through stressful job situations - working nights in dark factories for years on end and driving semis across ice-covered mountains, Wyatt created a mental way of escape - writing stories. He began to write film scripts and his friends found them to be worthy of the screen. After getting a feel for the new creative form, Wyatt took on the daunting endeavor: *The Whaler Fortune* - his first novel. Being pleased with its worth, and after a break in which he performed in several major stage plays, he followed with, *Revenge of the Wolf* – his second novel. He lives in beautiful North Carolina with his beautiful wife and beautiful daughter.

- Find Only Makebelieve online
- Find Wyatt on iTunes, Amazon, & Amazon mp3
- Twitter @thewyattmichael
- Find more of Wyatt's books on Amazon

www.ingramcontent.com/pod-product-compliance
Lightning Source LLC
Chambersburg PA
CBHW020904200626
46814CB00001BA/161